The Kab

Code

Nathan Erez

The Kabbalistic

Murder Code

Nathan Erez

Editor: Dorit Silverman

All of the historic events, the developments of the Hebrew scripts, and the customs of Kabbalah as described in this book are authentic and factual.

The Kabbalistic Murder Code\ Nathan Erez

Editor: Dorit Silverman

Translator from Hebrew to English: Ora Cummings

ISBN-13: 978-1499225723

ISBN-10: 1499225725

Contact information: nathanerezbook@gmail.com

The Spheres

The First Sphere

When The British Conquered Jerusalem

The British ascended to Jerusalem in 1917 of the Common Era, the seventh year of the reign of his exalted Majesty King George V. At first they camped on a high, unpopulated plane in the western part of the city, but after remnants of the Turkish Ottoman army had retreated, the Mayor of Jerusalem, Hussein Effendi al-Hussein and his deputy took it upon themselves to surrender. They picked up the keys to the city and set out in search of the British army, bent on swearing an oath of allegiance to their new rulers.

The first two British soldiers they encountered and to whom they offered to surrender happened to be cooks out on a mission to forage for vegetables for their commanding officer, a lieutenant. The cooks went to fetch their lieutenant, and the mayor and his deputy promptly surrendered. But the lieutenant was apprehensive about being the one to accept the surrender of the Holy City of Jerusalem and led the two dignitaries to his commanding officer, a captain who at first accepted their surrender, but then, feeling he might not be the proper party to accept the surrender of the City of God, he demanded that they re-surrender, this time to his commanding officer, a man with the rank of lieutenant colonel. However, after accepting their surrender of all the Holy Sites, the lieutenant colonel had second thoughts about his suitability for the task, and sent the bemused mayor and his deputy up the hierarchical line. After surrendering a number of times, the two finally came face to face with the Commander-in-Chief, General Allenby himself, but by now the mayor and his deputy categorically refused to surrender, arguing convincingly that they had already done so too many times.

Because of the numerous times the city fathers had surrendered and the lack of clarity as to who had been the one to liberate the city from the Ottomans, there is doubt as to the exact site where this took place. The soldiers of the Sixth London Division eventually erected a memorial to their fallen comrades, which states: "Near this place Jerusalem surrendered to His Majesty's gallant forces." Of course, this monument is unable to go into great detail as to the events leading to that surrender, since most of those who died in conquering the city did so as a result of inadequate diet or various exotic Oriental diseases, and not at the hands of the Turks.

Elijah searched for the place where his meeting was scheduled to take place. It was a meeting, which he did not know was to change his entire life, and it was somewhere in the vicinity of the Allenby Memorial. As he continued to search, he found himself once again staring at the memorial erected by the soldiers of the Sixth London Division to commemorate their fallen comrades. He kept coming upon the memorial from a different direction each time, after climbing down steep stairwells and entering musty alleys, all the while followed by the suspicious eyes of old women, tracking his every move. When he came face to face with the memorial for the fourth time, he decided he had no alternative but to ask for directions, but soon realized that everyone he approached was as much in the dark as he was.

"There is no Luzatto family," an old woman told him crossly, after he had explained, with great difficulty, that he was looking for the Luzatto Institute for Jewish Studies. An elderly fellow with a hearing aid stopped and thought at length while leaning on his cane. "Sorry, young man, I've been living in this area for forty years and I have to tell you that there is no institute by that name here." Elijah thanked him politely and moved away quickly. He had walked only a few yards when the man called him back to say, "It has just occurred to me that Luzatto could be an Italian name," said the old man. "Maybe you should check with the Italian Consulate." Elijah thanked him profusely and rushed off before the helpful old man could produce any more useful suggestions.

In the distance he saw a boy riding a bicycle and signaled to him to pull up. Elijah hurried over to the boy and again asked for directions to the Luzatto Institute.

"I don't know anyone called Luzatto," said the boy, "What street does the guy live on?"

Embarrassed, Elijah realized that he had not mentioned the name of the street to any of the people he had approached for directions. He looked inside the envelope and read the letterhead.

"It's 6 Judah Mani Street," he said. "Corner of Mani and Chelouche Streets and there's a bell on the mailbox."

"Well, you're on Mani Street," said the boy as he rode off on his bicycle.

Elijah looked up, amazed to discover that he really was on Mani Street. A quick walk brought him to No. 6 and, within seconds, he was facing the mailbox. The mailbox appeared new and locked and bore a small sign in English telling him that this was exactly what he was looking for: The Luzatto Institute for Jewish Studies. He glanced again at the note. Convinced that he passed this very spot at least twice in the last half hour, he couldn't understand why he had been unable to find the place before.

There seemed to be no explanation for his inability to find the address, but he concluded, logically, that the British, too, had most probably gone astray in this part of Jerusalem. Elijah smiled, recalling again how the British had conquered Jerusalem. His mind buzzed with thoughts of his favorite hobby, the various conquests of Jerusalem. Every nook and cranny in the city held a special meaning for him, every layer of stones brought to mind a different conqueror. When it came to the holy city of Jerusalem, Elijah was a veritable fount of knowledge, and his wife often asked herself if there was more to Professor Elijah Shemtov than met the eye.

It was almost 11:30 am and he was half an hour late for his meeting when he rang the doorbell, which was slightly hidden alongside the mailbox. A tinny voice with an indefinable accent emanated immediately from the speaker.

"Good morning, Professor. Do please come in. The gate is open."

It was very difficult from outside to discern the house, which was surrounded by a stone wall, topped by an iron railing that had seen better days. Together, the wall and railing were about five feet high and the lush climbing ivy, which covered them completely, obliterated any view of the house for anyone standing outside. Entering the gate, he was faced with a panoramic view of a garden, behind which stood what appeared to be a tower. Like most Jerusalem houses of that period, the first three levels were made of rough rock, while the stories above were hewn stone. The house had clearly undergone extensive renovations in the not-too-distant past; its roof had been tiled and a high porch was built onto the building. The garden appeared well tended, but it consisted mainly of perennials, with no flowers that might need constant care. The large, well established cypresses and pines in the garden were clear evidence that this house had stood there for a long time. Elijah walked up the path leading to the front door, which opened even before he reached it.

As he walked inside, the door closed silently after him. If the outside appearance of the house had surprised him, the interior design was totally mind-boggling. It had been totally demolished and rebuilt. If the house had once been three stories high, there was no longer any evidence of this. The entrance led directly into a large hall, which reached up to the roof. Up above, a gallery ran along three sides of the house, accessible by two separate flights of stairs. All the walls, except one, were lined with bookcases full of books, with some paintings interspersed among them. Here and there, square wooden beams served to prop up the bookcases. In the middle of the house there was a smallish sitting area, and on the wall next to it a huge window overlooked the garden. The impression of all this was not one of ostentation, but rather that the owner was a person of discreet aristocratic taste.

When The British Conquered Jerusalem

Elijah had never been one to walk by a bookcase
without examining its contents and now decided to check
through the books, while he waited for someone to appear. The
library was full of old and new textbooks, randomly arranged on
the shelves. The Babylonian and Jerusalem Talmuds lay beside
history volumes and research studies, Hebrew books next to
books in English, German, and other foreign languages. Large
and small books, thick and thin volumes, shiny covers next to
dull bindings stood side by side, emitting a somewhat dusty
odor.

A man entered the room, as quiet as a cat. He was
obviously Asian in origin - Japanese or Korean or Chinese–but
Elijah had never been able to distinguish between them.
Coming in from behind him, the gaunt man took Elijah by
surprise and promptly handed him one of two forms he was
holding.

In fluent English, with no trace of an accent, the man
said, "Good morning. You will need to fill in your personal
details before the meeting." Elijah could not take his eyes off
the man. He had many questions, but somehow they all stuck in
his throat. He glanced at the page; it was a standard form and
seemed to deal mainly with the number of the bank account to
which his salary was to be transferred.

"Are you sure you have no middle name?" asked the Japanese or Korean or Chinese robot. "Your first name is Elijah and your last name is Shemtov. Don't you have any other name?"

Elijah was taken aback by the very question, and took his time before answering. "As a child, I used to be known as Eli. I have no other name." That was his first lie, one of a long series of lies he would tell that summer. It would be several days before he realized its full portent.

After filling in the form, Elijah handed it to the man, who put it aside without so much as a glance. He handed Elijah the second form, and said, "This is the Institute's standard employment contract. I hope the provisions do not confuse you. It was, unfortunately, drafted by a lawyer, one of the necessary evils in our society, and it might appear somewhat threatening."

Elijah felt uneasy. The contract included a number of major provisions and he was to agree to them all. First, all the work had to be conducted within the confines of the Institute. It could be done at any time, day or night, but no material was to be removed from the premises. Second, the employee understood and agreed that he was forbidden to give out any information, either verbal or written, regarding his work, without the express permission, in writing, of the Institute's management. Third, he was aware of the conditions of employment and agreed to abide by them in full. The rest of the contract dealt with the financial aspects, specifying that he would be paid according to "the customary payment schedule".

Unable to pinpoint any specific problem with the contract, he signed and returned it. Only then did he realize that he had not even tried to find out what was meant by "the customary payment schedule" or, indeed, what kind of a salary he could expect to be paid. Before he had time to curse himself and his department head, Professor Landau, who had sent him to the Institute in the first place, the inscrutable robot disappeared. Again Elijah found himself in the high-ceilinged room, which reminded him of a church, but now he had already signed an employment contract without having so much as an inkling as to what he was doing in this place. He was angry with himself for having allowed himself to become the archetypal "absent minded professor". Whenever anyone broached him about anything beyond his own field of expertise, he would simply tune out and think of other matters instead, going back obsessively to the different conquests of Jerusalem or to his own work. Only when he realized that the other person had finished speaking and that he had no idea what had been said or required of him, would he ask the person to repeat himself. Such had been the case the day before, when Professor Landau had asked him to pay a visit to the Luzatto Institute at 11:00 am this morning.

Soon he would have to pick up his young daughters, and here he was with a signed contract and without the faintest idea of what he was supposed to do, what his employment conditions were, the size of his salary and - most important of all - if he could make it to the nursery school in time.

He knew only that Professor Landau had pounded on his door only yesterday afternoon and, quite uncharacteristically and without waiting for an answer, Landau had burst into the room. Landau, who was short and slim, had a shock of silver hair that added significantly to his height. Generally, he was a very soft-spoken man, who projected an aura of calm, but this time his behavior was totally at odds with his customary demeanor.

"Elijah, I need you to do me a huge favor."

"What's the problem?" asked Elijah, amazed at Landau's transformation, but also flattered by the request. After all, it was not every day that the department head asked a big favor of a minor lecturer who had not yet even been awarded tenure.

"They are looking for someone with experience in deciphering written texts, as part of a small project over the summer."

"All right, but why me?" asked Elijah.

Elijah had plenty of experience in this kind of work. He'd recently been assigned to decipher an illegible manuscript written by an 18th century Bukharan Jew. The manuscript, which had been written in a Spanish hand in its Persian variation, was an inferior commentary on the Book of Esther. However, the author's great-grandson, a building contractor who had recently struck it rich, wanted to have it published. The work had taken much longer than Elijah had planned, and the contractor felt that not only had he bought Elijah's expertise, but Elijah himself- lock, stock and barrel. Every day he would call Elijah's home to check up on his progress. Then, in what he thought was an act of supreme generosity, the contractor had presented Elijah with twenty copies of the printed work. Elijah had been unable to get rid of them, and now they would no doubt remain with him forever, taking up valuable shelf space. Elijah remembered that particular case ruefully; the last thing he wanted was to spend this summer plowing through another such experience.

"I did actually try to put forward other candidates, but they asked for you specifically. You may take that as a compliment." This, coming from his head of department, who was also the head of the tenure committee, left Elijah no choice.

Just as he was about to begin wallowing in self-pity, Elijah's reverie was interrupted by the arrival in the room of a thin man with a short beard and thick-lensed glasses. He was dressed in a neat black suit but wore no tie.

"I'm David Norman," he said, "and I'm happy to meet you, Professor Shemtov."

"Doctor Shemtov," Elijah corrected him, although he was quite flattered by the title by which he had been addressed.

"Have you ever seen the monument to General Allenby? The monument has never been completed, you know. The original plan was to have a statue of General Allenby astride a horse. However, as is the case with so many of Jerusalem's dreams, the monument is still standing there forlornly, waiting for its horse."

Despite his impatience and the need to learn what exactly he was being commissioned to do, Elijah restricted his response to a few polite words about the beauty of the house.

"You no doubt know that this house, in addition to its real estate value, is of great historical value as well. The house was formerly the property of Benzion Mammon, a Jewish magistrate at the time when the region was part of the Ottoman Empire, who had been finally able to settle a long-running dispute between the Arabs of two Jerusalem suburbs, Lifta and Sheikh Jarrah. In return, the Mukhtar, or head, of the village of Lifta, agreed to sell Mammon the land surrounding the monument in order to build a Jewish neighborhood on it. Parting with this land posed no problem to the Mukhtar. The land, being located on top of a hill and suffering fiercely cold winters, consisted of inhospitable terrain.

21

"Mammon, who was heavily involved in the community, carried a large gold pocket watch that he consulted often and ostentatiously to impress upon all what a busy man he was and how valuable his time was. Indeed, he never wasted any time and within the space of three years a number of sumptuous homes arose in the area. Some of the country's most notable Jews took up residence in these houses; among them were Judah Mani, the lawyer; Joshua Mansour, a well-known automobile dealer; David Valigo, a pharmacist; Rahamim Avikhazar, an importer of fish; and Rabbi Rahamim Chelouche, who had moved there from Egypt. The houses were all built around Mammon's residence, which was the largest and most opulent of them all. The new neighborhood was named Romema–'The Heights'."

"Are you a Jerusalemite?" asked Elijah, in an attempt to show interest in the other man.

"No," said Norman, leading him to the seating area. "I am simply quoting the agent who sold this house to the Luzzato Institute, and who demanded an outlandish sum for it. Do take a seat." Several elegant drinking glasses stood on the table. Norman opened what looked like a small bookcase and Elijah saw that it was actually a concealed refrigerator. He took out cold drinks and placed the bottles before them.

"Before we get down to business," said Norman, "I have to ask you a question which has bothered me ever since I read your article."

"Which one?" asked Elijah, impressed no end that someone outside the ivory tower of academe had actually bothered to read one of his papers. Academics are usually well aware that their papers are not written with the aim of being read.

"I've read most of them, but I'm referring to your famous article about the point on the Hebrew letter *Shin*."

Elijah promptly forgot about the nursery school and his daughters and the fact that he was supposed to be picking them up at midday. He orally summarized his latest article, on the developments in the research regarding the letter *Shin* from the time his previous article had been published. Norman listened attentively, devouring each word. There and then Elijah decided that he really liked the tall, thin man. Anyone who was so interested in recent research on the development of forms of Hebrew letters had to be a good person.

When Elijah completed his summation Norman sighed, "How brilliant you are, and so erudite," he said. "I'd love to continue this discussion, but you are no doubt pressed for time. Such is the curse of the modern era; so much we want to do, but the pressures of time never allow us to explore where our hearts would lead us. Meanwhile, has anyone explained to you the nature of the project we are here for?"

"Not exactly. I understood that you would be filling in the details for me."

"Not exactly," was a vast understatement. Elijah had absolutely no idea what the project entailed; indeed he had had no idea, when asked to come to the Luzatto Institute, that any kind of project was involved. In fact, his boss, Professor Landau had not even known Norman's name. "The Luzatto Institute has received a number of copies of an ancient document," Norman now told him, "and we are interested in a preliminary and fast decipherment of the copies. To tell you the truth, this will not be an easy task, but I believe it will be groundbreaking in its implications. I, personally, am very moved. We have heard that you are *the* expert in dealing with such manuscripts."

"I'm sure there are others who are better than I," protested Elijah weakly. He didn't understand why Landau had praised him so highly, but couldn't help feeling flattered.

Norman smiled again. "If you keep hiding your light behind a bushel, people will eventually begin to believe you. I'm sure you are curious about our academic connections. Simply put, the Institute periodically sends research grants to your Department, which, as a result, is nice to us. Sherry or diet cola, Professor Shemtov?"

"Diet cola, please, Doctor... Mister?"

"David will be fine."

"David, then. My wife Orna tells me that a single calorie is quite enough for me. She believes I'm a bit too chubby."

The old man got up from his chair, with the clear message that it was time to get down to business. He went over to a large, innocent-looking cardboard box, which sat on the desk behind him and pulled out a large photocopy of what appeared to be a manuscript of some kind. He sat down again.

From then on, Elijah noticed something peculiar about the man's body language. When he sat back down, he did not sit directly opposite Elijah, but to his side. At first, Elijah thought that Norman had done so in order to enable them both to look at the same document, but then, as they were seated next to each other, he saw that the lenses of Norman's glasses were very thick and realized that the man must have difficulty reading, which might have been why Norman looked straight ahead rather than at Elijah. Elijah was also forced to talk facing the wall opposite him, rather than directly to Norman. When he, nevertheless, turned toward Norman every so often - which caused him an immediate crick in the neck - he saw the man peering at him owlishly. It was like the weird staging of an avant-garde play, with both characters addressing the wall. Elijah tried to concentrate on Norman's accent, but was unable to place it as American or British. It was some type of bizarre amalgam, and Elijah could only see in his mind's eye the

25

surrender by Effendi al-Husseini and his deputy, as they bowed down to the British cooks.

After holding the document at an angle for a while, as if showing it to a man on the wall, Norman finally handed it to Elijah. After giving it no more than a cursory, vaguely disinterested glance, Elijah suddenly realized what it was - and was overwhelmed by what he saw.

"That simply cannot be!" he exclaimed, half to himself and half to Norman. "If this is what I think it is, it is a world-class discovery!"

He looked at Norman and mumbled, "This is unbelievable! If the manuscript is genuine, it will take the world by storm! It's the first time a text of this kind has been found, a text dating to shortly after the revolt of Bar Kokhba - and possibly only a hundred years later!"
Norman smiled. "It is possibly even from before the time of Bar Kokhba."

Elijah was engrossed in examining the text. "Indeed, it may be so," he blurted out. He examined it again. Of course, there were some misspellings, some sections that were smudged or faded, but it was unmistakable: this section showed unquestionably that the Kabbalistic work *Sefer Yetzirah*[*The Book of Creation*] was but a small fragment of a much larger work! He examined the photocopy carefully, totally oblivious to

Norman, who kept looking back and forth between him and the wall.

"Professor Shemtov, I'm sorry to disturb you," Norman disturbed him, "but you've been examining it for a quarter of an hour, and there are several technical matters we have yet to take care of. You are going to be able to examine it so much that your eyes will hurt."

Elijah looked up quickly and saw Norman, standing impatiently like someone waiting for a long overdue bus.

"I'm sorry, I'm afraid I didn't notice the time flying." Elijah had paid no attention to the time, or to the figure that flitted past the various open doors. It was a quiet figure, almost feline. Elijah had no way of knowing then that this photocopy would change his entire life. He was totally unaware of a whole series of almost imperceptible clues, which pointed to the true reason he had been chosen for this particular assignment.

"May I see the original?" asked Elijah.

"That," said Norman, as he inched his way slowly to the table, "is the million-dollar question."

Elijah realized that he had no idea how this photocopy had fallen into Norman's hands. But in no way did this dampen his ardor. At that moment, Norman appeared to be the one obstacle keeping him from his true purpose in life: to continue to examine the document before him.

"To tell you the truth, Professor Shemtov," said Norman, "I can understand why the formal arrangements don't concern you, and that my very existence annoys you."

"Heaven forbid!" Elijah replied, amazed at Norman's uncanny ability to read his thoughts.

"I noticed that you did not ask me at all how I received this copy, nor who the owner of the original manuscript is." Norman smiled, as if sharing a secret.

Elijah didn't answer. He thought he understood what Norman was getting at. According to the Israeli Antiquities Law, anything produced by anyone prior to the year 1700 was classified as an "antique". Moreover, every antique discovered after the law was passed automatically belonged to the State, and had to be turned over to the Antiquities Authority. Anyone violating the provisions of this law laid him or herself open to a potential two-year prison sentence and a very large fine. Nor was any person who'd acquired an antique before the implementation of the Antiquities Law immune. The government had the right to declare any such object "a national treasure" and could then force the owner to sell it to the State. It was thus not surprising that a considerable number of Israeli antiquities had "sprouted wings" and been whisked away to more favorable climes elsewhere in the northern hemisphere. Elijah wondered whether this law was based on a statute dating back to the pre-1917 Ottoman era, and was reminded again of

Effendi al-Husseini's surrender to the British cooks. He could not help but smile.

"The copy you see would, indeed, seem to indicate that *Sefer Yetzirah* was part of a larger text, which was destroyed," Norman went on. "According to *Sefer Yetzirah* the world was created out of the twenty-two letters of the Hebrew alphabet. It is a known fact that words have tremendous power, no less than reality itself. The proof of this is that the world was created out of God's utterances. God said, 'Let there be light,' and there was light. Certain combinations of the Hebrew letters, certain word combinations - a secret code by God – are the formula for our redemption. Legend has it that Rabbi Akiba ordered the *Sefer Yetzirah* to be destroyed because the Kabbalists feared that any slight error in the formula would bring about the destruction of the world. The risk was too great, and that is why, during the Bar Kokhba revolt, it was decided to have it destroyed.

"However, Nehemiah of Peki'in, a disciple of Rabbi Akiba, was bribed to copy the work, and he produced seven copies on parchment. The bribe he took, incidentally, was a guarantee that Peki'in would not be destroyed, and indeed that town was never demolished and its inhabitants were never exiled from the Holy Land. And it was the youngest son of Rabbi Simon bar Yochai, a famous Kabbalist, who offered the bribe."

Elijah poured himself another glass of diet cola, trying to process all the data. Norman assumed that he knew much more than was presented by the facts. Elijah dealt with the technical aspects of things. When he studied the dot at the top of the Hebrew letter *Shin*, he had absolutely no interest in thereby hastening this or that type of salvation. His interest lay in the addition, over the centuries, of this or that curlicue to the left leg of the letter, and the conclusions he reached were purely of an historical nature. Elijah was interested in the Hebrew script, which he studied hour after hour as if in a state of meditation that empties the mind of all other thoughts, and that was also the source of his livelihood. He was also interested in the various conquests of Jerusalem, but the Jewish Kabbalah was of absolutely no interest to him.

"The seven parchment scrolls were hidden away in Jerusalem, but as the city fell to one conquering force after another," said Norman, "the copies were dispersed to all four corners of the world."

Elijah was unable to understand how Norman could hone in on every one of the thoughts that passed through his brain. It was becoming increasingly disconcerting by the minute. He tried to blank his mind and think of nothing of his own; he tried only to listen.

Two points which were still unclear to Elijah, but once again Norman anticipated them.

"You may take it for granted that once conclusions on the seven scrolls are published, you will receive full credit for your work. And the second thing you want to know concerns your fee, which I assume you did not dwell upon when you signed the contract. We pay the accepted fee for this type of work."

The man must be a magician, thought Elijah, and felt a prickling sensation in his chest. Like every true academic, Elijah felt uncomfortable discussing financial matters. He was simply happy to be paid for his work, which made it possible for him to justify his absence to Orna, his wife. He assumed that he would be paid the same kind of money as he received at the university, in other words, starvation wages. It never occurred to him to complain, because he knew full well that this was a project he would happily have done for free, both because it had been assigned to him by Professor Landau and because of the nature of the project itself. When he saw the letter *Shin* in the document, decorated with a type of "crown" on its left leg, he realized immediately that this was a document that predated the Bar Kokhba revolt. He might even have been willing to pay for the privilege of working on the manuscript. Having such a momentous document published would almost certainly lead him to a "full professorship".

"How will I be paid?" Elijah asked hesitantly. "With a second job, I shall automatically be docked fifty percent in tax, which would leave me next to nothing. Orna, my wife, constantly complains about my inability to earn a decent living."

"You have nothing to worry about," Norman reassured him. "We will follow our standard procedures, and you will receive a net sum, after taxes. We pay 250 dollars per hour."

"Surely you mean shekels?" said Elijah, not believing his ears and trying hard to conceal his astonishment.

"No, no!" Norman exclaimed, elegantly disregarding the all-too-apparent amazement in Elijah's voice, as he began rifling through a pile of documents he had removed from a drawer. "I meant dollars. That is the net amount which you will receive per hour. We are not interested in having our scholars getting embroiled in problems with the tax authorities. We employ a law firm to deal with these matters. You will have the amount credited directly to your bank account. I want you to understand that it will be solely on your recommendation whether the Institute does, or does not, purchase the scrolls for hundreds of thousands of dollars. Given your background, I think the Institute will be getting an excellent deal."

The fee offered was more than satisfactory and Dr. Elijah Shemtov's motivation increased by the minute, and reached a level that matched Hasidic fervor. He tried to banish the few lingering doubts that continued to flutter through his mind. Of course, a number of unanswered questions remained, such as where would the hundreds of thousands of dollars needed to buy the manuscripts come from? Why buy them and bring them to Israel, when the State would only try to nationalize them? Also, if they were destined to become State property, why not have the government finance it? What had he not been told?

It was true that each manuscript would be worth a fortune, but Norman clearly had no intention of selling them. In terms of content, it should be enough to have just one of them if all were copies of the same original, what would be known as "backups" in modern parlance. All these intense thoughts pounding through Elijah's brain caused a neuron overload and everything seemed to blur together. What Norman saw were the blue eyes of a harmless dreamer, a person totally detached from reality, peering out from behind the computer. Elijah did not know it, but that was exactly what Norman liked about him. That, and of course his baffling ability to decipher ancient Hebrew texts.

"I'm happy that you're able to begin. There remain just a few minor technicalities to finalize."

The ring of a cell phone, playing the opening notes of the Unfinished Symphony, interrupted them. Norman answered impatiently, but almost immediately his tone changed to one of astonishment and apology.

"I'm very sorry. I hadn't realized that it's already two thirty. I know I should have been there at two. I'm on my way."

Norman turned off the phone. "It is important for me to sum up details with you, as I have to leave the country tomorrow," he commented. Accompanied by the Asian man, Elijah made another tour of the Institute. The man handed him a set of keys to the Institute and explained the order in which the doors must be opened. While the man showed him everything, Norman explained each item, the way a flight attendant would explain the use of life jackets and the location of the emergency exits.

His desk was on the second floor. Near the computer was a fax machine. The demands on Elijah were minimal: He was to go over each manuscript, type in the text in a simple word processing program, print it and e-mail it to an address Norman gave him. To ensure absolute secrecy, Norman told him, the computer would automatically delete whatever Elijah sent out by e-mail. Elijah did not hear the technical details, he was busy thinking once again of General Allenby, whose statue astride a horse has not, to this day, been placed on his monument. He did not understand how it was possible for the files which he prepared to be sent on without leaving any trace of them on his computer, but was assured that such would be the case. At the end of each workday, he would make use of the fax machine to report the number of hours he had worked. He was forbidden to call anyone outside the Institute or to smoke, and he was not allowed to use a cellular phone.

"It's the Institute's policy," said Norman apologetically.

He showed Elijah how to file a form recording the three hours of his first day of work. Elijah was stunned by how easily he had earned a sizable sum of money in one day.

He turned to leave. Norman picked up the keys Elijah had forgotten on the table and handed them to him.

"Please take down our telephone number," said Norman, "should your wife need to reach you." Elijah was confused. For some reason, he seemed to sense that Norman was delighted at his absent-mindedness. It was as if his confusion bore out exactly what Norman had expected.

Everything had happened so fast that Elijah felt himself in a dream, unable to absorb completely what had happened. He had managed to secure for himself a fantastically well-paid summer job, or, more accurately, it had been found for him. It was a job for which many people would have been willing to sell their souls to the devil. Truth be told, he may well have done just that.

But Elijah could think of only one thing and that with a distinctly victorious note: Orna.

The Second Sphere

When Hadrian Conquered Jerusalem

In the year 134 C.E. Jerusalem was conquered by the Roman Legions for a second time, following two years during which the city had been ruled by the forces of Simon Bar Kokhba, the Nasi *president of Israel.*

It is not entirely clear to this day why the revolt broke out. According to one school of thought, it was because Emperor Hadrian wished to turn Jerusalem into a Greek city, with a temple to Zeus. Another school believes that it was because the Romans imposed a ban on circumcision, under a law of the Empire forbidding all its residents from sterilizing or castrating anyone. What is abundantly clear is that this was not an easy battle for either side. The Jews prepared the revolt carefully, and secretly stockpiled a large supply of weaponry. They dug out an extensive and wide-ranging system of tunnels, reinforced walls and towers, and waited for a propitious time. When the revolt finally broke out, they had the advantage of taking the enemy by surprise, and defeated the Romans time after time. The XXII Roman Legion was totally destroyed, and was erased from the history books. The Romans were driven out of Jerusalem and all of Judea.

We are not completely sure about the position of the Jewish Sages during the time of the revolt. Some came out in support of it and others voiced their opposition. The most prominent supporter of the revolt was Rabbi Akiba b. Joseph, who said of Bar Kokhba, "A star [kochav]has risen from Jacob." Others, on the other hand, saw Bar Kokhba's actions as a revolt against Heaven itself and some attribute to Bar Kokhba the saying: "Lord of the Universe, do not help us, but also do not hinder us."

To aid the Roman forces, Hadrian summoned the heroic Julius Severus from Britain. Severus was wise enough not to confront the Jews face to face. Instead, he cut off their supply lines and captured one after another of their fortifications, and advanced slowly, step by step. Hadrian and Severus amassed a mighty army in Judea, consisting of thirteen legions, a force unparalleled in size at that time. Severus believed that the civilian population, with its women, children, and elderly would be unable to hold out for any length of time against a trained army. And he was right. After three years of fierce battles, the Roman army defeated the army of Bar Kokhba. Betar, the last

*center of the Jews, was annihilated, and with it most of the
Jewish settlements in Judea.*

*Many Roman soldiers were killed in the battles. In fact,
the losses were so great that, in writing to the Roman Senate,
Hadrian omitted the customary salutation, "If you and your
children are well, we are pleased. I and the army are well."
Nevertheless, the losses suffered by the Romans paled into
insignificance when compared with the destruction and
devastation in Judea. No fewer than a thousand Jewish
settlements were destroyed and 600,000 people were killed in
the battles and attacks. To this, we may add the numbers -
which we will never know - of those who died of starvation,
plague, fire, etc. So many Jews were sold into slavery that the
price of a slave in the Land of Israel dropped to that of a
portion horse fodder.*

*The results of the revolt were felt for many years to
come. Jerusalem was wiped out and was replaced by a Roman
city, Aelia Capitolina, in honor of Emperor Hadrian (Aelius
Hadrianus). Jews were forbidden to enter the city, a law that
remained in force almost until the Moslem conquest of the city.
Judea was ravaged. Those few Jews who remained either
moved to the Galilee in the north, or left the region altogether.
There was a mass migration to the land across the Euphrates
and Tigris rivers, and Babylon ultimately became the spiritual
center of the Jews.*

All the way home, Elijah rehearsed, to the minutest detail, what he would say to Orna to explain what had happened to him. Both he and Orna had doctorates, except that Orna was a world-famous ophthalmologist, while his doctorate was in the field of medieval Hebrew lettering. If anyone called and asked for "the doctor", there was no doubt as to whom the call was for. That night, though, he would demand equality! He would not tell her immediately about what he had accomplished. He would let her stew for a while, allow her to vent her accumulated bile. After all, because he had not picked up the girls, the nursery school teacher had been obliged to summon Orna from her hospital rounds. Indeed, by the time she had brought them home it was no longer worth her while to return to the hospital, so she was effectively stuck at home for the rest of the day. He would let her continue with her standard litany on how much longer would he continue to agree to work for the measly salary they paid him? And how much longer did he intend to fawn on Landau? He would listen to her patiently and after she finished, he would tell her everything that had happened to him that day, ending with the words: "From this day on, a meeting with me costs $750."

However, Orna had not even showered yet, as their daughter Michali had suddenly developed a high fever. And Elijah felt a sudden urge to refresh his knowledge on the Bar Kokhba revolt, which Norman had talked about in such detail as

39

if he were describing the latest suicide bombing. Elijah did not remember all the details regarding Hadrian, against whom the revolt had been waged and felt a special need to investigate the shape of Hebrew letters at the time of the revolt, in order to prepare for the delightful work that awaited him when he returned to the Institute the following day. He went over to his bookshelves, which were devoted primarily to the letters of the Hebrew alphabet and to his own personal hobby – from which he derived a great deal of pleasure, but which also aroused in him feelings of horror at the tremendous loss of life - the various conquests of Jerusalem. He opened up the chapter on Aelia Capitolina and read:

> "Why did the revolt break out? There are those
> who say that this was due to the attempt by
> Emperor Hadrian to build, as a replacement for
> Jerusalem, a Greek city with a temple to Zeus.
> Some say it was because of the prohibition
> against circumcision... "

"Elijah!" Orna called out in a tone of voice that was unmistakable. "Would it be too much of me to ask you for some help with the girls? After such a long day, I am at least entitled to take a shower, am I not?"

Elijah smiled, happy that at long last she would be going for a shower; afterwards he would be able to tell her his news. The Roman law had forbidden circumcision and castration.

With a smidgen of self-pity he thought of his own circumcision and for a fleeting moment he felt that the Roman approach had been an infinitely more humane one.

"Elijah, you are driving me crazy! How can you devote all your energies to reading about people who died centuries ago, but not so much as lift a finger to help your own daughters, who are very much alive? You'd better believe me that you're going to be the one taking the girls to school or the doctor tomorrow, whatever happens."

Bar Kokhba was a gutsy kind of guy. To say to God, "Lord of the Universe, do not help us, but also do not hinder us," was a very courageous thing to do. Just reading it gave Elijah the courage to take a stand.

"I'm warning you, Elijah! The only thing you are good at is messing things up! Come here this minute and help me!"

Elijah felt his wife had finally reached boiling point. He didn't want her to go beyond it, but he also hoped that her constant harping would end from that day on. He started toward the girls' room, still reading: "After three years of struggle, the Roman army vanquished the troops of Bar Kokhba."

"Damn it!" Elijah yelled as his foot stubbed the door-post in the hall. A sharp pain made him made him realize that he had miscalculated the turn and that one of the toes on his right foot had collided full-force with the door-post. His thoughts, which had been luxuriating over the different Hebrew letter-forms now focused solely on the agonizing pain in his foot. Holding the book open with one hand, Elijah bent down to rub the offending toe. It was one of those heavy picture-format tomes; all he needed now was for it to fall on his other foot.

"The number of Jews sold into slavery was so great that in the Land of Israel the price of a slave dropped to that of a portion horse fodder."

"Elijah! I am not your workhorse, when are you going to get that into your head?"

" ... There was mass migration to the land across the Euphrates and the Tigris Rivers..." Elijah pictured in his mind thousands of backpackers seeking out a spiritual center and finding refuge in the different ashrams of Babylon, which, in the latter part of the 20th century had become Saddam Hussein's Iraq.

"Well, well! Hello, Elijah! Have you just arrived? I've already put them to bed. Would be so kind as to read Michali a story before she falls asleep? I suggest that whatever you choose to read her shouldn't deal with conquests, disease, plagues, and death, as she lies there with a temperature of 104 degrees. I'm sure you'll understand and take that into account this time." Orna had reverted to cynicism, as she had no strength left to scream at her husband. Not that she had any need to scream, as Elijah was standing right next to her.

Elijah looked at his wife and noted with satisfaction that she was still beautiful, even after giving birth to two babies. To him, this was an objective appraisal, and not only because she was his wife. She had luxurious brown hair which fell in waves over her shoulders; even when she pulled it all up in a rubber band and went about devoid of makeup and dressed in rags, Orna attracted attention wherever she went.

Elijah could no longer contain his excitement and blurted out, "Orna, sweetheart, would you book us a vacation in the Bahamas for a week or two – or as long as you like?" Orna responded with a string of mocking insults; Elijah tried to convince her, in vain, of the seriousness of his intentions and in the meantime, Michali had fallen asleep. Orna went to take her shower, more put-upon and bitter than ever.

The next morning she drove off to work in the family's only car, not saying a word to Elijah before departing.

Elijah called an emergency babysitter to take care of his sick daughter and sent the healthy girl off to nursery school. He himself left home earlier than usual on foot; he loved walking and the fact that the Luzatto Institute was within walking distance of his home pleased him immensely. He started pondering on the enormity of the calamity that had occurred in the very place where he now walked. Nineteen hundred years ago, you could have heard the cries of the wounded, and from afar you could have seen the city going up in flames. No, he corrected himself in his mind, ever the exacting scholar, it was actually about 1870 years ago. One of the most significant effects of the defeat had been the sudden disappearance of the flowing post-Herodian script.

In every written form and every language there are two primary types. Nowadays, they are referred to as square and cursive. The first is the official letter shape used for printing books and newspapers. The second refers to handwriting, which evolves from the first. When you write something by hand, you tend to want to write more quickly. The letters used in cursive script are affected by the environment, the types of writing instruments available, the paper, the ink, etc. Gradually, over time, letters are shortened, lines are joined, and a new style of handwriting is eventually created, which differs from that of the official letters and that is known as cursive handwriting.

This also applies to Hebrew. The official Hebrew script is what is known as square script. The letters are composed of horizontal and vertical lines, with a few diagonals. Religious works and especially Torah scrolls, are generally – but not always – written using this square script. Letters and other works are written using cursive script, which changes from one era to the next and from one country to another.

At the end of the Hasmonean era and during the Herodian, a unique cursive script began to evolve, an indication of wide-ranging cultural activity and of the fact that more people were literate. This cursive script attained its highest degree of perfection toward the end of the first century C.E., but the manuscripts of the post-Bar Kokhba era, a few decades later, show no trace whatsoever of that script. No sign of it appears on any fragment of parchment, papyrus, or stone carving of that time. People suddenly stopped using the style. They reverted to square script, and developed other cursive scripts. Scholars see this as another sign of the grave calamity that had befallen the Jewish people. Mentally, Elijah had already composed the title of his next article: "The Disappearance of the Post-Herodian Cursive Script."

Elijah needed only a single glance to identify the different styles of Hebrew cursive script. Within seconds, he could tell if a document was from Spain or Provence, from 19th century Morocco or 14th century Egypt; whether it was from the Crimean Peninsula or had been written by one of the members of the priestly clan of Djerba, Tunis, who according to Jewish tradition had been exiled there after the destruction of the First Temple. There was not a single known form of Hebrew cursive script with which he was not familiar. He enjoyed his expertise, and knew that he was good at it. He had no interest in the contents of the various documents. To him, it was all the same whether a document was a deed of sale for a field, a divorce document of a woman who had infuriated her husband, a letter from a father to a wayward son, or a wearisome commentary on a forgotten work. What attracted him was the form of the letters, the style of the script, the spaces between lines and pages, the type of paper and ink used, and the words as such.

"Never ask me about the content," he would say. "I can tell you what words were used in this document or that, but as to who wrote them and why, I suggest you check with experts in that field." Content was simply something that never interested him.

Prof. Adir, a tenured professor in his department, had once told him, "I understand you, Elijah. You are one of those lovers to whom his partner is totally irrelevant, be it the Queen of Sheba or a rubber doll. All you care about are procedures."

At the time, Elijah had been taken aback by the analogy. However, as Prof. Adir had uncharacteristically made that particular comment to him in private, Elijah chose to ignore it. Instead, he preferred to regard himself as an expert in the history of art, and he considered the manuscripts brought to him as works of art.

Arriving at the corner of Mani Street, Elijah saw from a distance that a man standing next to Norman was locking the doors of the Institute. Close by stood a large black Mercedes taxi (for many years Israeli taxi drivers had a penchant for large black Mercedes cars) with its trunk open. Elijah assumed that the man, who then carried a small suitcase from the Institute and placed it in the trunk of the taxi, was the driver.

"Good morning, Prof. Norman," Elijah called out, quickening his pace.

For a moment, Norman was taken aback, and his body language seemed to indicate that he wanted the car trunk closed before Elijah could see what it contained. Norman made a sharp turn toward Elijah, and Elijah had the distinct impression that he had not expected to meet him that morning.

"Thanks for the compliment, Prof. Shemtov. To what do we owe the privilege of your arrival so early in the morning?"

Elijah noted that Norman was rather pale and sickly looking. Elijah was confused and felt he had done something wrong.

"Should I help the driver with the suitcases?" asked Elijah guiltily.

"There's no need," replied Norman. "Everything has been taken care of. I'm afraid I have to leave; but do keep up the good work. Let me tell you what my father used to say to me: 'You will bring the fountain.' Goodbye, Prof. Shemtov, I'll be in touch with you."

Elijah had no idea what the reference to "the fountain" was about, but thought this might not be a good time to go into such a question.

Elijah noted the trace of a smile on Norman's lips, like a weak flashlight on a dark night, or a wayward cloud on a summer's day. He realized that he had blundered again, but couldn't understand how. The taxi driver whispered something in Norman's ear.

Norman turned to Elijah and said, "We are late. Be well." It was clear that he had difficulty getting into the car, and was only able to do so with the driver's aid. The taxi drove off.

For the first time, Elijah used his own keys to enter the Institute. The Luzatto Institute was the dream of every scholar. Elijah stationed himself at the table in the lower hall, it was a gigantic mahogany table that was totally empty except for the materials he needed for his work. He was amazed at the pastoral quiet in the Institute and found it hard to comprehend that this building, which was but a short distance from the bustling and vibrant Jerusalem Central Bus Station and its loud sounds, was a haven of tranquility and quiet. Birds chirped, and from his window, he could see trees all around. From one of the balconies, you could see clear across to the abandoned Arab village of Lifta, at the entrance to Jerusalem.

Elijah thought of calling Orna to tell her about the magnificent mahogany table, the vast library and the quiet surroundings, but when he tried to do so a recorded feminine voice noted that it was impossible to dial outside. As the rules forbade cellular phones, the scholars of the Institute were effectively cut off from the outside world. And since Elijah had forgotten to give Orna the Institute's phone number, there was no way she could call him.

"Not a bad way to ensure that your employees do what they're paid to do," he thought to himself. He decided to wander around the Institute for a while before settling down to work.

The gallery, which overlooked the main hall, was accessible by two separate staircases. This time, Elijah chose the right-hand staircase, and out of curiosity tried all the doors on the way. Most were locked and appeared to have been that way for quite a while. "I wouldn't mind living here myself," he thought. A library and computer downstairs, a bedroom and bathroom upstairs, and total peace and quiet - what more does one need?"

One of the doors was unlocked. He opened it and saw that the room it led to contained a single piece of furniture - a desk. He opened the drawers out of curiosity, but they all seemed to be empty. At the bottom of one drawer, though, he saw what looked like some writing. He looked again and realized it was a piece of paper, which had somehow become stuck and was of a shade close to that of the wood the drawers were made of. He pulled out the paper and was surprised at what he found.

The paper itself was quality stationery stock and had the letterhead in English of a company named "Luria Investments

Ltd." The address was in St. Kitts. Where in blazes was St. Kitts? Below this was a list, evidently of things the person needed to do.

The first line contained an academic quote in English, from an article entitled "Movement with Words", which had been published in an American journal named *The Struggle for the Future*. The article was written by one Odell Weiss. Elijah had never heard of such a journal, but the unusual name Odel Weiss caused him to smile. The rest of the page was in Hebrew.

The second line began with "Visit Gardi in the hospital" while the third was the address of a company named Texas-Com. The CEO was listed as Dr. Shalomo Nehorai, whom Elijah knew personally.

The fourth line dealt with the Kim Foundation, which offered grants.

Elijah looked at the page. He was not interested in the to-do list, but what did interest him was that it was written in the Hebrew known as *Rashi* script, a script that has not been used in handwriting for hundreds of years.

What fool would use that script today? he thought to himself. The writing was clear and precise, and showed that whoever had written the note felt totally comfortable in using that particular script.

He was startled by a noise from behind the door and wanted to leave the room as fast as he could, before anyone knew he had been there, but he was unable to do so. Someone had locked the door from the outside! He began sweating profusely and didn't know what to do, as he stood helpless in the locked room. He decided to call for help. At first he called out quietly, but as the minutes passed and there was no response, he began shouting louder and louder. He was panic-stricken. Finally, after several minutes of mental agony, he heard footsteps. Someone jangled a bunch of keys, and the door eventually opened. In the doorway stood the young Chinese or Korean man.

"What are you doing in here?" the man asked.

"I was looking for some material," stammered Elijah.

"Did you find anything?" The tone was again metallic, robot-like.

"No, no, I..."

"Everything you need is on your desk. You have no cause to search here." The man was distinctly unfriendly.

"I'm terribly sorry," Elijah mumbled contritely.

"There's nothing to be sorry about. Just do what Mr. Norman expects you to do."

Elijah returned to his desk and placed the paper he had found in the drawer on the corner of the table.

He did consider tossing it into the wastebasket, but decided in the end to follow a dictum he had learned from his father: there is always time later to throw something away; he accepted the logic of that saying.

Elijah began working, concentrating on the photocopy in front of him. An hour later he went to the bathroom, and when he returned the slip of paper was no longer there. It had been removed from his desk. This really bothered him. He asked himself what else there was at the Institute, how many people worked there, and why he had not met a single one of them during all the hours he had been there. In fact, the Asian man only appeared after he had been obliged to yell for help. He tried to reassure himself with the idea that the paper had nothing to do with his work in any case, and made a determined effort to again concentrate on the task at hand.

However, one thought kept running through his mind: if someone had taken the trouble of removing the paper, it must be of more importance than he had imagined. Moreover, the unusual use of the *Rashi* script must be somehow significant. Fortunately for him, he had the gift of total recall and, in a short while, he managed to reconstruct the entire note, complete with an exact duplication of the script involved. He forced himself to ignore the note and continue with his work. To assist him, he examined each letter of the photocopy individually with the help of a large magnifying glass, which he had spotted – and coveted – the previous day. The work, which exhausted his eyes, was uplifting to his soul.

Again he read the text:

"The stone was very precious, the very essence of all beauty and treasure. It was known as *Even Shetiyah*. In this world, the stone was located beneath the place of the Holy of Holies, and from it, it spread along all types of tracks and paths to all of creation. For this stone stands at the heart of the entire world, and at that point all are joined and gathered together... "

The letters were totally consistent with the era in question. What is the "*Even Shetiyah*"? Where is it now? Was Norman's interest in it due to its great value? Elijah had no idea. In any event, as far as he was concerned, these questions were irrelevant. Pleased with the day's progress, he sent the results of his work by email, and turned to the no-less-pleasant task of recording the time he had arrived at the Institute and when he would be leaving, which he sent off by fax. He noted that he had no idea which country was represented by the country code in the fax number given him by Norman. He would have checked this out, but there was no telephone book at hand and he soon forgot all about it.

The night was dark and gloomy, and a thick fog enveloped the city as he trudged wearily toward his home. As he walked an idea occurred to him, as sharp as a knife: the missing paper must be the clue to the entire riddle, and deciphering it would lead to a hidden treasure. Even if it did not lead to a treasure, it would at the very least enable him to understand the strange things that had occurred since the previous morning.

In his mind's eye, he visualized again the photocopy of the scroll on the desk in front of him, and wondered if anyone was capable of understanding what was meant by "tracks and paths in all directions". He agreed with those mystics who felt that language simply does not have the ability to convey supreme truths, and all the more so when attempts are made to put these down in writing. All his profound thoughts came to an abrupt halt when he opened the door to his home. Here he was met by a jubilant welcome from his daughters who fell upon him like two small, love-starved animals.

"You owe us a story from yesterday," Michali and Efrat squealed. Michali was feeling a lot better and her temperature had dropped.

The girls were fully aware that their father's skills lay in storytelling and certainly not in cooking, washing, dressing, fixing, sewing, etc., and that was why this was their standard request. That night Elijah chose to tell them the tale of the *Golem* of Prague:

"The Kabbalists of Prague knew how to make themselves a *golem*, a human-shaped figure, made of earth and water, in other words, mud. Whenever they completed the study of that week's portion of the Torah, they would gather around a bonfire and spend the whole night fashioning little men out of mud. Then they would write on the forehead of each such 'creature' the Hebrew letters, *Alef, Mem, and Tav.* Would you girls know what that stands for?"

"It stands for the Hebrew word '*emet*' - truth," the little girls cried in unison.

"Yes, and these are also the first, middle and last letters of the Hebrew alphabet. On the other hand, the word '*sheker*' - a lie - is composed of three consecutive letters towards the end of the alphabet.

"The whole night, next to the bonfire, the Kabbalists would pray and dance, and would infuse life into these 'little men' that they had created out of mud in their own image. From then on, each new creature acted like a robot. Although it could not speak, it had a certain degree of understanding, and was primarily useful for carrying out household chores. It grew and grew without end. It became a mighty giant and could be extremely dangerous. That was why, before a *golem* became too tall and strong, the Kabbalists would take its spirit away from it, and it would revert to being earth and water.

"The *Maharal* of Prague, the rabbi of the community, did not want to part from his *golem,* because it was very helpful and dedicated. He refrained from doing anything, and the *golem* grew larger and larger, until it was an enormous giant. The rabbi realized that this could not go on, so he waited for an appropriate time. One day, he asked the *golem* to remove his boots. When the *golem* bent down to do so, the rabbi was able to reach its forehead. He reached out and deleted the first letter, the *Alef.* And what was left?"

"*Met*," Efrat, the older, answered immediately. In Hebrew, the word *met* means "dead".

"That's right," said Elijah, "the *golem* died. He immediately turned into mud, and the water evaporated, leaving a pile of earth at the rabbi's feet. The problem was that the *golem* had been so large, and the pile of earth was so big, that it completely covered the rabbi and he, too, died. From that time on, it has become customary to talk of 'the *golem* that arose against its creator'. Now, girls," he concluded, "Do you understand the power of the single letter *Alef*?"

Michali couldn't bear it any longer. "I don't like stories like that. I want you to tell us the story of Little Red Riding Hood."

Elijah agreed to tell them the story, but the Jerusalem version of it, a version that had an educational message. The wolf ran after Little Red Riding Hood, not because he wanted to catch her, but because he wanted her grandmother's freshly baked cookies. He did not devour the grandmother, but the cake she had prepared for the Sabbath. The hunter did not kill the wolf, but captured him and returned him to the Jerusalem Biblical Zoo. The wolf was punished by not being allowed to watch television for a full week, and regretted having stolen the cookies. Elijah ended the story on a triumphant note, that the wolf still regrets his actions.

And together, the little girls added: "To this very day!"

The little girls finally fell asleep, and Elijah silently went to his computer. He sent an email to Ziva Elitzur, a renowned librarian, asking her to locate the article by Odel Weiss that was mentioned on the paper he had found. He felt that he had taken the first step toward finding the lost treasure. The original Odel had been the daughter of the saintly Baal Shem Tov, founder of the Hasidic movement, and the grandmother of Rabbi Nachman of Bratslav. Who, but a hippie, born-again Jew would go about with a first name like that? He was curious.

First thing the next day he went to the library to seek out the article. On the way, he saw Prof. Ashuri about to enter the cafeteria and waved to her. Instead of going straight to the library, he decided to speak to her first. Prof. Ashuri always looked like a rather chubby, old grandmother on her way to babysit her grandchildren. Legends flew on campus about the brown beret Prof. Ashuri always wore. According to some, she wore the same beret each day; others insisted that she had a number of such berets and wore them consecutively. But, notwithstanding her dowdy appearance, Prof. Ashuri was an extremely important, world-renowned scholar of Kabbalah.

"What does the *Even Shetiyah* mean to you?" he asked her and immediately saw her light up.

"I'd like to tell you a story about Rabbi Nachman of Bratslav," she began. "There is a mountain, and on that mountain there is a stone, and from that stone a spring flows. The mountain and the stone and the spring all lie at one end of the world, and the heart of the world lies at the other end. The heart lies on the other side of the world from the spring, but is longing to come to that spring; at the same time the spring wants to come to the heart.

"Now, you may ask, 'If the heart is so desirous of coming to the spring, why doesn't it simply go to it?' The problem is that when it tries to approach, the incline of the mountain is very steep, and as it climbs the mountain it can no longer see the spring. And if it does not see the spring it will die, because its life force comes from that spring. Thus, as soon as it comes close to the mountain and can no longer see the spring because of the incline, it is forced to retreat. Should the heart cease to beat, heaven forbid, the world would be destroyed, because the heart is the life essence of every living creature. That is why it cannot go to the spring, but must stand opposite it, pining for it."

"What, then, is the *Even Shetiyah*?" asked Elijah. On the tip of his tongue was something else very important that he wanted to ask, but he couldn't remember what it was. When you want to say something that you know is important, but that you cannot for the life of you remember what, it is almost impossible to concentrate on anything else.

But the question had already been asked, and Prof. Ashuri replied, "This goes back to the original sin and the Kabbalistic concept of 'breaking of the vessels'. The world somehow became messed up and turned into what it is now, but that is not its natural and desirable condition.

"Now, as to *Even Shetiyah*. It can be translated as the Foundation Stone, in that all of foundation begins from it, or, alternately, as the Watering Stone, which 'waters' the whole world with its largesse. If the *Even Shetiyah* were to cease to exist, the world too would cease to exist. Unfortunately, the *Even Shetiyah* has become dislodged from its normal place, and the whole world must seek to put it back in its proper position. This is what the story of Rabbi Nachman of Bratslav is all about."

Elijah asked himself why he needed all of this; why had he allowed himself to be involved in the text; a thing he always steered well clear of? But, since Prof. Ashuri was providing him with a full dissertation, he felt that at a certain point he might have to respond; so he listened attentively.

"The Kabbalah is based on a theory about the structure of the world. At the apex is the Creator. In His desire to do good, He produced a perfect creation, which is obviously a spiritual world which is better than the one in which we live. From that world derived other worlds, one from the other, until we come to the coarse world in which we live."

Elijah sighed, "I am quite confused by all this. One world is derived from another. How do you explain this to your students?"

"What do you know about computers?" Prof. Ashuri asked him, appearing to change the subject.

"Very little," Elijah answered. "I've gotten to the stage where I write my articles by myself. I even took two compulsory courses in programming and actually enjoyed them. I also surf the internet, but how is all this relevant?"

"You'll soon see. Do you have any idea what happens inside your computer when you use it?"

"Let's not get carried away," said Elijah.

"I'll explain to you about your PC and then we'll come back to the worlds of the Kabbalah. Did you ever wonder how it is that a computer, which is nothing but a bunch of wires and electronic parts, produces what we want of it? The answer is that it does not do so directly, but via a number of different layers and intermediaries.

"In the final analysis, all the information which is processed is relayed through a series of transistors which can either be in the ON or the OFF mode. The question is whether they are carrying an electrical charge or not. It is this division, into the ON and OFF modes, which is the basis of our computers, which work on a binary system. At the core, computers are run by computer languages known as assembly languages. They only accept zeroes and ones, and their response is also based solely on zeroes and ones.

"The computer manufacturers have written various machine programming languages which are more amenable to people. These languages are called 'higher-level' languages, but they too can be very complex. For average people like myself, these, too, are far too complicated. For us, there are computer languages that are of an even higher level. Let us assume, for example, that I have a program on my computer that stores all my telephone numbers. I enter the data into the computer, and my program translates this into a lower-level, more complex language, and then this is translated into an even more complex language, until eventually the translation is into machine assembly language. After a series of such transformations, we end up with a language that translates everything into electrical signals of pure machine language.

"A simple act of entering telephone data is ultimately translated into thousands of actions, which act on many thousands of transistors. When I try to retrieve data from my telephone database, the computer works in the other direction, with thousands of actions taking place before the data is delivered to me.

"Practically speaking, there never has been, and there never will be, a way for us to carry out the most elementary action on a computer without our affecting all these different 'worlds' and 'layers' which separate our world from the world of the computer.

"For the average user, all of this is totally irrelevant. The average user has no idea what happens every time he uses the computer. He knows that he performs a certain action and receives a certain result. For the average user, who may at best have a vague idea of how computers work, the different layers involved in operating the computer simply do not exist."

Elijah remained silent, for he was beginning to understand the basic ideas behind the Kabbalah. Afterwards, to ensure that he had digested the information correctly, he asked, "Does that mean that we can compare the world in our Kabbalistic interpretation to the world of the computer? We have a central Creator, whose influence is felt via many worlds, and through them He reaches our world. These layers of worlds descend from on high, downward through many intermediaries until they reach our world and influence it. Is that what you meant?"

"Would you like to sign up for my course?" Prof. Ashuri asked, laughing.

"You have many students."

"Many," sighed Ashuri, "and from various faculties. A considerable number of them are not even registered at the university. They come to register, and I ignore the fact that they are not on the roster. This year, I closed registration after seventy-five students had signed up, but in reality over a hundred attended each lecture. For purely selfish reasons, because of my age, I suppose, I refused to accept any more. I have found lately that Kabbalah has shown signs of a resurgence of interest. As a result, many charlatans earn a fine living from it."

Elijah remembered that he was really on his way to the library. He parted from Prof. Ashuri in his normal awkward, hesitant and apologetic manner, thanking her profusely no less than three times; he would even have bowed down to her if that was what would have enabled him to expedite his exit. However, Prof. Ashuri had one more important observation to make.

"I hope that your interest in the Kabbalah will not infect you with that dreaded disease..." she smiled.

"What disease do you mean?"

"Kabbalistic literature is generally divided into three major streams. The first and most important one is the cosmological, mission-oriented one. Here we find a direct line between ourselves and the Master of the Universes, by way of His influence on all the intermediate worlds. Note the term,

'Master of the Universes' in the plural. In this view, there are mutual influences, going from the upper worlds to us, and from us to the upper worlds. All the commandments and all the proper intentions and all the prayers are ultimately aimed at mending those spheres, which were damaged at the time of the Creation. In the language of the Kabbalah, this means repairing those vessels which were broken.

"The second stream is Kabbalistic-prophetic. It is an attempt to attain what is known as cleaving to God and to achieve spiritual elevation. This can be accomplished by internal meditation, which includes reciting the Holy Names, internal and external purification, combining sacred letters and repeating them over and over, singing and moving the head, and breathing techniques. This can unite one with the higher worlds. One who does this properly can reach the level of prophecy. There are even books with detailed instructions on how to actually accomplish this and how to ascend to a higher spiritual level. I often hear of students who have embarked on such a course, and it is, indeed, a disease."

"Don't worry about me. And what about the third stream?"

"The third stream is the one which has elicited the most criticism. It is referred to as Practical Kabbalah. By that, we mean people who use the Kabbalah for their own personal purposes, as a way to exploit the secret knowledge to which they have access in order to control nature and man's fate. Practical Kabbalah appeals directly to supernatural forces and sometimes even makes them solve the problems of the one calling upon them. These include attempts to foretell the future, to converse with the dead, to heal the sick, to banish evil spirits and the evil eye, and of course to acquire wealth, respect, and/or the love of a man or a woman. That, too, is a dangerous game to play." Prof. Ashuri laughed, but Elijah could not tell whether or not she was serious.

When he walked on, the spell was broken, and he remembered what else he had wanted to ask her. He remembered something Norman told him before he set off on his travels that he claimed to have heard from his father: "You will bring the fountain!"

The Third Sphere

When The Israelis Conquered Jerusalem

In 1967, the nineteenth year of the State of Israel, the Israelis took the Old City of Jerusalem. After a number of battles, the Israel Defense Forces broke into the Old City via the Lions' Gate. The original plan had been to conquer the walled Old City through the Dung Gate, which appeared to be less fortified. However, the senior paratroopers refused to enter the Old City via the Dung Gate and demanded that the entrance to the sacred city be through the Lions' Gate. As they explained it, the very name Lions' Gate was more in keeping with their own view of themselves. This choice received considerable criticism once the battle had been won, with claims that it would have been preferable militarily to attack the city through the Dung Gate. The officers in charge of the operation, who saw such carping as no more than hindsight, rejected this criticism angrily. Another factor, which was not considered at the time by *those involved, was that there was a certain poetic justice in the choice of the Lions' Gate. In Arabic, the gate is known not as the Lions' Gate, but (more properly) the Leopards' Gate, so named because of the stone animals engraved above it, but as "The Gate of the Tribe" (*Ashibat*), a word reserved for the "Tribe" of the Jewish people, whereas an Arabic tribe is referred to as a* Kabilah. *The name is an indication that - for reasons which are not clear - the Arabic tradition is that this is the gate through which the Jews will enter the city.*

As a result of this war, the Hebrew University of Jerusalem underwent its third major transformation. Originally, when the university was founded in 1925, the dedication ceremony, attended by the British High Commissioner for Palestine, Sir Herbert Samuel, took place at the site where the original campus on Mount Scopus was later built. During Israel's 1948 War of Independence, the Mount Scopus area was one territory in which battles were fought over. While the campus was ultimately retained by Israel, it became an enclave, entirely surrounded by Jordanian territory. Under the terms of the cease-fire reached between the two sides, Israel was granted limited access to the campus and was permitted to post a small contingent of people there. Only once a month, and this by means of an armed and armored convoy, were the contingent's provisions brought in for the following month. That, of course, rendered it valueless as an educational institution. To meet the needs of the university, a new campus was built in Givat Ram, in the western part of the city.

When the entire city of Jerusalem was liberated in June 1967, the government immediately decided to return the Hebrew University to its original site. As a result, a major concrete complex was built on Mount Scopus, planned by a top architect who had won numerous prizes for his distinctive work and exceptional talent. What no one had foreseen when viewing the blueprints in the abstract, but soon became apparent in reality, is that the layout was so complex that neither the students nor the lecturers could find their way around, and people who had been using the facilities for years would often find themselves lost.

As he drove to the university library in Givat Ram, Elijah kept mulling over what Prof. Ashuri had said. However, as usually happened when the logic in his mind was confronted by material that differed from it on the emotional level, there seemed to be a short circuit, and his mind went blank. Why the hell did one have to drive from one campus to the other just in order to access the library? On a rational level, he knew the answer, but that did not make it any more palatable. Life has a dynamic of its own. Thus, even though the campus on Mount Scopus was again accessible and in use, the campus at Givat Ram was still there. In the end, it had been decided that the university would function with two campuses, divided by faculty: the exact sciences would remain in Givat Ram, while the social and behavioral sciences would be located on Mount Scopus. The result was that students and lecturers whose program included elements of both would be forced to commute between Mount Scopus and Givat Ram.

Elijah loved his office on Mount Scopus. From his small window, he could see the Temple Mount and the Old City. However, the manuscript collections were kept in the Givat Ram library, and so it was that he, too, joined the numerous commuters between the two campuses.

Added to the time wasted in driving between the two, was the fact that there was a chronic shortage of parking spaces. He did eventually find a space, but it was a long way from the university entrance. Wearily, he walked from his car to the library, where Ziva, whom he had asked to find the article by Odel Weiss, was the librarian.

"Since when are you interested in the supernatural?" Ziva asked him in a stage whisper. A number of professors looked up, and Elijah felt very ill at ease. He had no idea how Ziva could have known about the conversation he had just had with Prof. Ashuri.

"What are you talking about?" he said, trying to appear indignant, but feeling guilty for doing so.

"Just take a look yourself," said Ziva, pointing to a computer screen near her. Elijah sat down and looked at the screen. He had no idea from which database the information on the screen had come, but he understood that it must be from some journal entitled *The Struggle for the Future.* The display showed that the journal had been catalogued under four headings: Social Justice; the Radical Left; Interdisciplinary Studies, and Supernatural Phenomena. There was a note that this particular issue of the magazine was devoted entirely to the supernatural. There was also a note to the effect that the actual content of this issue was not available on the Internet, and that anyone who wished to read the articles in question should obtain the print version.

Elijah relaxed. One's personal rights were still respected by the university, and Ziva's comment had nothing to do with his conversation with Prof. Ashuri.

"I was sure this was an article about manuscripts. Where is the actual journal, so I can read the article?"

"It might seem rather strange to you," said Ziva, "but that particular issue is missing. What's even stranger about this whole business is that three months after we received that issue, the publishers contacted all the universities and asked that it be returned. The official reason they gave was that there were a number of editorial errors. The scuttlebutt, though, was that some of the authors were nonplussed by what they themselves were supposed to have written. They claimed that what they had submitted had been substantially modified by the editors without their permission, and accordingly they demanded that the issue be withdrawn. Our university, as all the others, returned its copy."

Here Ziva grinned, a grin that spread over her entire face, and she told him conspiratorially, "However, we still have part of it."

"How did you manage that?"

"Actually, you can thank a miscreant for that. Some man evidently tore out two pages from the journal, and after we had returned the journal itself, those pages were found lying around elsewhere in the library. Now, whenever we return anything for replacement or whenever we find something missing, we place a cardboard marker in its place, to remind us that we are waiting for the replacement. Here, we simply pasted the two pages to the cardboard marker. These pages are still here, and I've photocopied them. They consist of the editorial page with an advertisement on the other side, and two sides of an article by Ms. Weiss which you asked me to find for you."

Elijah wanted to say something, but Ziva didn't give him a chance. "Since I know how your mind works, I have already tried to find out if Ms. Weiss has any other publications to her name in any other magazine, but I lucked out. This is the only article she's written. I tried to find out more about her, but again, got nowhere. There's no address given for her, nor any other way to contact her. I figured you'd be interested in reaching her, so I sent an e-mail to the journal editor. He replied very politely, but told me he had only been editor for a year, and that this article was from before his time. Since that particular issue was published, there had been three different editors, and the entire format and content had changed. Now it is no longer called *The Struggle for the Future*, but *Societal Justice*. The new editor also told me that there were no any extra copies available of that particular issue."

"That's not what I wanted to say," remarked Elijah defensively. "First of all, what makes you think that a man tore out the pages? Couldn't it have been a woman? Be that as it may, my more basic question is: What would I do without you?"

"You'd probably do all the work on your own, or find someone else to butter up," Ziva replied.

"No way! There *is* no one like you. You're absolutely unique." Elijah took the envelope containing the pages that Ziva had prepared for him, while she returned to the line of people waiting patiently for her assistance.

Elijah decided to check out the new issues of *Societal Justice*. On his way to the stacks, he noticed a magazine entitled *A Different Existence*. After his conversation with Prof. Ashuri, he thought this magazine might also be of interest. He leafed through it and was amazed at the plethora of treatments and workshops offered. He read the names to himself: aromatherapy, Reiki, and various names he had never encountered. On every page he was accosted by names: Feng Shui, Tao-Shiatzu, Anthroposophy, Yura Veda, I-Ching, Deepak Chopra, Magnetotherapy... he was quite relieved when he finally saw an ad for a familiar treatment: acupuncture.

"At least that's one I've heard of," he murmured to himself.

One of the ads he noticed, for a workshop, completely floored him. He read and reread it a few times to be sure he had not misunderstood what it said; the workshop was one which led its participants to learn the spiritual laws for achieving success.

Elijah was exhausted. He felt as if he had fallen out of the frying pan and into the fire. It seemed to him that there were far more professionals offering salvation and justice than there were takers of such services and decided it was time for him to get back to reality and the demands made of him by his daughters. He returned home and forgot about the envelope in his briefcase.

After three full hours of work the next day, he finally remembered the envelope and decided to read the pages of the mysterious - and missing - journal. Seating himself on a comfortable sofa, he began reading. The first page consisted of the editor's declaration:

I am afraid that many of you have preconceived notions about supernatural phenomena. The source for this is probably the Marxist tendency to relate only to the material. Every hint at any phenomenon which they cannot understand is rejected scornfully, as if it was nothing but opium for the masses. This issue seeks to confront these views. All the authors are individuals who have had to deal with supernatural experiences in their own lives; not through any angel or other intermediary, but they themselves. All of them are partners in our quest for...

And that was where the page ended.

Elijah stretched out comfortably and began reading the article by Odel Weiss, a name probably chosen to add a further dimension of mysticism. Both the beginning and the end of the article were missing.

One must remember the era. It was at the end of the '60s and the place was the San Francisco area, which was full of all sorts of hippies. Bespectacled young men with long hair and young women with and without tight-fitting blouses indulged in long and wild conversations into the small hours of the night about what is above, what is beyond, and what is between the two. All types of weird hypotheses dealing with UFOs, death, religion, and politics wafted through the air. Economics majors held earnest debates on subsidizing marijuana and weed's effect on the world economy. Plus, of course, we had the era of sexual liberation, unhampered by such problems as herpes or AIDS. Some of those involved knew the zodiacal and astrological signs of the night better than they knew the moldy apartments in which they lived. The air was dominated by scents of hashish and marijuana, and these were the spiritual guides of the more conservative students. In this atmosphere of total intellectual inebriation, every irrational idea was greeted enthusiastically, and the crazier a person was, the greater he appeared to be to those around him.

On one of the days when I was starving, I agreed to come to my parents for a meal. I brought along my new friend, John McDonald, a man in his late fifties, whose every sentence totally fascinated me. My parents did not ask who he was. It was not considered appropriate to ask visitors where they came from and where they were going; the turnover was too great. John was thin, tall, had thick lenses in his glasses and a strong desire not to stand out from the crowd. My uncle, a real estate broker, who was regarded in our family as more tolerant and liberal toward young people such as us, was also at the meal. After the meal, rather than embarking upon the customary rave of his generation about the crisis the country faced with its youth, my uncle began to discuss with my parents the value of real estate in the area, and claimed that the large influx of hippies had brought down the value of real estate. John asked politely to add some comments of his own on the issue.

"That's only a temporary decline. In the long run," he claimed, "there's no doubt that an investment in this area will offer an astronomical yield. I have no doubt that thirty years from now the entire area will be the creative center of the United States."

John went to explain, in elegant English with an impeccable Oxford accent, why. I learned later that this was one of his remarkable talents: the ability to adopt whatever accent he wished, so that no one could guess his origins.

"Mark my words, thirty years from today all those restless souls out there will have realized at least a small part of their dreams. After all, by then, the person to be elected President of the United States will have been one of them. They will bring about changes in basic concepts and managerial techniques, will smash the prevailing hierarchies, will mock all the accepted traditions and sacred conventions, and will come out on top."

We listened to him bewitched. Years later, my uncle told me that as a result of that

conversation, he had bought up a substantial
amount of property in the area:

> "It was the best advice I ever
> received. My only mistake was in
> not following his advice to the
> end. John spoke about thirty
> years, and I sold all my property
> after twenty years. I was simply
> afraid to wait any longer, but,
> believe me, I still made enough
> money. Who would have guessed
> that this area full of wild-haired
> youngsters would one day come
> to be known as Silicon Valley?
> Properties that were then going
> for a song are now worth
> millions. Believe me, that guy of
> yours was really something
> special."

My uncle never forgot John, and he wasn't the
only one; no one who met John could ever forget
him. There was a kind of massive "presence" or -
in mystic terms, "karma" - about him. He had to
make contact with you, but if he did, you fell

78

into his trap and could never, ever get away from him.

After that meal, I remained glued to him for three solid weeks and I have a feeling that I learned more from him in those three weeks than I learned in all the rest of my life.

In the spirit of the time, we spoke about the future of the world. John explained to me in great detail the theory of Malthus, the English priest who had become a professor of economics. As early as the end of the 18th century, he foresaw a global crisis. Based on his analysis, the number of people in the world increases geometrically every few years. In contrast, the amount of food grown is limited to the amount of available arable land. As he saw it, there is no way for us to escape the total famine, which will bring about political and social chaos, and this, in turn, will bring about a drastic decline in the world's population. John explained to me that this crisis will have to come eventually, but can be delayed by the development of new technologies to make the land more productive and by the destruction of many species of animals in the search for more cultivable land, but it is unavoidable. The resulting famine, along with the political and social chaos, can bring about the destruction of mankind. This, of course, is predicated on there not being a drastic revolutionary change in mankind and its needs. John sometimes would refer to this as "the Nash point of equilibrium".

John's life had been a remarkable one. He had fought in the Spanish Civil War, had barely escaped execution and had only survived due to the intervention of a woman named Rosa and her daughter, Maria. That enchanted summer we spent together, he taught me a few of his talents. He had the ability to move objects merely by saying so. He told me which words to say, and I followed his instructions. I believe the words were in Hebrew, Arabic, or Aramaic. However, that was not where his real ability lay. Making objects move was just a by-product of...

Here the page ended.

Elijah finished reading and closed his eyes. What conclusions could be reached from what he had read? It seemed at first, that there weren't any. On the other hand, there was one, albeit rather far-fetched, conclusion to be found - although as an academic he tried very hard to avoid wandering off into the realm of speculation. Still, what he now realized was that if, before, he had believed that Norman's interests evolved around ancient manuscripts, it seemed now that other matters held the man's attention as well. Elijah took a short break and returned to work. Having, at first, thought that his working conditions were superb, now, after only four days, he was overwhelmed by a sense of loneliness. He would have preferred to work in his office at the university, where he always had the option of walking into a colleague's office to disturb him.

He came back to the reconstructed page, which he had already cataloged in his mind as the to-do list. He crossed off the line relating to the article he had just read. Any further attempt to obtain the entire article, he felt, would be a waste of time. He looked at the other lines of the reconstructed form, about the Kim Institute, which offered scholarships, and the note to visit someone named Grady. Elijah was not sure why, but somehow he felt it was important to uncover the meaning of these lines.

He reconstructed the note in his mind and was again struck by the fact that the writer had used the *Rashi* script. The first printers of Hebrew books were Italians. Generally, the text of the books used a fancy square Hebrew script. In order to differentiate between the main text and the commentaries on that text, they printed the commentaries in a different and simpler script. The most popular script for these commentaries

81

was a Spanish semi-flowing script in a southern Italian style. The most popular commentator on the Bible and the Talmud was Rabbi Shlomo Yitzchaki, known universally by the acronym of his name, *Rashi*. His was also the first commentary printed. As this script was the archetype for future commentaries, it became known as *Rashi* script. Ironically, we are absolutely sure that *Rashi* never used such a script in his own writings, rather a flowing Ashkenazic script. It is more than likely that, had he been given a document printed in this script, *Rashi* would have found it difficult to read.

Reluctantly, Elijah returned to the text he was supposed to be working on for Norman. He completed his immediate task without coming to any definite conclusion. Here and there, he was unsure about certain words or letters; there were a number of possibilities, and all were legitimate. He wrote down all his uncertainties, explaining where necessary what and why his doubts were, and sent the document out. While faxing the record of the day's work, he checked to see if Norman had replied to him about the previous day's fax, and was disappointed that no response had been received.

The phone rang suddenly. Elijah couldn't make up his mind whether he should answer it or not, but did pick it up in the end.

"Orna?"

"Elijah? Hi, it's Norman."

"Dr. Norman!" Elijah cried out, truly happy to hear Norman's voice again.

"We read what you sent us yesterday, and we've decided to send you to see one of the originals. How do you feel about that?"

"Are you kidding?" replied Elijah jubilantly. "That has to be the ultimate dream of every scholar!"

"Great! We'll pay at our standard rate for all your work, including your flying time."

"Flying? Where to?" Elijah asked. He had been convinced that the original must be locked away in some safe within the confines of the Institute.

"The original is in Hong Kong," Norman told him, and waited for his reaction.

Elijah was stunned. Of all the places in the world for a Hebrew manuscript to be found, why would it be Hong Kong?

"Elijah, are you still there?" he finally heard Norman asking anxiously.

"I'm sorry. I've been thinking about what you just said. As you can imagine, I hadn't expected this. I'll have to ask my wife, of course."

"The entire trip will take you two days. Most of that time will be spent flying, and you will be spending a few hours studying the manuscript itself to better check out those letters about which you were unsure. This manuscript belongs to a Mr.

Wang. In an hour or two you will receive a fax with all the details about the flights, the addresses, and your contacts."

And indeed, before he left for home, Elijah received a fax detailing the entire trip.

At home, he was nervous. How would he break his news to Orna? What would she say? And what should he do if she vetoed the trip? Should he go anyway? And who would take care of the children while he was away? In the end, though, his problem solved itself. After they had finished eating and before he had mustered the courage to broach the subject, the phone rang.

Efrat answered the phone. "Yes, I know you asked for Dr. Shemtov, but which one? My father or my mother?"

"No, my father is not a doctor; my mother is. My father knows how to read things. He is very good at reading things. He can even read handwriting which isn't clear. His job is to teach big children how to read."

No one was surprised when Efrat put down the receiver and called out, "Mommy, it's for you!"

"Yossi from the bank," Orna repeated aloud. "Yes, I can hear you. This is Doctor Shemtov. No, you're not the first one to be confused."

As she listened, her face turned solemn. For an instant, Elijah was concerned, but soon he could see that Orna was smiling again. "Excellent! We'll deal with it. We simply forgot.

You're right - in the next few days. Meanwhile, there's no reason to do anything."

Orna came back to the table, clearly pleased, as she explained what she had heard.

"At first I was concerned, because the bank generally calls us only when our overdraft is getting out of control. For the first time since we've been married, this call was the exact opposite. Yossi from the bank noticed that a couple of days ago a sizeable sum of money was deposited in our account by the Luzzato Institute and listed as 'salary', and he wanted to know what to do with it. It seems, Elijah, that you were actually telling the truth two days ago. Who would have imagined - an expert in languages earning that kind of money?"

"So, are you ready to take a vacation?"

"Yes, Elijah, I'd like that very much. Here in Jerusalem all we get to breathe is the holy air of the Holy Land. I'd like something more prosaic for a change."

"That's just what I wanted to discuss with you," said Elijah, grabbing the bull by the horns. "Some of that money is supposed to cover a trip I need to take on behalf of the Institute. It's just a short trip to Hong Kong, to check something out."

"What do you mean, 'to check something out'? You're hardly anyone's idea of a sleuth. How insidious can a manuscript be? Or is it just that you've managed to nab a free trip? As far as I'm concerned, you can fly to the moon if it's part of your job description."

Elijah felt instant relief. What it all boiled down to was money.

According to the faxed itinerary, the flight would leave Israel Saturday night and arrive in Hong Kong at lunchtime on Sunday. His airline ticket would be waiting for him at Ben Gurion International Airport. In Hong Kong, someone would pick him up and drive him to the New City Hotel, where a room had been reserved for him for two nights. A sentence in the fax, which had been underlined twice for emphasis, stated that everything had been paid for and that he had no need to pay for anything.

Only when he reached the airport, where his airline ticket was indeed waiting for him, did he realize that he was traveling first class. Elijah had flown many times, but this was the first time he was going first class, and he had no idea what to expect. When the flight was called, the flight attendant at the door chided him gently for having waited in the regular departure lounge rather than the VIP lounge. He felt strange entering the first class compartment. The flight attendants all smiled and went out of their way to be helpful. His seat was more like a royal throne than an airplane seat. Next to the seat was a whole array of buttons, with which he could order delicious meals, the latest movies that had not yet been shown in Israel and all kinds of tools and accessories to help him sleep. After finally falling asleep, he awoke shortly before the plane started its descent to Hong Kong airport.

The airport was by far the largest one he had ever seen. He sailed through passport control expecting someone to be waiting for him, but there was no one. Following the signs, he started wheeling his suitcase toward the train that would take him to the city center, where his hotel was located. Suddenly he noticed a taxi driver who seemed very agitated. The man was going from one westerner to another with a crudely hand-lettered sign, and kept receiving negative responses. Elijah glanced at the sign and saw that it was for "Professor Simtov". In a brilliant flash of intuition and using all his language and anthropological skills, he assumed that the man was looking for him. He beckoned to the taxi driver, who ran over, holding a copy of the fax that Elijah had received. Elijah nodded, and the relief on the man's face was palpable. He looked like he had finally reached the Promised Land.

The trip took about forty-five minutes and they finally arrived at a very elegant hotel in the center of Hong Kong.

Elijah's joy knew no bounds when an immaculately dressed man came over and introduced himself as Mr. Lee, assistant manager of the hotel, and insisted on giving Elijah his business card with his personal, hand-written, cell phone number.

"Feel free to call me at any time and about any matter," the assistant manager assured him in English with such a strong Chinese accent as to render it nearly incomprehensible.

As they moved toward the elevators, Elijah saw a woman who looked like a nurse, with an open case that looked as if it contained first-aid equipment. The woman suddenly stopped and stared intently at the woven carpet, like an eagle picking out a wounded dove as its prey. Elijah followed her gaze, and saw a stain on the floor. The woman, who was evidently a maid, came over with a cleaning cloth, and soon the stain was a thing of the past. Elijah noticed that the maid then continued around the lobby, cleaning and removing other stains.

Elijah entered the gold-colored elevator and pressed the floor number - 31. In his room, he was greeted with a large complimentary basket full of fruit and chocolates. Next to it was a short printed note in English, along with a business card. Glancing at the business card, he saw that it was from the same Mr. Lee, again with a handwritten note to the effect that if he needed or wanted anything, all he had to do was call.

His window faced the bay separating Hong Kong from Kowloon. The skyline was filled with one skyscraper after another, reminding him of New York. He tried to open the window to get a better view, but soon realized that the window was not meant to open. A wave of claustrophobia hit him, and he decided to go outside.

Outside, there was a large square, with a statue of an illustrious-looking man in its center. Under the statue was the inscription, "Sir Thomas Jackson". Elijah assumed that Jackson must have been the admiral or general who had liberated Hong Kong from the Chinese, but then, when he read the full inscription, he realized that he had been an English banker who had been the head of the Bank of Hong Kong. Couldn't they find some author, poet, or at least a general to whom to dedicate this monument? How grandiose to erect a statue to a banker, when, in Israel, there isn't even a simple one to commemorate General Allenby's conquest of Jerusalem!

He continued his walk and came to an old church, Saint Patrick's Cathedral, which had been built in the 1840s. Almost all the other buildings in the area had been torn down to make room for skyscrapers, which had sprouted up all over the place in recent years. Not far from the church, he was delighted to find the Ohel Sarah synagogue. It, like the church, looked old. Elijah thought of going in, but was dissuaded from doing so by the fact that it was locked.

Finally, he entered a large shopping mall near the hotel. One of the stores there had all types of unusual electronic devices. He noticed that he was the only westerner there and his presence had evidently caused a stir. There were microphones that could pick up a conversation from afar, miniature cameras that could be attached to a flowerpot or picture, invisible ink for marking one's property, fingerprinting kits, cameras disguised as pens, and many other such esoteric devices. Suddenly, he saw the Chinese or Korean man whom he had seen at the Luzatto Institute, standing near one of the cameras! He wanted to call out to the man, but the shock of seeing him there had left him momentarily breathless. Besides, he had no idea what the man's name was. Pushing his way through the crowd, Elijah saw that the man had made for the door and, before Elijah could reach him, had disappeared. The crowds were so dense that Elijah found it difficult to make out the direction the man had taken. Eventually, he saw him darting out in front, and Elijah ran after him, shouting, "Hey! Luzatto! Wait a second!" The man appeared to slow down for a while, but he did not even look back and continued to walk quickly as if nothing had happened.

"Damn it! All these Chinese look alike! I bet it wasn't him at all," Elijah muttered, as he tried to catch his breath. He must have been experiencing an adrenaline rush, causing him to imagine finding someone familiar so far from home among so many million people in Hong Kong.

Disappointed, Elijah returned to the store with the cameras. He decided he deserved to reward himself after the wild goose chase and started to check out a camera that had caught his attention. It looked like a simple flashlight, and indeed it did cast a light, similar to any other flashlight. There was one difference, though: when you pressed a button on the side, it took a digital photo of whatever the flashlight was shining on. Then, by attaching it to a computer's USB port, the photo could be downloaded to a computer.

"Would this be used for photographing documents?" he asked the salesman.

"Oh, yes! For documents. Especially at night when you don't have much time. Just for that." While the salesman's English was halting, he did manage to make his point clear.

Elijah was curious why the salesman had made a point of talking about taking photographs at night, but listening to how the salesman struggled with English, he decided to forgo any further questions. Credit cards speak all languages, and he charged the camera to his account. Only after he had bought the camera did he notice that the store was called "Spy Master".

A man who came running after him out of the store and said, "Hey, Mister, if you need anything, I can help you. Hwa-Sung, specialist in private investigations. I have to warn you that Europeans who conduct their own private investigations in Hong Kong are making a big mistake. They sometimes even endanger their lives." He took out a business card and handed it to Elijah.

Elijah laughed and told the man he was a university professor and had no need for any such services.

"I'm sorry," said Sung, "I thought you were a colleague. I thought you must be a private investigator, and I was surprised that you would be working in Hong Kong on your own. Everyone knows that the Chinese organized crime syndicates in Hong Kong are very powerful, and have strong ties to the government."

Amused by this encounter, Elijah returned to the hotel and waited for his contact to take him to the place where the document was kept.

The phone rang at 7:30 p.m. Elijah picked up the receiver and was surprised to hear a female voice with a reasonable English accent.

"Prof. Shemtov?" the voice asked hesitantly.

"Yes, how can I help you?" Elijah asked.

"I believe that I am to drive you. Can you make your way to the hotel's rear entrance?"

He agreed, and set out immediately.

Outside the door, a young Chinese woman waited impatiently. Like most westerners, Elijah was unable to estimate the ages of Chinese women. She looked to be somewhere between twenty and thirty, but he was not willing to state so unequivocally.

"Prof. Shemtov? I'm Wang Mei-Ling," the woman introduced herself. "I am to take you to my grandfather, Mr. Wang."

They walked to her car, which he saw was parked quite a distance away. It seemed to him that Mei-Ling was checking to see if anyone was following them. He was perturbed. As they drove, Mei-Ling seemed to be very preoccupied and uncommunicative, and Elijah grew increasingly concerned. They started driving uphill.

After a while, in an attempt to obtain at least a minimal amount of information, Elijah asked, "What does your grandfather do?"

"You don't know?" Mei-Ling said, very surprised. "He's an antiques dealer."

"Oh, I knew that, of course," lied Elijah, "but how does one get rich doing that?"

Mei-Ling laughed. "His grandfather bequeathed him a fortune, but please don't discuss money with him. He is very sensitive and does not want to attract attention to himself. It was only with great reluctance that he agreed to buy his home on Victoria Peak. In Hong Kong, the higher up a building is, the more expensive it is."

They came to an eight-story building. At the entrance stood a doorman, who greeted Mei-Ling effusively. The apartment itself was on the eighth floor. Mr. Wang, dressed in a traditional Chinese robe, opened the door himself and welcomed them in. He bowed down deeply and Elijah, confused, did the same.

Wang led Elijah into the living room. It was quite a large room and had a huge picture window overlooking the bay. In front of the window stood a traditional Chinese writing table with a single manuscript on it, which Elijah saw immediately was in the same script as the photocopy he had been given in Jerusalem. He identified the handwriting as that of Nehemiah of Peki'in, and was exhilarated at the thought of being able to handle the original. Wang pointed to him, but did not speak. Elijah sat down and took out the various items he needed - a magnifying glass, pens, paper for drafts, and the photocopy he had brought from Israel, and he laid them all out on the table. Wang sat down on a couch behind him.

"My grandfather would like you to work on the manuscript now. He has a very high opinion of you, and appreciates that you made a special trip to his home in order to examine the manuscript. My grandfather invites very few people, besides the immediate family, to his home," Mei-Ling pointed out.

"Please tell him that this could take hours. He might prefer to leave me here alone, and to rest while I work."

Mei-Ling answered him without bothering to translate for her grandfather's benefit. "Prof. Shemtov, I believe that my grandfather insists on seeing how you deal with the manuscript and will be terribly hurt if you ask him to leave. The manuscript is worth a fortune, and he hopes to sell it after receiving your assessment of it." Mei-Ling left the room.

Elijah was confused. He nevertheless began to work and soon totally forgot that Wang was sitting behind him. The work was easier than he had anticipated. He became totally engrossed in the letters before him. Suddenly, he found himself jolted, as if he had inadvertently touched a high-voltage wire. Even though in theory the two documents were supposed to be identical in content, on the seventh line of the manuscript the language differed from that of the photocopy with which he had been working. Moreover, this version gave the exact location of the *Even Shetiyah*. "It stands at the heart of the world, on the Temple Mount, fifteen paces north of the Holy of Holies, with an infinite number of roads connected to it." He assumed that this had to be the line which interested Norman, and that if Norman became aware of the change he would be prepared to pay an enormous amount of money for it - in fact whatever sum necessary in order to obtain this copy.

Elijah thought about copying the text, but rejected the idea out of hand. He remembered the flashlight with its built-in camera that he had just purchased and decided to use it. He photographed the text twice, and saw that Wang had gotten up to see what was happening. He smiled at Wang and showed him the flashlight. Wang left the room, and a few moments later returned with Mei-Ling and a stronger flashlight.

"My grandfather is surprised that you need more light," said Mei-Ling. "He specifically set up the table by the window. In any event, this is a more efficient flashlight."

Elijah went back to work. It appeared that whoever had written this document must have been in a hurry, because in most such cases the writer would first etch lines in the parchment to ensure that his writing was straight. Here, though, there were no such lines and the writing was sloppy. When he finished, Elijah looked up with a sigh of relief. Just as he was going to signal to Wang that he had finished, he turned over the parchment and was astounded to find parts of letters there. He rolled up the parchment, and when he had rolled it as tightly as possible, he saw that the parts of letters now joined together, and it was possible to read them. The writing was evidently in Arabic, accompanied by a short sentence in Hebrew, in a rabbinic Sephardi script. The ink used in the writing seemed to indicate that it had been done with a fountain pen-early 20th century, Elijah surmised. It also bore the stamp of the Ohel Sarah synagogue in Hong Kong. There was a signature, but he was only able to make out the word "Batzri".

"I understand that this manuscript comes from the Ohel Sarah synagogue, and once belonged to someone named Batzri," he said half to himself.

When Mei-Ling translated his comment to Mr. Wang, the old man replied and Mei-Ling translated back: "My grandfather is delighted that you know them. He was a young child when the distinguished Mrs. Sassoon died, and... how do you call a Jewish priest?" she asked, somewhat embarrassed.

"A rabbi," Elijah volunteered.

"Yes, of course, right. He remembers Rabbi Batzri to this very day, even though about eighty years have passed. Rabbi Batzri had a full white beard. My grandfather loved to look at him. In those days he used to spend hours in the synagogue with his grandfather, who was the synagogue's caretaker."

"I'm surprised they haven't moved the synagogue elsewhere. It is surrounded by skyscrapers, and no longer belongs in that area."

"That's just the point," said Mei-Ling, in an almost simultaneous translation. Wang interrupted her; he appeared upset. Mei-Ling looked at him, surprised, but Wang recovered immediately and suggested they drink tea in his workroom.

They walked behind him. "He evidently likes you," said Mei-Ling. "Very few people ever enter his workroom. I never dare to go in without being invited to do so."

Over tea in the workroom, Wang told them that there had once been an older wing to the synagogue, but this had been torn down when he was still a child. His grandfather had managed to salvage an old crate of religious items and manuscripts from the demolished wing, including this one. That was evidently the fortune that his grandfather had bequeathed him. As they sat there, Elijah noticed a business card in English on the table. Glancing at it, his curiosity was aroused by the name "Kim" that he saw written on the card. He was reminded of the handwritten list he had found in the Institute, which included a mention of a scholarship fund by the Kim Foundation.

As they were talking, Elijah casually stretched out his hand to the business card and asked, "Is this yours?"

Wang looked at the card, snatched it away, and hid it in his hand. They continued talking, Wang was obviously very upset about the business card.

A few minutes later, Wang exchanged a few words with his granddaughter and she translated to Elijah that her grandfather was tired and it was time to end the meeting. Elijah began to mentally process everything he had seen. The Arabic writing on the manuscript would seem to indicate that it had been brought to Iraq after the Arab conquest. He remembered, of course, that the Mongols had captured Iraq, and assumed that when various Jews had come from Iraq and settled in Hong Kong, they had brought the manuscript with them. Elijah was, of course, deeply interested both in scripts and in conquests. He was aware that neither of these fields would interest Norman,

but was happy that his mission was a success in terms of
Norman's needs. This, then, could have been the reason why he
agreed to Mei-Ling's suggestion that she show him Mrs.
Sassoon's club.

"You will be able to enjoy a relaxing massage," she told
him.

"Me? A massage? Never!" He was quite convinced that
any contact with a strange woman in the Orient was sure to
leave him infected with one or other infectious disease.

They returned to the bustling city center, where the neon
signs and skyscrapers reminded him of Manhattan. After they
had reached the entrance to Elijah's hotel and parked the car, he
stopped suddenly and did a double turn; a small sign had caught
his attention: "Madame Rachel Sassoon, 1835-1921." The
woman's name appeared in both English and Hebrew letters.

"Mrs. Sassoon is a madam?" Elijah asked Mei-Ling,
surprised. Only now did he realize that Madame Sassoon's
"club" was what, in the west, would be referred to as a brothel.

"The fabulously wealthy and famous Sassoon family
produced philanthropists, distinguished rabbis, noted
businessmen, and there is also Rachel Sassoon, who moved to
Hong Kong. Members of the Sassoon family lived in Iraq since
the fall of the First Temple, in 586 B.C.E.," Mei-Ling told him.

Elijah was not sure how Mei-Ling had been able to
choose the correct words, but she had managed to bring up the

conquest of Jerusalem by the Babylonians. And this, for Elijah, set the wheels in motion.

The Fourth Sphere

When The Babylonian Conquered Jerusalem

In the year 586 B.C.E., the Babylonians conquered Jerusalem. The previous winter they had laid siege to the city, and a year and a half later the walls were breached and the city vanquished. The conquest generated a wave of panic throughout the nations of the region, ranging from the kings of Aram and the inhabitants of Edom, through to Moab, Ammon, and the remaining Philistines. Then, as now, there was a prevailing belief that it was not possible to take Jerusalem from the Jews. None of the kings of the surrounding lands had even imagined that an enemy could as much as set foot in Jerusalem, not to mention actually conquering it. Nebuchadnezzar utterly destroyed the earlier conception.

King Zedekiah, a man of weak character who had allowed himself to be led by his ministers and his wives when he should have been resolute, attempted to flee. Like all the rebels of Judea and the kings of Jerusalem who had needed to flee,

Zedekiah sought sanctuary in the east, in the Judean desert. However, Zedekiah was no David, and did not even get as far as the desolate stretches where he might have found refuge. In the Jericho area, the Chaldean army pursued him and his army fled, leaving him to be captured by the Babylonians. Zedekiah was hauled in chains to the Babylonian king. There, the king forced him to witness his two sons being killed before his eyes, after which he was blinded in both eyes. Blind, he was dragged to Babylon, where he was thrown into a pit, a lesson to all the other kings of the region on the futility of trying to resist Babylon, and a powerful disincentive to trying to throw off the Babylonian yoke.

Not content with a mere military victory, the Babylonian king sent Nevuzadran, the captain of the bodyguards, to Jerusalem to utterly crush any possibility of a revolt. Nevuzadran burned down the Temple, the royal palace, and every large and important building in the city. The Babylonian army tore down the outer, protecting wall of the city, destroyed all other remaining houses, and plundered whatever it could lay its hands on.

Even that was not enough for Nebuchadnezzar. In order to prevent an alternative leadership from arising, he forced many of the leading figures into exile in Babylon. These included the royal officials, army officers, metalworkers, weapon makers, scribes and priests, and all military personnel.

This exile of the elite was the second one imposed on the country within a short period of time. About ten years earlier, there had been an abortive attempt at revolt led by King Jehoiachim, who died in the siege of Jerusalem. The previous revolt had ended with the surrender of the king's son, also called Jehoiachin, and was followed by the exile to Babylon of Jehoiachin, his officials and military officers. The revolt by Zedekiah ended Jerusalem's role as the spiritual and governmental center of Judea.

The cultural results of the Babylonian invasion were catastrophic. Considered an integral part of the structure of the country, the prophecy came to an end and all subsequent attempts to resurrect it ended in failure. Because of the fact that the prophecy ended over 2500 years ago, we are not quite sure of the type of role it played at the time.

Because of the vicissitudes of the time, the literacy rate plummeted, and many books which had been handed down for generations simply disappeared. There are many and varied stories and legends regarding the fate of the Ark of the Covenant, which all sources agree was located in the First Temple and which seems to have simply disappeared in some inexplicable fashion. This ark contained the tablets received by Moses at Sinai, together with various scrolls whose content we cannot even begin to surmise. The ark survived all the wanderings of the Israelites in the desert, the reigns of the different judges, capture by the Philistines and being transported from one city to another, as well as the various revolts and alien strains of worship that had coursed through the land at different times. And now it had suddenly disappeared, leaving no hint in the Scriptures as to where it was taken. Both the Bible and the Babylonian chronicle of the Babylonian victory list the enormous quantities of the spoils taken by Babylon, including an itemized record of instruments, large and small, used in the Temple, some whose purpose we do not even understand. For some reason, though, the Ark of the Covenant simply does not appear in either list. Some people surmise that, fearing for the future, King Josiah hid it. According to this view, therefore, the Ark is still to be found somewhere on the Temple Mount. The more widely accepted explanation is that the Ark, being made primarily of wood, was burned in the great fire that destroyed the Temple, and that purely by chance this was not listed in the Bible. Its disappearance, though, was the final blow to the history of the First Temple.

This Babylonian exile also brought about the birth of a new cultural center for the Jews and ultimately competed with Jerusalem and Judea for supremacy in the spiritual realm of the Jewish people. Some of the greatest works in Jewish thought and law originated in Babylon, beginning with the prophecy of Ezekiel ben Buzi, who prophesied on the Kebar River in southern Babylon, through to the Babylonian Talmud and the Jewish law rulings of the Geonim, the preeminent Jewish spiritual leaders in the generations following the Talmud.

"How could a member of such an illustrious family turn out to be so unsavory a character?" Elijah asked. Mei-Ling had a ready answer, and defended Madame Sassoon to the fullest.

"For many years Madame Sassoon worked as the assistant of the previous Madame. When the previous Madame died at a ripe old age, Madame Sassoon naturally inherited the position from her. There is universal agreement about her wonderful business acumen, with which she transformed brothel into the most lavish one in Hong Kong, if not the entire East. In her old age, she expanded into other lines of work, by taking advantage of all the contacts she had made over the years; she eventually became one of the richest people in Hong Kong." Turning to Elijah, she suggested, "Let's go in and take a look."

Disconcerted by the very thought, Elijah launched a defensive attack: "I don't suppose I can expect any more from a city that erects statues to bankers rather than to generals." His scorn was quite transparent.

"Oh, don't be so high and mighty," said Mei-Ling. 'In her last years, the rabbis here also were willing to accept Madame Sassoon's money. Not surprisingly, she was not particularly close to the Jewish community, and there was a mutual distance between them."

"I would have expected as much," said Elijah drily.

Mei-Ling continued. "In her old age, when she had become queen of the local nightlife, it was impossible to ignore her. But credit where credit is due: she bore no grudge against the local rabbis and she used her extensive list of contacts to help many people overcome all types of bureaucratic and other obstacles. Would you like to meet her granddaughter, Lynne Sassoon?"

Given Elijah's fascination with Jewish history, Mei-Ling had pushed just the right button in arousing his curiosity about a member of the Sassoon family, and he decided, despite his misgivings, to go in. Never in his wildest dreams, could he have imagined what he would see upon entering the building, but the one thing he noticed immediately was that whatever was there had no connection whatsoever to Judaism. Behind a massive glass window sat twenty-five to thirty women in three groups. They were dressed like members of a beauty pageant, each with a diagonal sash upon which was printed a number. Clients were evidently required to "order" them by that number. They all wore high-heeled shoes and their bare legs were stretched out in front of them. As to what they wore underneath their sashes, let us say that whatever it was would barely have excluded them from a nudist beach. Elijah was dumbstruck by what he saw, and was literally speechless for quite a few minutes. After this assault on his vision, the next attack was on his hearing. He had assumed at first that the glass was a one-way mirror, allowing the men to see and pick out the woman of their choice, but preventing the women from seeing the men making their selection by number. It seemed so inhuman and depraved!

That illusion, too, was shattered, when he started to hear various voices calling out from beyond the glass, at first individually, but then in unison, "Madame, Madame, Madame, Madame." The women were all trying to outdo each other in attracting Mei-Ling's attention, each of them wanting to be the object of selection. The women clearly assumed that Elijah and Mei-Ling were a couple, which meant, of course, that they should appeal to the wife. Elijah was glued to the spot and totally unable to look at any one of the women. The only association to come to mind was when, as a third grader, his class had visited a turkey farm. The teacher had told the class that these were highly educated turkeys. To prove her point, she had yelled to the turkeys, "In which Hebrew month is the festival of Purim?" The turkeys had all gobbled back with what one might - by a very long stretch of the imagination - construe to be the word "*Adar.*"

Eventually Mei-Ling took pity on the poor man and said to him softly, "Dr. Shemtov, please come with me." Even though he felt as if his legs had turned to lead, he somehow managed to drag himself behind her.

He was brought into a large and well-lit office, which looked no different from offices of countless businesses throughout the world, totally sterile and utilitarian. An office is an office regardless of what business it represents, he thought to himself.

Seated behind a desk, Lynne Sassoon looked like one of a number of variations of Oriental women and quite unlike any of the Iraqi Jewish women of Elijah's acquaintance in Israel. He assumed she must be of mixed parentage. She smiled and was about to greet Elijah when, as he looked around the room, his eyes fell on an open door which led to a conference room; in the conference room, four men sat talking. While he could not hear what they were saying, one thing was clear: the man facing him was the Chinese or Korean man he had met at the Luzzato Institute. This time, there was no doubt about it! Elijah could not take his eyes off him. He was vaguely aware of Lynne addressing him, but couldn't concentrate enough to hear what she was saying. For all he knew, she could be listing the various types of massage and other "services" on offer by the establishment. He was very keen to ask her about her ancestry and hoped to be able to trace it as far back as possible, even to the time when Babylon - now Iraq - was the spiritual center of the Jewish people.

Just then, from behind, two men dressed in black, with black neckties, entered the room and took up positions behind Elijah. They had entered so silently that Elijah was not even aware of their presence. However, Lynne's evident confusion made it clear to Elijah that something must have happened. Before he had managed to react, the Chinese or Korean man burst into the room with a gun in his hand, and fired. At first, Elijah thought the gun had been aimed at him, but when he heard what sounded like the angry growl of a hungry leopard behind him, he turned around and saw one of the two men falling down bleeding, while the other drew his gun and managed to shoot the Luzatto Institute man in the chest. Even in the throes of death, the Chinese or Korean man motioned to Elijah to run into the inner rooms of the brothel. One of the men who had been sitting in the conference room followed him. Without thinking consciously about what he was doing, Elijah ran in the direction he was shown, followed by Lynne Sassoon and Mei-Ling. He lost the man who was in front of him at a bend, and started running even faster.

Totally lost, he wandered into a room where a very portly westerner, completely covered with lather, was being mounted by a slim young woman, who was sliding all over him. The excessive heat, the fact that the Oriental man who had evidently been shot was the one he had seen in Israel, as well as all the things he had seen since entering the building, left him utterly disoriented, to the extent that he became dizzy and saw black circles dancing before his eyes. He rushed out of the room and kept running until he was brought to a halt by stumbling over a body lying on the floor. He had evidently come full circle

110

The Kabbalistic Murder Code

and was again in Lynne's office. He fell on top of the Chinese man, who was bleeding profusely from his wounds.

"Luzatto!" screamed Elijah, his face almost touching that of the mortally wounded man. The man was clearly breathing his last breath. Elijah tried to stand up, but kept toppling over. Suddenly he felt an outstretched hand pulling him. It was the one of the men he had seen earlier in Lynne's office.

"Hurry! Come with me! You are in great danger!"

The man grabbed Elijah's jacket and dragged him into a small room, occupied by a woman. Throwing the woman out of the room and sending her to the manager, he grabbed a container and shook it before spraying Elijah from head to toe with a white foamy substance, making it impossible to identify him.

"What the hell is going on?" Elijah shouted, using the most vulgar language he could muster.

"Mister, they wanted to kill you. Kim tried to protect you, and paid for it with his life."

"Who is Kim? Is he the man I met in Israel?"

"Yes, he was sent to protect you."

"To protect me from whom?"

"From the White Lotus gang."

"And who are these 'White Lotus' guys anyway? What on earth would they want from me?" The questions kept tumbling out.

"They are what you would call the Chinese Mafia."

"But why would the Chinese Mafia care about me? Orna is never going to believe this!"

"They believe that you bought the manuscript for your wealthy employer, and decided to take you hostage so as to blackmail him."

It all began to sink in, although Elijah was still not quite sure what was really happening. "So how much could I possibly be worth to him?" he asked.

"To him, you are not worth a thing. He is interested only in the manuscript. Kim loved that manuscript, and was willing to forfeit his life to protect it. We'll hide out for a while and then we'll take you to a safe house. There is no way we can go back to your hotel, because I'm sure they're there waiting for you."

"What will happen to Kim? I think he's still alive."

"There's nothing we can do about him. His lungs are filling up with blood so fast that he will be dead by the time we get him to a hospital."

Elijah remained frozen in place, with the foam all over him. He was afraid even to breathe.

Finally, at 2:00 am, Lynne came in and said to him, "We can take you now. You will be going to Batzri."

They left by a little-used side entrance. He never saw Mei-Ling again. They entered a small black car which had been waiting for them, and the driver took them, following a circuitous route with many detours, to a house at the edge of the city.

A smiling, cheerful man who looked surprisingly like an old Yemenite that Elijah knew in the Israeli town of Rosh Ha'ayin, opened the door. The man appeared to be very alert, and in spite of the late hour he acted as if he had been anticipating visitors.

"I'm so pleased to meet you," said the man, holding out his hand. Elijah automatically shook the outstretched hand.

"I'm Rabbi Solomon Batzri," the man introduced himself. Elijah had heard the name Batzri at Mr. Wang's home, but had no way of knowing if this was the same man, or a descendant. Wang had described the other Rabbi Batzri as an old man many decades earlier, and he was no doubt dead by now.

"It's a pleasure. I'm Elijah," he replied mechanically. He was totally numb after all he had gone through that night.

"Here you can feel totally secure. Please take a seat. Would you like clothes that are not quite so wet?"

"No, no, I'm fine," replied Elijah, and he realized that this answer guaranteed him lower back pain for weeks to come. "Could you possibly explain to me what is happening here?"

"Yes, I can. I am the grandson of Rabbi Judah Batzri, who was a friend of Madame Rachel Sassoon. When Lynne contacted me an hour ago to host you in my home, I was more than delighted that I could be of service. In order for you to understand why you're being hunted and how much money is involved, let me tell you a little about my grandfather and Lynne's grandmother.

"In spite of my grandfather's name, which would seem to imply that his family hailed from Batzra in Iraq, he was actually of Yemenite origin. There are those who say that my grandfather's father did not leave his home voluntarily, but was forced to do so after having been excommunicated by the noted rabbi, Rabbi Joseph David HayyimAzulai, who was the author of the *Ben Ish Chai* series. He appears to have been excommunicated for teaching Kabbalah to those who were unworthy of learning it. According to the letter of excommunication, he had no part in the people of Israel or in the city of Jerusalem. He was forbidden – as were the next three generations succeeding him - to set foot in Jerusalem. My grandfather was of the first generation to which this edict did not apply. He lived in Palestine in abject poverty, and became a friend of the Kabbalist Rabbi David Moreno, who took him under his wing. My grandfather had wealthy relatives here in the East, and even though the news that he was seriously involved in Kabbalah greatly disturbed them, they invited him to move here so he would be able to spend his last days in comfort. In order for him not to feel that he was living off charity, he was put in charge of the '*Genizah*', the old book repository, and it was there that he met Madame Sassoon."

"I understand," said Elijah, all the while understanding absolutely nothing at all. If anything, the only detail he did understand was that the more time elapsed, the more deeply involved he was becoming - and he saw no way he could extricate himself from the mess he was in.

"My grandfather was always considered to be something of a strange bird and he kept to himself. Here, too, rumors were rife with regard to his study of the Kabbalah and that made people wary. Once, when I was small, I heard him repeating a series of Hebrew words and verses, like a mantra, and I could see that he was in ecstasy. I was too young to understand what he was doing, and if anything, I was scared. I finally mustered the courage to ask him what he was doing. He told me that he was trying to recall a child of my age, the son of David Moreno, who had disappeared or been kidnapped. His dealings and meetings with Madame Sassoon were strange and evoked all kinds of questions. However, because of their advanced ages and public status, no one said a word. It was Madame Sassoon

115

who supported him in his old age, and it was she who insisted on being the one to organize his funeral service and choice of headstone. It was she, too, who executed his will, which was not a difficult thing to do, considering that he owned almost nothing. Madame Sassoon continued to have an interest in Judaism even after my grandfather's death and, rumor has it, she even hired private tutors to teach her Judaism and mathematics. She died about three years after he did. Since her only daughter had severed all ties with her and the rest of her family had not been especially fond of her during her lifetime, the Hong Kong Jewish community was not surprised to learn, when her will was read, that she had left the brothel to her daughter, while the rest of her estate, which included real estate, stores, shares and a great deal of money, was to be used for the construction of the Third Temple in Jerusalem, no more, no less. The Jewish community in Jerusalem was appointed to oversee this.

"Based on British law, which states that where the provisions of a will cannot be enforced as such, the estate is then apportioned for similar aims, the judges in Hong Kong ruled that since, at present, there is no way for the Third Temple to be built, in the interim the interest was to be used for religious and charitable purposes. Note the judges' use of the phrase 'in the interim'. In other words, the capital remains available for if and when the Third Temple is built."

"And where is the capital at present?"

"There was no simple answer to this when it was in probate. The judges ruled that the capital be transferred to the Jewish community of Jerusalem. But which one? The Sephardi or the Ashkenazi? There was an all-out battle between the two groups. The Sephardic community claimed that since Madame Sassoon came from a distinguished Iraqi family - and the Iraqi Jews are all Sephardi - the money should go to them. The Ashkenazi Jews claimed that since all Jews are brothers, the money should be divided equally between the two communities. During her lifetime, she had been shunned by all, but after her death people suddenly declared themselves her best friends. This dispute dragged on for years, and both sides periodically sent representatives to Hong Kong – their traveling expenses to be deducted from the inheritance once the claims had been settled. In the end, it was decided that the Sephardic community would receive 70% of the interest and the Ashkenazi would receive 30%."

"While all of this is fascinating," said Elijah - his scholarly patience wearing dangerously thin - "how does Norman fit into the picture?"

"The heads of the Chinese crime syndicates, which are very much a part of Hong Kong as well, heard about the manuscripts which had somehow or other found their way here. These manuscripts are worth a fortune. My grandfather and Mr.

Wang's father once found an old crate full of manuscripts. You and Kim were merely messengers. Since your arrival, the situation has become too dangerous for you to remain here and finish your work."

"One second, please. You're under a totally mistaken impression. I'm not a businessman and don't have the authority to negotiate with Mr. Wang or with anyone else. I'm a scholar of manuscripts, and was merely sent here to examine the manuscript and report my findings to Norman."

"Indeed? And what conclusion have you reached?"

"The manuscript is a forgery," Elijah lied.

"I knew it! I knew it! I've always known that the real manuscript was in my grandfather's possession. Wang found a number of valuable manuscripts in the crate, but my grandfather had one manuscript of his own. He gave it to Rachel Sassoon for safekeeping. This manuscript had never been in the crate and was handed down in our family for four generations until it was given to my grandfather. My father told me it had been stored inside a silver sphere to keep it out of the hands of the fanatical Khalif Omar, the same khalif who had burned down the library in Alexandria. My father also told me that he had seen the place where Rachel and my grandfather had hidden the silver sphere, and he spelled out to me exactly where it is to be found. For years I thought it was nothing but a legend, and when I became a rabbi I believed it inappropriate for me to delve into the Kabbalah. And of course, as a rabbi, I could hardly go to the brothel and look for the silver sphere. It is possible that I am the only one alive today who knows where they hid the ball."

"And I'm the only person in the world who can tell you if the manuscript is genuine or not," responded Elijah, throwing out the bait.

"Let me call Lynne. We can drive there if it's not too dangerous."

"Back to the brothel?" said Elijah nervously. He knew about the criminals and their rule of always returning to the scene of the crime; and he was terrified of going back there. All he wanted was to head for the airport and take the 7:00 am flight out of town.

At the brothel the phone rang and rang, but no one answered.

"The place is obviously closed. There is no one there," Rabbi Batzri said sorrowfully. He was consumed with the desire to get his hands on that manuscript, but of course it was only worth the effort if the manuscript did not turn out to be a forgery.

"I think I'll take a cab to the airport," proclaimed Elijah. "I'm so tired I'm afraid that if I fall asleep now I won't get up in time for the flight. I might as well go to the First Class lounge and sleep there."

"I'll go with you," said Rabbi Batzri, even though it was close to 4:00 am. He called a taxi service and ten minutes later a cab arrived. Rabbi Batzri mumbled something in Chinese. Elijah had no idea what he said, but he noticed that they stopped a few minutes later at the rear door of the brothel.

"I'll be right back," said the rabbi, as he swiftly climbed up the fire escape leading to the roof of the building. He came back down a few minutes later; he was obviously tense. The veins in his neck protruded angrily, and he was breathing deeply but unevenly. He had a package with him. In spite of the coolness of the night, he was perspiring. He ordered the driver to set off.

Elijah understood that there must be some major problem, but had enough sense not to engage Rabbi Batzri in any conversation. When they reached the airport, Rabbi Batzri paid the driver and got out of the cab with Elijah.

"I have the equipment to examine the manuscript with me," said Elijah quietly.

Batzri responded immediately. "You have it with you? As you saw, I have my grandfather's manuscript, and would like you to examine it. I'm willing to pay you whatever you ask."

"You saved my life tonight. I wouldn't dream of asking you to pay. It's the least I can do for you." Elijah knew that, if anything, he himself was willing to pay as much as was demanded just for the chance to examine the manuscript.

"Let's go into the men's lavatories. You can go into one of the stalls, while I stand guard outside."

"Are you sure it's safe here? I'd hate to be caught with my pants down."

"While we're in the airport we're totally safe. That's why I jumped at the opportunity of accompanying you here. The members of the Chinese Mafia are known to the local security forces. They do not find it easy to enter the airport."

Once inside the stall, with the manuscript in his hands, Elijah forgot about the world outside. He was snug in his own little world. He peeled off the white cloth in which the manuscript had been wrapped. Fighting the manuscript's tendency to curl itself up, he was able to spread it out before him. Yes, this had definitely been written by Nehemiah of Peki'in. He knew this script well by now and, to him, it was like receiving a letter from the past. He began to examine the script line by line. The first few lines were identical to those of the photocopy he had received at the institute and to the copy in Mr. Wang's possession. Here again, there was a change in the seventh line! Elijah began to understand what was involved: each copy provided another hint. Elijah had no idea what it was, though, as he had not been educated on the Kabbalah. Up to now, there had been something about the *Even Shetiyah*. And there was an allusion to the heart of the world and to the spring. Here, though, the text was totally different.

By now, he was convinced that each of the seven copies contained a different hint, and that was why it was vital for Norman to acquire all of them. Only by obtaining all seven copies and comparing the seventh line of each could a full picture emerge. Now he understood why Norman was willing to pay any amount of money to obtain all seven manuscripts! Elijah photographed the manuscript, making sure to focus on the seventh line, and then rolled it up, wrapped it carefully in its cloth, and came out. Rabbi Batzri was waiting anxiously.

"It's genuine!" ruled Elijah, and Rabbi Batzri almost kissed him in gratitude.

"I suggest that you offer it for sale to Norman," said Elijah, as he handed the rabbi Norman's business card.

Only once the plane had taken off and was safely in the air, was Elijah able to unwind a little. Now he was free to think back to the to-do list which he had found in the desk drawer. It seemed that days before Kim died, whoever had written the note had mentioned the need to take care of the Kim Foundation. That was the end of his tranquility!

The Fifth Sphere

When The Arabs Conquered Jerusalem

In 638 C.E., which is the year 17 of the Hegira, the Arabs
conquered Jerusalem, which was still called Aelia Capitolina. It
was a bloodless conquest, in which Patriarch Sophronius
surrendered without a fight. Sophronius, though, was only
willing to surrender to the head of the Muslims, Khalif Omar
ibn al-Khattab. Omar had arrived in Jerusalem from Syria,
riding into Jerusalem on a camel and dressed simply in a
camel's hair garment, to show the modesty of a devout Muslim.
According to Christian history, on the other hand, the garments
he was wearing were filthy.

In consultation with a Yemenite Jew who had converted
to Islam, Ka'ab al-Akhbar, the khalif decided to build a prayer
hall on the Temple Mount itself. Ka'ab asked that it be built to
the north of the Even Shetiyah - so that when the Muslims
prayed in the direction of Mecca they would be facing the Even

Shetiyah. After all, by tradition, that is the Foundation Stone of the entire world and it is from it that the world was formed. Thus, when Muslims bowed down in prayer they would be bowing down to the Temple Mount, where the Second Temple had stood. Omar was opposed to this idea, and mockingly claimed that Ka'ab was still thinking like a Jew.

In Omar's days, Jerusalem's lot improved tremendously. Omar destroyed nothing. He even permitted seventy Jewish families from Tiberias to settle in Jerusalem when they wished to, a decision which was praised by the Jews and condemned by the Christians.

The fate of Alexandria was different. Its library contained 700,000 books, or more properly, scrolls, for in those days there was no such thing as bound books with writing on both sides of the page. By all accounts, this was the largest, most comprehensive, and most famous library in the ancient world. Anyone who came to Alexandria was searched. If it was found that he had a scroll with him that did not exist in the library, it was confiscated and copied. The copy would be given to the owner, while the original would become part of the library. Most of the books in the library were in Greek, but there were books in other languages as well. The library did not merely collect books - the first translation of the Bible was undertaken under the patronage of the library's wardens. The library also conducted many studies. One of its librarians was the first person to attempt to establish the size of the earth. Even though his calculations were wrong, they were relied upon by Christopher Columbus when he tried to persuade the King of Spain to underwrite his voyage. The library collected scrolls for about a thousand years, from Ptolemy I through the Roman governors and then the Byzantines.

Omar, who was evidently illiterate, was not impressed: "If whatever is found in these books is in the holy Koran, there is no need for them, and all we need is the Koran. If what is found in them is not in the holy Koran, there is certainly no need for them. In any event, the scrolls are to be burned."

His orders were heeded and executed almost in full. For six months, hundreds of bathhouses in Alexandria were heated by the scrolls, which were used as fuel for their ovens. These included scrolls on mathematics and medicine, maps and drawings, letters and poetry. Hundreds of thousands of items went up in smoke. A thousand years of man's quest for knowledge were destroyed in this unmitigated act of vandalism. However, the one minor consolation was that, as is so often true with any bureaucracy, the bureaucracy here was not overly efficient. Not everything went up in flames. A number of scrolls somehow survived the conflagration. For reasons unknown to us, one of the copies of the present scroll was not destroyed and was hidden in a silver sphere. The silver sphere was transported to Damascus, along with other valuables, and was

*added to the treasury of the Ummayah Khalifate, which then
ruled the city.*

*The Ummayah Khalifate did not rule there for long. In
747 C.E., a freed Persian slave revolted against the khalif and
installed his own family, the Abassids, as rulers.*

*The first Abassid ruler carried out a number of standard
Middle Eastern practices to assure his rule. First, he had the
freed Persian slave and a number of other radicals executed.
Second, he strengthened his army, and third, he proclaimed
Baghdad his new capital and transferred all the treasures he
had looted from his predecessors to that city. Included in this
was the silver sphere, which had been taken from the treasury
in Damascus.*

*The khalifates were replaced by independent rulers, but
Baghdad remained the cultural and social center of the entire
Middle East. In its days of glory the population of Baghdad was
in the millions, and it was known for its fabulous wealth. One of
the khalifs had no fewer than four thousand concubines, while
another had a carpet made which measured four hundred
meters on each side, and was woven with gold, silver, and silk
threads and embedded with rubies and diamonds. It was this
legendary city that was ruled by Harun al-Rashid, he of the
1001 nights.*

*Baghdad's luster was destroyed in a single month. In the
1250s, the Mongol tribes united under Hulagu Khan, grandson*

of Genghis Khan. The bearded, long-haired Mongol warriors rampaged through what is now Iran, moving westward. Within a few months they had crossed rivers and trampled, smashed and destroyed anyone who tried to impede their progress. Even the Assassins, in their mountain strongholds, were unable to hold them back. In January 1258, the Mongols advanced on Baghdad. The last khalif begged for fair terms of surrender or for mercy, but his request was rejected out of hand by the Mongols. On February 20, the city was taken by storm. It was burned to the ground, and all its wealth plundered. The emir and his entire family were executed. All the inhabitants of the city, numbering about a million at the time, were either slaughtered or sold into slavery. The fabled palaces were looted, the libraries destroyed, and all the houses torched. Whatever Omar had done to the library in Alexandria was amply repaid by what the Mongols did to Baghdad.

Among all the booty was the silver sphere. It was brought to Beijing, where Kublai Khan had established his new capital. Together with silver jewelry, gold platters, and dazzling silk paintings, the globe remained in its new abode for more than 700 years. Untouched, it survived rulers and dynasties. At first it was the Mongol dynasty, followed by the Ming and finally the Manchurian. In the Forbidden City, the beautiful sphere intrigued weak emperors, plotting eunuchs, and sly women of the court. However, its tranquility eventually came to an end.

In the days of Emperor Pu-Yi, the last emperor of China, many items of the royal palace vanished in a mysterious fashion. Often they disappeared along with the people who had been entrusted to guard them. The silver sphere somehow found its way to Hong Kong, where it was to be melted down for its silver content. However, the silversmith realized that it was hollow, and somehow, miraculously, the scroll was found before the sphere was placed in the furnace. The silversmith had a Jewish friend who bought the manuscript for a princely sum, and thus the scroll wound up in the colony's Sephardic synagogue.

Elijah slept through most of the flight back to Israel, in spite of attempts on the part of the cabin crew to ply him with all the goodies they had on hand for their privileged first class passengers. He arrived home, smiled wanly at his wife and daughters, dutifully handed over the gifts he had bought at Israel's Ben-Gurion Airport before taking off for Hong Kong, and fell asleep for another day and a half.

He awoke at 3:00 am and decided to make himself a cup of tea and read about the different conquests of Jerusalem. This time, his choice of a conquest was not random. In order to better understand what had happened to the scroll he needed to learn more about Khalif Omar; it was his way of trying to come to terms with the fact that he had survived an attempt on his life. He still believed, naively, that in books he would find the answers to all the important questions in his life. He pulled out one volume about conquests, and before settling down to read, sent an email to Mei-Ling with a short question: "What can you tell me about Kim?" He eagerly awaited her answer.

He knew little about Omar's conquests, because basically, Jerusalem had enjoyed a period of calm during Omar's time. He eventually got around to pouring the hot water over the teabag but forgot to take out the teabag before drinking. When he finally did try to remove the teabag, only the label came out, while the teabag itself settled at the bottom of the cup. However, so preoccupied was he that he also forgot to take out the spoon.

He remembered the fate of the library in Alexandria and thanked the god of bureaucracy, through whose divine intervention, together with that of weary officials and corrupt military men who were not above accepting bribes, the scroll had survived. Elijah also found a reference in a scientific work to the silver sphere. He even found a photograph of it, before the silversmith in China had mangled it in preparation for the furnace. And he recalled with satisfaction the privilege of handling the scroll that had been contained in the ball. Meanwhile, he absent-mindedly reached for the teacup, picked it up, and the spoon hit him straight in the eye. Instinctively he recoiled, and in the process the tea splashed all over the book he had been reading. As the teabag had remained in the cup all along, the tea was very strong, and he was afraid that the dark stain now spreading over the page he had been reading would make it illegible.

Elijah ran to the kitchen, making such a din in the process that Orna cried out anxiously. He returned with a towel to sop up the tea and enable him to read the part of the page that concerned him. The sphere itself depicted the world and the stars around it, and had traveled from Alexandria to Baghdad. It had remained there until the Mongol hordes ransacked the city and carried off all its wealth. It did not require a great historian to know that the devastation of Baghdad was so great in that single month that the city has simply never recovered from it, even though more than 700 years have elapsed since that time.

Elijah closed his eyes and dozed off. He dreamed he had sprouted wings and was flying in the general direction of Beijing. Mei-Ling joined him as he flew over Hong Kong, but they suddenly found themselves flying over Jerusalem. "Why Jerusalem?" he asked himself. He looked down upon the Temple Mount, as Mei-Ling flew alongside him. Mei-Ling suddenly shoved him, and he plummeted down to the ground.

He awoke in a cold sweat and got up feeling edgy; impatiently he waited for the sun to rise, so he could go to the Institute and demand an explanation. No one had told him that the large sums of money flowing into his bank account were meant to cover the seriously great risk to his life involved in taking this job. No one had offered him the option of deciding whether to sacrifice his life so that Orna and the girls could live comfortably for the rest of theirs.

It was 5:00 am, still too early to go to the Institute, and even if he did go - and of course he had the keys to let himself in - he would find no-one there. He checked his email and found Mei-Ling's reply to his letter. She wrote: "Kim Su-Yan was born in South Korea. His mother was a teacher and a devout Buddhist, while his father was a bodybuilding instructor. His childhood was spent in army camps in communist North Korea.

131

Those who knew him as a child remembered how, at the tender age of eight, he had fought full-grown soldiers with the tenacity and ferocity of a pit bull. He studied various styles of martial arts, and for twenty years had been involved in learning and teaching both ancient and modern methods of martial arts, an activity at which he spent twelve hours a day. He specialized in the flying kicks of Tae-Kwan-Do, the long throws in Judo, the twisting of the hands in Jiu-jitsu, the falls and rolls of Aikido, the head butting of Korean Pachigi, and others that I cannot even remember.

"The soldiers among whom he had grown up with had taught him to use various kinds of personal weapons, from the nunchaku sticks with their two wooden staffs joined by a chain, to modern-day police batons. His father had tried to temper Kim's aggressive nature, forcing him to learn techniques that emphasized the more spiritual aspects of life. Thus he learned the techniques of the monks of Shaolin, which were based on the movements of animals in nature, the breathing exercises of the Yoga masters, and the exercises of the Tai-Chi elders."

"Dear Mei-Ling," he wrote back, "That was very impressive indeed. You have no idea how shaken up I am by what occurred, and now that I read about Kim's background, I really mourn his loss keenly. Why was he the one to die?"

It took a mere seven minutes for Mei-Ling to answer him.

Filipinos, and all other Asians. They had not the slightest suspicion that the bespectacled Japanese gentleman in a business suit and tie was the same one who had physically beaten them in hundreds of protest rallies and demonstrations. His remarkable escape, given the massive manhunt that had been launched to catch him, merely added to his legend.

"However, after the freedom to which he had become accustomed in Teheran, Kim found it impossible to adjust to military life in Korea. He moved to Los Angeles and opened a martial arts academy under the traditional name of Dojo. His school became known because of the great number of injuries suffered by his students. His students remember the frequent wail of ambulance sirens, more than once a night. To receive a black belt, the initiate had to snap four blocks of wood with his feet, three with his hands, and two with his head. He had to jump from a ladder to the ground and fall on his back, with only his feet and hands absorbing the fall. In spite of his extreme demands - and probably even to a certain extent because of them - Kim won the adulation of his students. The feeling was that for anyone who had received a black belt from Kim's Dojo, nothing in the world could present a greater challenge and everything else could only be much easier. If you're interested in more details, you can check out a US site about karate and the martial arts, where you can read all about him. Write me. In friendship, Mei-Ling."

Elijah thanked her and tried various search engines until he found the site to which Mei-Ling referred. One of the articles on Kim was very interesting, and Elijah printed it out.

"Kim Su-Yan - A Legend in his Time," he read.

"From his balcony on the third floor of an apartment block in Los Angeles, Kim often leaps into the adjoining swimming pool. We should stress the word 'leaps' rather than 'dives,' because the pool is not directly adjacent to the building. When he leaps, he must move off a number of feet from his building so that he can land in the pool. Otherwise, he would fall to his death on the concrete deck surrounding the pool.

"Kim Su-Yan is an honest man with principles. He attributes this to the pedantic upbringing he received from his mother. Thus, for example, he has never been late for a scheduled class and has never expelled a student for failing to pay the fees. Kim seldom makes any promises, but those he makes, he never breaks. To date, there has never been a recorded instance of Kim harming someone who trusted him. His license was revoked because a death took place in his Dojo. All his students are invited to sign up here in protest against that revocation. We intend to fight it!"

This article was signed by three of his students.

Elijah's belief that Norman was backed by big money was clearly reinforced by what he had just found out about Kim. The same source that financed the Institute must have been the

The Kabbalistic Murder Code

one to arrange for Kim'sescape from Teheran, although Elijah could not quite figure out the connection between the two. He guessed that Norman had known about the scroll in Hong Kong and thought that Kim would be able to get it for him.

"Then why did he have to send me?" Elijah asked himself. "Ostensibly it was to have me check the authenticity of the scroll and that it was worth its asking price. Now I'm not even sure if he wants to buy it. The photocopy should be enough for his purposes, as I saw when he showed me the first photocopy. Norman is interested only in finding the clues in the seven different manuscripts. All the hints together are supposed to lead him to the end of his search, at the point where I put all the clues together and come up with the complete sentence."

Elijah rushed to the university. At the Faculty of Computer Sciences he found a lab assistant and asked him to download the photos he had taken with the flashlight-camera. The young man had never seen such a gadget, and for two hours he sweated at connecting it to a computer, using the cable that came with it. He worked silently, and Elijah did not try to disturb him with any idle prattle, lest he ruin the young man's concentration. Eventually, the lab assistant got the hang of it and the first photograph appeared on the screen. While the edges were somewhat blurred, the seventh line had come through crystal-clear. Now he could read it:

137

Just as pregnancies decreased among the
Israelites when they were enslaved in Egypt, so
too will they decrease under the servitude of the
foreign regimes, until the King Messiah comes
and the redemption will come at the appropriate
time, which is one of these.

Elijah no longer trusted Norman. Before he would tell
him about the contents of the third manuscript and his
unexpected success in obtaining the clue in the seventh line, he
would need to understand what was behind all the sentences and
what Norman was actually searching for. He would find an
immediate answer to that, so he believed, if he had a chat with
Professor Ashuri.

And indeed, Professor Ashuri took one look at the text
and immediately identified the issue involved. The question
deals with the problems involved when Passover, which is the
festival of spring, occurs in the summer. Briefly, she explained
it to Elijah. The Hebrew calendar, which is theoretically based
on the lunar month, consists of twelve months. That, however,
only adds up to 354 days, whereas the solar calendar consists of
365 days, making a discrepancy of 11 days a year. In order to
align the two, an extra month is added to some Hebrew years,
for a total of seven months, over a cycle of nineteen years. The
years in which a month is added are referred to as "pregnant"
years. This calculation, however, is not totally accurate. If we

average out the length of the Hebrew year, it is slightly longer than the solar year. The difference is only one of minutes, but over a very long period the difference accumulates, each time making Passover start a little later on the average. Over a very long time, this can, eventually, in theory, result in Passover taking place in the summer. Scholars have been aware of this problem for quite some time. The change takes place so slowly it cannot be sensed in any one person's lifetime. Nine hundred years ago, when first discussing this discrepancy, the scholars of the time decided that problem was so far off in the future that it could safely be assumed that the Messiah would have arrived by the time it became acute, and he could deal with it. In any event, there are years where the problem is more noticeable and others when it is less so. The accepted assumption has always been that the Messiah will arrive during one of the more problematic years, and will promptly set about solving the problem. Those years in which Passover is later than usual are referred to as the years of the Concealed and the Revealed and it is during these years that the Messiah could make an appearance, bringing with him the ultimate redemption. Various Kabbalistic works have used different calculations to try to plot out which years are more likely to bring the Messiah.

"According to some calculations," said Professor Ashuri, "the Hebrew years 5508, 5512, and 5558, or in secular terms, 1748, 1752, and 1798, were especially propitious. I have to give a class right now," she continued, "but if you have any more questions, feel free to call me at home."

"I really appreciate your help," said Elijah, nonplussed yet again, as he left her.

Elijah decided to do something concrete. He took a bus to the Institute for Practical Kabbalah on Agron Street, where he asked if they had any information on any descendants of Rabbi Batzri, the noted Kabbalist who had lived in Jerusalem. The people there were all very familiar with Rabbi Batzri, and were amazed that Elijah knew anything about him. The institute head advised him to contact a Rabbi Zanani, who - while not a descendant of Rabbi Batzri - was definitely a descendant of the holy *Ari* - Rabbi Luria. Elijah immediately traveled to the address given to him and found himself in a waiting room, where he sat for three hours surrounded by barren women seeking the rabbi's blessing to combat their infertility, women whose husbands had disappeared, and people with various life-threatening diseases. There was nothing mysterious about the waiting room: it was not in some dank cave or old house. It was a simple waiting room, not unlike those used by regular physicians, with plain, whitewashed walls. Two or three people circulated among the men and women waiting in the room, collecting money.

"I must admit," Elijah said to himself, "that mysticism is a desirable profession in Jerusalem, and all of these people are definitely consumers of mysticism." Indeed, mysticism had become a product like any other, and a very lucrative one indeed. Could that be what interested Norman?

Finally, it was Elijah's turn. He was ushered into an almost bare room, where an elderly rabbi sat on a couch; indeed, it could almost be said that he was sunk into it. Behind him was a photograph of a man who appeared to be of Yemenite extraction, and Elijah asked the rabbi if this was a photograph of the same Kabbalist Rabbi David Moreno, whom Rabbi Batzri had mentioned in Hong Kong. Elijah was not interested in trying to impress the rabbi with his knowledge, and was afraid that his question might have touched a sensitive nerve. The rabbi was clearly taken aback, but did not venture an answer. Elijah then showed him the sentence fragment from the manuscript: "The redemption will come at the appropriate time, which is one of these." He asked the rabbi if this year was a propitious one. It was a shot from the hip, without any attempt at weighing the possible consequences. The rabbi gave him a penetrating, serious look, and remained silent for a time. He remained deeply engrossed in thought and mumbled certain words that Elijah could not fathom.

He twisted his fingers, pulled the hair of his long beard, and finally answered, in a guttural Hebrew that Elijah could only understand with great difficulty, "The last time was eleven years ago. This year will be propitious and the next propitious one will be nine years from now." Elijah did not want to reveal his motives in asking, and left the aged rabbi's presence.

"How much do I need to pay?" he asked the man in charge of finances. "A thousand dollars."

Taking $1500 from his wallet, Elijah gave him the entire amount and dismissed the man's attempt to return the extra $500. He hurried out of the house. At such high prices, he was grateful that his Luzatto salary had enabled him to pay without putting himself into debt.

He hurried to the Luzzato Institute, as if to signify that nothing had changed and it was "business as usual" and was soon engrossed in studying the texts on what he now regarded as "his" desk. The telephone rang; in the utter silence within the Institute's walls, the ringing of the phone was a totally unexpected intrusion, and Elijah jumped from his chair, startled. He picked up the phone and heard the voice on the other end of the line. It was Norman.

Norman heaved a deep sigh, clearly audible over the phone, and noted: "I've heard all about the terrible tragedy. Kim was a very close friend of mine, and I shall miss him deeply. I hate to think of what you must have been through. I was afraid someone else might be interested in so valuable a manuscript and as you can see, I took the proper precautions. I always knew that, on a one-on-one basis, there was no one who could defeat

Kim. Although I really hope you haven't decided to quit, I'll fully understand if you have."

For a second, Elijah was thrown off balance. Norman's voice sounded so warm, so caring, and so convincing. Elijah realized he needed to play for time and if that meant lying, that was the way to go.

"On the contrary, Mr. Norman, I am particularly keen to stay on now, in memory of Kim. What would you like me to do?"

"We've uncovered another manuscript, which requires your authentication, and that means you're going to have to take another trip to examine it thoroughly. That is, if you're willing to do so, of course."

Elijah felt a familiar knot in his stomach, a common occurrence when he was tense. He assumed Norman must have found out about the Batzri scroll, which Elijah had not even mentioned.

Norman continued, "It is vitally important this time, too, that the owner remains unaware of the fact that we are so intent on getting our hands on the different manuscripts. The financial arrangements will be the same as last time."

"I thought you'd like me to work here. I don't think I'll be able to fly to Hong Kong again."

"I wouldn't send you there for all the money in the world. This trip will be to Istanbul."

Elijah sighed what he hoped was an inaudible sigh of relief. That meant that Norman did not yet know about the scroll in Batzri's possession. He decided not to say a word about it - at least not at this time.

"Don't worry. The 'White Lotus' is only active in its own territory."

"OK. I see no problem with flying to Turkey."

"I don't know what I can do as a memorial for Kim. I'm thinking of setting up a research fund in his memory," said Norman.

Elijah paled. He felt fortunate they were not using videophones, so that Norman could not see all the color draining from his face. He was sure now that Norman himself must have written the Rashi script list he had found. After all, one of the items on that list, which was written before Elijah had even begun to work for the Institute, was to set up a research fund in memory of Kim. Elijah remembered being utterly astounded at his first meeting with Norman at the man's evident ability to read people's minds and to know in advance what was going to happen. He began to have doubts about Norman's ethics. As far as he was concerned, Norman could well be an evil man; if he knew that Kim was slated to die, why didn't he do everything in his power to prevent his death? Furthermore, although he was aware that Kim would die, Norman had been cold-hearted and emotionless enough to plan

144

a research fund in his memory. The memorial fund now seemed to Elijah no more than sheer hypocrisy.

Elijah got up and went to stand by the window. It was getting late, an hour at which he could easily decide to go home. But he needed time to gather and galvanize his thoughts. He regretted greatly that - unlike in any other of the other projects he had worked on - he had allowed himself to become involved in the content of the manuscripts, rather than merely their letters and shapes. Elijah was amazed at himself. Even the study of the texts in terms of their meaning seemed to him bizarre. Usually, he stayed away completely from the implications of the meaning of each text. He loved what some might call the "mechanical" aspects of dealing with text, working extensively with the physical structure of each item - its paper or parchment, the ink used, the writing instrument involved, and of course the style of the script. As to the meaning of each document, he left that for others who specialized in different spheres. Once, in a fit of anger, Orna had taunted him by claiming that his obsession with the physical aspects of decaying documents was really no more than an escape from reality. But, like every experienced husband, Elijah had learned not to enter into confrontations with Orna when she was upset, but rather to agree with whatever she said. Deep down, however, he felt that what he was involved in was the real world. Now he had a golden opportunity to deal exclusively with manuscripts. One day he might be able to forget everything that had happened in Hong Kong and return to his earlier, uncomplicated lifestyle.

He returned to his desk and tried, as a way of preparing for his trip to Istanbul, to review the script used in the late Ottoman era. But he soon lost patience and stopped working. He sat there doing nothing, but tried to find some sort of explanation for everything he had gone through since beginning to work for the Institute. He reviewed the day's events and remembered the holy *Ari*, Rabbi Luria. But it occurred to him that this name was familiar in a different context! The letterhead on the piece of paper, which had been removed from his desk, was that of the Luria Investment Company. Maybe the time had come for him to look into that company. He gathered his personal items, locked up behind himself, and left the Institute. As he searched for something in his pocket, he realized that he had Orna's cell phone, which she had given him the day before to take care of, and which he had forgotten to return to her. He had the perfect means to conduct a little investigation.

But he soon realized that what in theory seemed a simple, straightforward task was, in practice, one of great difficulty. Elijah's knowledge of finance was probably on the same level as a caveman's knowledge of advanced nuclear physics. Or even less. When he came to the part of the daily newspaper that related to stocks and share prices, he turned the page with no interest whatsoever in checking anything out. He had never invested in any stock, and he kept as far away as possible from anything to do with the stock exchange. His only savings were in a study fund, for which a regular sum was deducted from his salary every month. For the first time, he found himself handicapped by total ignorance. He had no idea whom he might call about this "Luria" company. At first he thought he might approach an economics professor with whom he was friendly, but then another name popped into his head: Gabi Moldovan.

"I wouldn't say that Moldovan isn't honest," Professor Adir once said about him, "but he's the kind of person who, if you wake up in the morning after having to share a blanket with him on a freezing night, you'll find that he hogged the whole blanket for himself. Everything is totally legal and aboveboard and he will be apologetic in the extreme, but the same thing will happen every night, with the same result."

Gabriel Moldovan went to school with Elijah, and was two years his senior. During their school years they had lived near one another. His father owned the local fruit and vegetable store, and from an early age Gabi had worked for his father, showing some serious business acumen. He was forever trading in marbles, buying and selling used textbooks, working with various boring groups and getting paid, and everyone predicted that he would be a millionaire by the time he was twenty-five.

147

At university, he studied Economics, and after graduating became a rising star in one of the many investment houses that mushroomed during those years. Once, Elijah and Gabi had bumped into each other on campus and embraced like old friends. Gabi told him that he was now giving an extension course on "Initiatives in High-Tech Companies - From the Initial Concept to Making Profit." He was lecturing already, even though he had never even finished his Ph.D., and Elijah had to admit that he had felt a twinge of envy when he heard this, both for himself and for all the others who had finished the course.

"Elijah, what you've got to understand," Gabi had once patronized him, as if he was a kid, "is that there is absolutely no difference between selling fruit and vegetables and selling real estate or even selling high-tech companies, except for the profit margin. In every case, if you want to make a sale you have to overlook defects, hide problems, make light of flaws even when they are obvious, and sell the apples before they rot."

Elijah called Gabi's office and asked if he was in.

"Who's calling, please?" Gabi's administrative assistant asked, without answering his question.

"Dr. Shemtov," replied Elijah. He didn't usually bother using his title except when talking to administrative assistants. Even then he felt ill-at-ease in invoking it, but he had learned the hard way that a title often has a magical way of allowing

148

him to speak to someone, probably, he figured, because the "administrative assistant" would realize that there would be hell to pay if the doctor in question turned out to be his/her boss's personal or family physician.

"Just let me check," said the assistant, without waiting for Elijah's response. He found himself on hold, with the local news channel blaring from the receiver. There was some item about what the prime minister had said – or maybe it was something the prime minister had not said. Elijah didn't have time to clarify the point, when he heard Gabi's sonorous voice on the other end of the line.

"Well, well, if it isn't Dr. Shemtov, custodian of all our manuscripts. To what do I owe the pleasure of this call?"

Elijah chuckled. Say what you might about Gabi's morals and questionable business ethics, it was always a pleasure to speak to him. "Hi, Gabi. I hope I'm not interrupting anything. I know how valuable your time is. I have a simple question for you. As an international expert on investments, I wonder if you could tell me anything you might know about the Luria Company."

There was dead silence at the other end.

Finally, Gabi asked him, "What exactly is it that would you like to know?"

Elijah began stammering, a clear sign that he was nervous. He had not thought out exactly where he hoped his line of questioning would lead. He tried, using his all-too-limited experience, to recall what one asks about investment companies.

"Nothing in particular. I'd just like to know if it's a good idea to invest in the company. Do they pay a decent dividend? Is the management sound? What's their background? You know - just the standard background information."

"Why would you consider investing in them?"

"Well, it's not that I'm seriously considering investing, but I wanted to know if I should even consider them as a reasonable prospect," replied Elijah cautiously, inwardly praising himself for how he had weaseled out of revealing anything while at the same time posing the question that he wanted answered.

"Elijah, that's not something I can answer just like that over the phone," said Gabi. "Come on down to my office and we can really discuss the question properly."

"When would be a good time?"

"Now would be great. Why don't you come over right now and I'll be waiting for you. I have a couple of very important meetings, starting in an hour and a quarter from now. How long will it take you to get here?" Elijah said he would set out directly.

Elijah flagged down a passing cab, and was in Gabi's office twelve minutes later.

Gabi was a partner in the firm Kaufman, Eichler, and Moldovan. The scuttlebutt was that Kaufman had contributed the money left him by his father, a noted diamond merchant; Eichler, the contacts he had made while working at the Finance Ministry; and Moldovan, the business sense and silver tongue.

The offices were in a refurbished old Arab building in central Jerusalem. The entry hall led to a magnificent, large lobby, adorned with paintings by modern artists. Plush wall-to-wall carpets covered the entire floor surface. A few clearly expensive couches had been placed at various strategic places in the lobby. The overall impression was one of affluence, of partners who had "made it" and who would be as successful on your behalf if you entrusted them with your money. A corridor led to the enclave of the "holy of holies" where the offices of the high priests of investment were located.

Elijah had not yet reached the receptionist's desk when Gabi burst into the lobby.

"Elijah!" he yelled out, taking Elijah by the arm and more or less dragging him into the corridor.

Amazed, Elijah noted the elevator that went up a single floor to the partners' offices and those of their senior employees.

"Why bother going up a single floor?" asked Elijah. "Why don't we just climb the stairs?"

"How would people know that we are senior executives if we did that?" Gabi smirked.

With his shock of fair hair and smiling face, Gabi radiated an aura of sincerity, like a naive farmer's son. That and his vaunted sense of humor were enough to captivate widows with large estates to invest. Elijah noted that Gabi's legendary shock of hair had begun to thin with age, and he took a furtive look at his own hair in the mirror in the elevator. He was not exactly impressed with what he saw, and quickly turned back to Gabi, who was addressing him.

"Elijah, what's the sudden interest in investments? What do you know about stocks and futures?"

"Sorry," said Elijah as he realized that Gabi was speaking to him. "Could you repeat what you just said?"

"Well, when you asked me about investing in Luria, I figured you must have finally given up on earning a decent salary at the university. I thought you must have joined the many university lecturers and professors who have seen the light and have left academia. I believe that Luria is staffed by just such people. They were highly intelligent and probably unparalleled in their knowledge of what makes things tick - or alternately, they had exceptionally good inside contacts. In any event, they excelled in their performance on the market."

Elijah noted the use of the past tense, but decided not to say anything. He would first see where all this was leading.

Still groping, Elijah asked: "Could you explain to me their exact line of work?"

"Luria specialized in futures, and was known for the meteoric rise in the value of its portfolio. In the futures market, both sides agree that one will sell the other a specific commodity at a specified price on a specified date. For example, I might sign an agreement to sell you a hundred kilos of gold at a specific price six months from now. In other words, we agree on the quantity and the price today, but the deal will only be consummated in six months' time. At that time, I will hand over the gold and you will hand over the price we agreed upon. *Capisce?*"

"I understand," said Elijah, "but what purpose does it serve? Why can't I buy it now or wait six months and buy it then?"

Gabi laughed. "Eli, where do you live? In the stratosphere? Come back down to the real world. Your comment shows me how abysmal your knowledge of finance is."

"Well, you know my background. Start with the assumption that as far as I'm concerned, everything you have said makes about as much sense to me as if you'd been speaking Akkadian."

"Where do they speak Akkadian nowadays? In Pakistan?"

"In Pakistan they speak Urdu, an Indo-Iranian language which was originally written in Arabic characters. There's no place where it's spoken these days. Akkadian came from Akkad, an empire in northern Iraq. It's the first written Semitic language, and was originally written in cuneiform. Although that empire was only in ascendancy for about a hundred and fifty years, between 2350 and 2200 B.C.E., Akkadian served as an international language in the Mesopotamia region, and in actuality was still used as late as the 6th century C.E. Eventually, it was replaced by Aramaic."

Elijah hadn't planned it that way, but from the way Gabi looked at him, he could see that his answer was a retort to Gabi's gratuitous denigration of academia. The answer surprised Gabi somewhat, but at the same time caused him to have a certain amount of respect for his learned friend, as if his extensive knowledge of extinct languages made up for his almost total ignorance of economics.

"It's always good to learn something," said Gabi. "I get your hint, and I promise to improve. Let me explain to you in simple terms about the futures market and how it operates. Let us assume, strictly for argument's sake, that I am a company that represents orange growers in Israel. We are interested in growing oranges for sale in the winter, but are afraid of the price dropping by then. Nowadays, there's a futures market where one can, for example, sell a ton of oranges at $1000 a ton. As it's possible to have a rough idea of our anticipated crop yield, we would like to sell fifty tons of oranges right now, at today's price. If torrential rains in Morocco or Spain cause a reduction in their crop yield, the global price of oranges will rise six months from now, in which case we will not have earned as much as we could possibly have earned had we waited until then to sell. If, on the other hand, the other countries have a bumper crop and flood the world market with oranges, the price will drop. In that case, our decision to sell at a fixed price now will be very much to our advantage and will save us much grief. If our company prefers stability and isn't interested in surprises – either good or bad – we'll prefer to sell our crop in the futures market. This way, we can plan our production goals without having to worry about unexpected surprises.

"Of course, you can simply insure your crop. As you know, nowadays you can insure anything, from a football player's feet to a singer's voice, but insurance is more expensive and can only compensate you for a bad crop without giving you the oranges you might need."

"I understand, but who'd be willing to buy tons of oranges months in advance?"

"That's a good question. Suppose, for example, that you have a factory that produces orange juice, and you know that you need a certain quantity of oranges each summer. You need to buy the oranges in the winter in order to manufacture orange juice and orange concentrate. Here, too, you don't know what the future price will be, and you want to avoid unpleasant surprises. The best way to do this is through the futures market, by purchasing a specified quantity of oranges at $1000 a ton. The advantage to you is that you guarantee delivery of the oranges to you six months from now at a price you already know, even though in actuality you will only pay for and receive the oranges at that time. In a futures transaction, we match up a person who wants to buy in the future at a fixed price to a person who wants to sell in the future at the same fixed price."

"I still have a few questions," said Elijah. "First of all, what happens in the event of a crop failing? Or if the buyer goes bankrupt? In such a case, the sides have not guaranteed anything for themselves."

"Also an excellent question, but in reality such futures transactions are not really made between two parties – the seller and the buyer – but through an agent, who is like a middleman or a broker. It is he who is responsible to both the seller and the buyer. The buyer buys from the broker, and the seller sells to the broker. The broker receives a percentage for his work and is responsible for having the terms of each contract carried out."

"But how does he ensure it?"

"The fact is that anyone who enters into a futures transaction has to put down security for part of the amount. Let's take our example. Let's say the price of oranges right now is $1000 a ton. We can be almost positive that the price per ton will not go up or down by more than $200. In such a case, the broker will require both parties to the agreement to offer a security of $200 per ton. Let's say that you go bankrupt and cannot buy the oranges. The broker will sell the oranges in the summer at whatever the market price is. The most the price can go down is $200 a ton. If the broker can only sell the oranges for $800 a ton, he'll use the buyer's security of $200 a ton to pay the seller, so the seller gets the $1000 he was guaranteed.

"Let's say someone has $1000 to invest and the price of oranges is $1000 a ton. He's convinced that the price of oranges will go up within six months to $1200 a ton. He can buy a ton of oranges now and store them for six months. He'll then gain $200 when he sells them at $1200. Still, there's an alternative. He can take a risk and with that $1000 he can buy five tons of oranges on the futures market, for six months from now. In such a case, each $200 of his money serves as security for a ton of the oranges that he guarantees to buy. In six months, if the price goes up to $1200, he can sell the five tons for $6000 and wind up with a $1000 profit – not bad for a $1000 investment!"

"Yes, but what happens if the price drops below $1000?" asked Elijah.

"Then he'll lose his entire investment," Gabi replied. Investing in futures offers the prospect of making a sizable profit – but also of losing your entire investment. Life is hard."

"And can one actually buy oranges in Israel on the futures market?" asked Elijah.

"Funnily enough, to the best of my knowledge one can't buy oranges on the futures market in Israel. You have to realize that the Israeli market is small with only a few big players. On the other hand, there are many other commodities that can be bought or sold that way. Throughout the world there are markets for platinum, gold, silver, and many other metals. Also many agricultural products, such as wheat, barley, coffee, sugar, flour…there are also markets for shares, various currencies… all based on the same principle.

"If, for example, you're a US company that sells goods to Thailand and your contract specifies that you will be paid in bahts, which is the national currency of Thailand, in thirty months from now, how can you be sure that the baht doesn't suddenly depreciate? You can take out insurance, which will guarantee that you receive a certain exchange rate, but an easier way is to enter into a futures transaction for the money you will receive, and sell it now. That way you can protect yourself against any depreciation. Theoretically, you can regard a futures transaction in currency as a way for your company to protect itself from any danger in the future."

"I understand," said Elijah, "but who are the buyers and sellers in these deals? Are they the people who need the goods? Or just speculators? Or gamblers?"

"Not necessarily. Most of those involved don't really want the items themselves. When the time of the actual sale arrives, the buyers and sellers pretty much balance one another out, and only a few percentage points change hands. Most of those in the futures market are businessmen and risk-takers. I don't think the word 'speculators' is appropriate here. We're dealing with businessmen who see which way the market is moving and act accordingly. The market needs these businesspeople and investors in the futures market. They can be regarded as a certain kind of insurance agent."

Elijah looked at Gabi but said nothing. To him, they were all speculators and gamblers, and he couldn't understand why Gabi would want to defend them. Gabi continued to expound on the importance of those investors.

Finally, Elijah asked him, "By the way, do you personally invest in futures?"

"Oh, no! I don't even have enough funds to invest in many more certain ventures. However, I must admit that if a client asks me, I would invest in futures on his behalf. I suppose that's the whole point, isn't it?"

Gabi pushed a button and called out, "Rina, could you bring us something to drink?"

Rina, dressed in tight-fitting jeans that left very little to the imagination, came in and took their order: two cappuccinos and croissants.

"What point is that?" asked Elijah, surprised.

"The point, Eli, in case you've forgotten, is the Luria Company."

"So I am to take it," said Elijah, "that that company invests in futures."

"That has to be the understatement of the year. Luria was by far the biggest player in the field. It had become a legend, until it suddenly dropped right off the radar."

"Are you telling me that it no longer exists? I don't understand..."

"Eli, let's stop playing games here. I'll give you a brief review of what I know about Luria and then you will tell me what you know. Is it a deal?"

Elijah nodded, although he had no intention of keeping his part of the bargain.

Gabi smoothed down his remaining hair, and Elijah smiled.

"The company was established in the mid-eighties. In the nineties, when everyone started taking an interest in it, they realized that in the eighties alone it had earned over a billion dollars, all of which was available in cash. What infuriated everyone was that it had done so totally within the law and

160

absolutely aboveboard. The process it had used could be seen easily and clearly. Its original capitalization was about two or three million dollars, and all it did was buy and sell futures. It might buy sugar and sell gold, buy gold and sell diamonds, unload cocoa and buy wheat.

"All these were small transactions in terms of the market - maybe two- or three-million-dollar deals, sometimes even smaller. It didn't even have its own offices. Instead, it worked with a number of small agents in various locations worldwide. We have no idea how many such agents there were and where they were located. Luria never took out a bank loan, and as a result was never subjected to an in-depth investigation."

"So what went wrong?"

"The truth is that, had there not been computers, no one would ever have even taken an interest in Luria. However, at the beginning of the nineties the company bought two supercomputers in the United States. At the same time it ordered highly sophisticated, state-of-the-art encryption tools, the best the market had to offer. At that time, the only ones who needed such computers and encryption tools were members of the defense establishment, and anyone desiring to export either of these from the United States would need a specific export license issued by the Defense Department. It soon became known that these items had been shipped without any such authorization. Purely by chance, some of these components were found in a shipment sent to Luria, and everything came crashing down."

"Where were the computers meant to go?"

"That is a question to which there is no clear answer. Some people claim that the computers were meant to go to St. Kitts, which was where the company had been incorporated. Others say that they were destined for Spain, and there are even those who say they were being sent to Israel."

"To Israel?"

"Yes. The computers were impounded without a struggle. Luria lost hundreds of millions of dollars, and simply seems to have disappeared. The Defense Department did not complain, because the amount that Luria paid in fines was way beyond what it had expected to get. Had Luria gone to court it would have stood quite a good chance of having the fine reduced substantially, because it could have used the computers in the United States or sold them within that country. The press had a field day, and there were all sorts of hypotheses as to why the company acted as it did, but Luria remained silent. There was no press release, no authorized spokesperson, not even the venting of a disgruntled employee. Nothing. *Nada*."

"One second," said Elijah. "Isn't it possible to find out who signed the incorporation papers and who the directors were?"

Gabi smiled forgivingly. "Elijah, between the two of us, do you know St. Kitts? Do you even know where it is?"

"Well, not exactly," Elijah admitted.

"St. Kitts is one of a series of islands, whose total population is about thirty thousand people. There's no income tax there, because so many companies are incorporated there."

"And where does Gabriel Moldovan fit into the picture?"

"About three months before the company collapsed, in 1992, I happened to be at the office of Joshua Abadi, an investment adviser from a competing investment house. He left the room for a while, and I was in the room by myself. I saw an open envelope on the table and looked inside. It contained an order to buy five million dollars' worth of Japanese yen at a date three months hence and to sell them at noon exactly forty-one days later. The risk was enormous, as the five million dollars were only meant as security on a figure fifteen times as large, seventy-five million dollars. I had to replace the paper in the envelope immediately, so I couldn't read all the details. You have to understand that in the futures market, prices change from hour to hour and often from minute to minute. The most sophisticated computers in the world can only provide investors with marginal help. Investment counselors change their recommendations on the spot, and here we are, finding out about someone asking for an investment three months in the future? Has someone gone crazy here? The order was on Luria stationery!

"When Abadi returned, I tried in every way possible to get him to talk about the contents of that envelope. On the envelope there was a picture of a lighthouse. If I remember correctly, it was white with silver print. I asked him jokingly if he was suddenly involved in shipping companies. He said, 'No way! That's a personal letter from a relative in Spain.' From that point on, I followed what Luria was doing. I kept tabs on that particular transaction, and found that on it alone Luria had made twelve million dollars. I went nuts. There was no possible way to forecast changes like those of the yen that far in the future. Two days before the buy date, the Japanese government fell after a major scandal. The yen took a nosedive. Three weeks before the sell date, the yen began climbing, reaching its highest value an hour before the scheduled sell time. After that, it started dropping. There's never been a case like that in the history of the stock market..."

Norman! Thought Elijah to himself. *How come I didn't realize it? A man who can read people's thoughts, who can forecast events and foresee the different possibilities, why shouldn't he be able to use these same powers in the world of finance?* Suddenly, another thought occurred to Elijah. It was on the tip of his tongue, but he couldn't quite formulate it. Gabi's voice receded into the background, and he appeared to be some alien creature whose lips were moving, with a hand that every so often pushed back its hair from its forehead. What was the thought? What was the thought? Elijah did everything possible to retrieve it, but without success. It irked him, like a pebble stuck in his shoe. There was another man he knew, who could foresee where to invest. The man had made millions. Who was that man, darn it? Where had he met him? Or had he just read about him? Or was it a movie he had once seen? He decided that his search through his mind was fruitless at that time, and decided he'd come back to it after the meeting.

Now he suddenly saw that Gabi was silent and was looking at him. Was he waiting for an answer? In order not to appear to have lost the thread of their conversation, he went on the offensive.

"OK. We agreed that you would tell me everything you know about Luria. What else is there that you haven't told me yet?"

"Nothing," replied Gabi.

"Gabi, I want the truth. I have no doubt that after what you saw, you spied on Abadi."

"I guess I should tell you about that as well. But heaven help you if you repeat so much as a word of what I tell you to anyone. It appears to me that Luria Investments has not really vanished. It simply changed its name and is now known as

Cordoba Investments. OK, I've come clean. Now it's your turn.
What can you tell me about Luria Investments?"

"Actually, it's a very simple story," said Elijah, playing
for time. He was able to spot a red flag whenever a person says,
"it's really simple," or "trust me," or "to tell you the truth," and
knew that you should be all the more suspicious of what that
person has just told you. However, he could not think of a better
opening. He realized that whatever he said from that point on
Gabi would regard with suspicion, but he felt he had no choice.

"As part of my work, every so often I have to deal with
ancient manuscripts. By their nature, in most cases these
manuscripts are owned by extremely wealthy people. Who else
can afford a medieval Italian handwritten Megillah scroll with
gold-leaf adornments? However, these people are not able to
judge the authenticity of these   manuscripts, and that's where
we come in. In short, I did someone a very big favor, and by
doing so I saved him a fortune and he really likes me. He gave
me a big tip, and he suggested I invest it in Luria Investments.
And now I have just realized that I helped this guy so much, and
his advice to me turns out to be worthless, as Luria Investments
no longer exists."

Elijah left the office, heard Rina mumbling something,
and only after he was on the stairs did he realize that she had
said goodbye to him in a very friendly manner, while he had left
without even acknowledging her, treating her like nothing more

than a piece of furniture. At that point it would have appeared silly of him to return and say goodbye to her, so he simply forgot the whole episode. He was totally engrossed in trying to decipher what made Norman tick, and tried - unsuccessfully, as he had to admit - to make sense of the man and his powers. Norman seemed far too intelligent to be a run-of-the-mill businessman. In Elijah's world, businessmen were basically illiterate, knowing very little beyond a smattering of arithmetic. And the few that were not illiterate confined their reading to boring material like balance sheets, over which they could pose for hours. The first thing they did when they got the newspaper was to open it to the dreary financial pages, where they showed a sickening obsession for news of which communications company is merging with another.

Norman, on the other hand, read academic treatises for pleasure, and in fact had been one of the few who had read Elijah's published articles. Norman was too good to be an ordinary businessman and Elijah assumed that he had to be one of the investors or even one of the owners of Luria Investments.

When he reached the street and had put some distance between himself and Moldovan, he finally remembered the name he had been seeking, the other man who had been able to predict what would happen in the future, the man who had predicted that land in Silicon Valley would be worth millions: he was the man mentioned in Odel Weiss's article which

Norman had noted in the list. The man's name was John McDonald, and there had to be a tie of some kind between the two.

The Sixth Sphere

When The Ottoman Empire Conquered Jerusalem

In 1516, about twenty-four years after the Jews had been expelled from Spain, Sultan Salim I, also known as Salim the Grim, took Jerusalem. It was a relatively easy conquest, because the remnants of the Mamluks, whom he had defeated near Aleppo in Syria, offered no resistance. Salim visited the Temple Mount, donated large sums of money to the Al-Aqsa mosque, and reduced the poll tax that was levied on Jews and Christians.

Scholars agree that Jerusalem flourished in the first century after the Ottoman conquest. Salim's son, Suleiman the Magnificent, refurbished mosques, built marketplaces, repaired water conduits, excavated new water reservoirs, and set up a soup kitchen for the poor. The crowning glory of Suleiman's work in Jerusalem was the building of a large wall, which encircled the city. In order to build the wall, Suleiman brought in the noted architect Mimar Sinan from Istanbul. It took years for the wall to be constructed, but it still stands to this day.

The Jews greeted the Turks enthusiastically. They had already learned from their coreligionists in Istanbul, Salonika, Izmir, and throughout the Ottoman Empire that the Turks treated the Jews fairly. Jewish historians note regretfully how different Jewish history would have been had the expulsion from Spain taken place after the Ottoman conquest of Jerusalem. Many of the Jews who had been expelled were afraid to go to Jerusalem under the Mamluks, but they would have had no such reservations under Ottoman rule and would have settled in the city joyfully.

The Ottoman conquest strengthened the region's Jewish population and many Jews were drawn to it, primarily to Safed. Some of the greatest Kabbalists and Halakhic - Jewish law - geniuses were active in the country during that era, including the Kabbalist Rabbi Isaac Luria, known as the Ari, *and Rabbi Joseph Caro, author of the Code of Jewish Law, the* Shulhan Arukh. *There were even those who wished to restore the ancient institution of the Sanhedrin - the supreme Jewish court of law - but internal conflicts prevented the pursuit of this idea.*

The Ottomans ruled Jerusalem for just over four centuries. From time to time, emissaries of the Turkish sultan would visit Jerusalem to impose order on the city, but their efforts were generally unsuccessful. This was primarily due to the vehement opposition of the local leaders. Ottoman rule in Jerusalem was characterized by a slow but steady decline in the control exercised by the central government. The Ottoman Empire finally came crashing down with the defeat of the Turks in World War I.

Elijah hurried home. Orna was on duty at the hospital that evening, and Elijah had to take care of the girls. Orna, who tended to distrust Elijah's decision-making processes, had left out some watercolors and paper, so the girls could paint. Elijah arrived home a few minutes before the babysitter was due back with the girls from the amusement park. He arranged the table carefully so as to make it easy for the girls to paint, and he placed his favorite colors close to the paper. However, as his mind was preoccupied, rather than leaving paintbrushes for the girls to work with, he placed a silverware setting alongside each of the paint sets, as if they were to have supper there. Metaphorically, he had merged the two functions.

Spain. Spain. Gabi had mentioned Spain twice. Once he had mentioned Spain as a possible destination for the supercomputer, and again he had noted that the letter with the lighthouse on it had arrived from Spain. Elijah made a mental note to see if he could find a link to Spain. He also sent a request by e-mail to his favorite librarian asking her to dig up information on Luria and Cordovero, as well as to try to track down the origin of the name "Luzzato". He was convinced that all three names were of Jewish origin, and finding out more about them might help him to learn more about Norman.

Efrat and Michali burst into laughter when they saw their worktable with the silverware along with the paints. To them that served as inspiration and they painted pictures of plates full of food, placing the paint containers on the drawings as "items" in their "meals". The red paint represented ketchup, while the yellow was mustard. They had the time of their lives. Each in her own way expressed the thought that it was much more fun to be with Daddy than with Mommy, their nursery school teachers, or their babysitters. Elijah looked at the drawings as objectively as any parent can, and thought to himself - objectively, of course - that their work was way above average for their age.

He was amused by his daughters' high spirits, brought about by his absent-mindedness, and was intrigued at how creatively the girls had dealt with the situation. He tried to concentrate as he scrambled eggs, cut up some vegetables, toasted bread, and removed a packet of sliced cheese from the refrigerator. He was again rewarded with compliments; how much more fun it was when Daddy prepared a meal.

After supper, the girls made no fuss about taking their showers and were soon ready for bed. Any time friends called Orna at that time of day, she would hang up abruptly, telling them, "I have to get the girls ready for bed." It was a major project each night. Elijah was delighted at how easy it was to "get the girls to bed". He would have time to study the Ottoman conquest of Jerusalem. In other words, he needed to prepare for a flight to Istanbul. Actually, there was very little for Elijah to catch up on with regard to the Ottoman conquest of Jerusalem.

173

It was one of his favorite eras, and he was very familiar with it. He, nevertheless, decided to look through some of his books in order to remind himself of any isolated fact he might have overlooked.

He was soon deeply engrossed in reading about the construction of the city wall; suddenly he heard a plaintive voice:

"Daddy!" It was Michali. And here he had thought he had gotten them off safely to bed.

"Yes, Darling?"

"Could you come here? I've got a tummy ache."

"Lie on your tummy. It will soon pass."

Elijah wondered what type of local discord had led to the Jews of that era to abandon the idea of reconstituting the Sanhedrin.

"Daddy!"

"Yes, Michali?"

"I want you to come here. The door is bothering me."

"What?" Elijah was not sure that he had heard correctly.

"The door to my room is bothering me."

"Oh, all right... I'm coming." Well, he could see that his was not the only creative mind in this house.

What does it mean when we are told that the sultans were unable to impose order on the city? How could they permit such a situation to continue?

174

"Daddy!"

"Yes, Michali?"

"You told me that you were coming already!"

"Mommy will be home soon. If you lie quietly, she will come and give you a kiss."

"OK."

"Good night, my precious."

Elijah surfed the Internet. He found that the Kabbalist Luria was none other than the saintly *Ari*. The information on the Internet was very minimal, merely noting that the *Ari* was the founder of the later stream of Kabbalah. Unlike the earlier Kabbalah - that of the *Zohar* – the Kabbalah of the *Ari* offered redemption for the entire nation and not only for the individual. Elijah devoted some time to rethinking what he could remember about Norman's mysticism. What was Norman seeking in the Kabbalah? Was it merely a business proposition, given the worldwide interest in it? Were its financial rewards so great that he was willing to sacrifice people's lives in order to attain his goals? Or did it involve something so much more profound, something that Elijah had not yet discovered?

About five hundred years after the Turks came from Istanbul and conquered Jerusalem, Elijah was on a plane flying in the other direction, and he visualized to himself the causes for the disintegration of the Ottoman Empire. It had probably fallen for the same two reasons that all empires fall. First, it had grown so large that it was impossible for the central government to control its far-flung territories. Second, it had become internally rotten, with the primary preoccupation of its bureaucrats being self-preservation, with little regard for what was good for the empire. In today's world, no one country rules a distant land, with the locals administering it on behalf of the central government. Elijah found himself with plenty of time to dwell on this subject.

For some unfathomable reason, the Turkish customs officials appeared to be on a working-to-rule strike and it took him longer than anticipated to leave the airport. The long wait gave him time to glance through his guidebook and he even managed to catch a few winks in the First Class lounge.

Only when he finally arrived in Istanbul did he realize that the customs officials had not been the only ones on strike. The country, on the whole, had a rhythm and tempo that were geared to doing everything slowly. It was simply the way the country was run. The contrast to Hong Kong was incredible. It seemed that no one in Turkey was ever in a hurry to get anywhere or do anything, and every line and queue inched along at a snail's pace. There was a long row of taxis waiting, and when Elijah's turn came, the taxi driver, who had been busy playing backgammon, begrudgingly rose to help him with his luggage. It was clear that the driver mightily resented this unwelcome and uncalled-for intrusion into his leisure time.

The hotel was in the middle of the Old City, and the driver had to perform various acrobatic stunts just to end up parked outside the hotel entrance. It was a luxury, square-shaped hotel built around a massive atrium. In the atrium, a giant fountain sprayed colored water. The elevator was encased in glass, and it, too, was located inside the atrium. Totally at variance with the elevators in Hong Kong, the elevator in this hotel just crept its way up and down. It was clear to Elijah that if he wished to save time he should use the stairs, but the lethargy of the country had already infected him, and he waited patiently for the elevator.

Elijah's cover story was that he was an Israeli professor in Istanbul on a short, private vacation, and had only come upon the manuscript by chance. That was why the trip would last but three days, and most of the time he would indeed be touring. To him, this did not exactly present any hardship, especially given the amount of money that would accrue to his account for these three days. In fact, after discovering the ties between Norman and the Luria Investment Company, he had no compunctions about bankrupting Norman.

After a brief tour of the city and of the Emir's palace, he returned to the hotel, ate an early supper, and went to sleep happily. Those who do not have small children cannot imagine the joy of being able to sleep through an entire night without being disturbed even once. And a person with two small children knows very well that either or both of them would be sure to wake him at least once a night, and that the best one can hope for is that if both children wake him up in the course of a night, at least they should do so at the same time.

Luxuriating in his temporary freedom, Elijah got up later than usual the following morning. He had to be at the book bazaar at noon and passed hundreds of stores selling gold and silver jewelry in order to reach it. He wandered around the book bazaar, cast an eye on the store where his meeting was to take place, and continued strolling around. He spotted a very old *Ketubah* - a Jewish marriage agreement - which had evidently been copied from an even more ancient one. It was obvious to him that whoever had done the copying was not too familiar with the writing style he had tried to copy.

Soon it was time for his meeting. He returned to the store. Someone behind him appeared to have said something like "*donmeh*", and it sounded as if the person was speaking to him. He entered the store with trepidation, and was relieved to find that the salesperson was a young woman. He wanted to explain what he was doing there, but before he could say a word the young woman said, "Good morning, Professor Shemtov. I am delighted that you came. My name is Ozlem." Her English was impeccable.

The young woman could not have been more than twenty-three years old. She was thin and wore very old-fashioned glasses. Her hair was short and she had a very pleasant voice. Although she was not beautiful in the conventional sense of the word, there was something exotic and captivating about her looks.

"I thought I was supposed to meet Mr. Alfred," replied Elijah, somewhat confused.

"Alfred is my brother. He should be here any moment," said Ozlem with a smile. "He asked me to entertain the distinguished professor from Israel until he arrives. We are delighted that you found time to come to us during your vacation."

Elijah sat down and enjoyed the apple-flavored tea that Ozlem brought him. He enjoyed talking to her, especially as she seemed to know everything that there was to know about Turkey and Istanbul. The name of the bookstore would translate as "the Tradition of the Book" and she mentioned to Elijah that it had been in the family for five generations and that it dealt with an eclectic selection of books and manuscripts. The family also owned an antique shop in the city's commercial center.

A young man of about thirty entered the store as they were speaking and Elijah guessed correctly that it was Alfred. Alfred, too, wore glasses, and was somewhat overweight. He sported a short beard and an obvious tendency to baldness.

"Professor Shemtov," exclaimed Alfred loudly, as he grabbed Elijah's outstretched hand and shook it enthusiastically. "I'm really sorry about the delay. I hope that Ozlem treated you well." Like his sister's, his English was as good as that of a native speaker.

"Ozlem treated me very well indeed, and I learned a great deal from her," said Elijah.

"I'm sure that you didn't expect to see the manuscript here," said Alfred with a smile. "The conditions here are deplorable. In order to see the manuscript, you'll have to accompany me to our home in Asia."

"In Asia?" blurted out Elijah, but he immediately recovered from his initial shock. "You, no doubt, mean the Asian section of Istanbul."

"Right. Istanbul is the only city in the entire world built on two separate continents. The Bosporus Straits separate the two parts. Our European side alone has a greater population than the entire country of Belgium, but for some reason Europeans still look upon us as Asians."

Ever the scholar, Elijah immediately countered, "Pay no attention to them. The so-called 'Asians' included people like Moses, the prophet Isaiah, and Jesus. And they are but a minuscule sample of the many 'Asians' who made it in life. After all, they wrote the greatest bestselling book of all times - the Bible."

Alfred laughed, and went outside to find a cab. Their conversation was stilted throughout the trip and provided Elijah with no information as to how Alfred would have anything to do with the manuscript. Could he be a Jew?

As if reading his thoughts, Alfred suddenly volunteered, "You know, I visited Israel about five years ago, and it never ceased to amaze me that the second or third question everyone asked me was whether I am Jewish."

"Yes, to Israelis, being a member of the Tribe is an important element," Elijah said apologetically, although he didn't fail to notice that Alfred never did tell him whether or not he was Jewish.

The cab made so many twists and turns that Elijah lost his sense of direction altogether. At one point, it took them across a long suspension bridge.

"We are now crossing from Europe to Asia," Alfred noted.

Elijah wasn't particularly competent geographically and had only just scraped through his navigation tests in the army. Even as a tank commander, he had never bothered to use maps and would always tell the unit leader, "You need to make sure I can always see your tank. If you ever disappear from my line of sight for two minutes, I'll become hopelessly lost in the Sinai Desert, and I'll wander about for forty years until they find me. It's your responsibility."

When The Ottoman Empire Conquered Jerusalem

Even after they had crossed over to the Asian side of Istanbul, the cab drove for about half an hour until there was a notable change of scenery; high-rise buildings gave way to private homes, all enclosed by fences. Alfred told the driver to stop next to one of them, and Elijah saw that the cab driver was impressed with the house. A woman with Slavic features, who seemed to work there, opened the door for them. However imposing the outside of the house appeared, it was nothing compared to what lay beyond the fence. The house itself was surrounded by a magnificent garden, with a private swimming pool at one side. Inside, all the floors were covered with exquisite carpets, and the furniture was elegant and obviously expensive.

Elijah was led immediately to the study, which overlooked the garden. On the table was the original manuscript and next to it were all the tools of his trade: a magnifying glass, a special thick needle, a set of pens, and paper. At his request, Elijah was allowed to get straight to work. He was grateful that Alfred did not insist on standing by him the whole time. Withdrawing from the world and its problems, Elijah concentrated solely on the manuscript before him. The manuscript appeared to have originally been a scroll consisting of parchment sections sewn to each other, but over the ages the linen thread that kept the different sections together had rotted away, and now each section was separate from the others.

182

He was pleased to see that his original hypothesis had been correct. The manuscript had evidently gone through three separate stages; it had been difficult to see this on photocopies, but to his practiced eye, seeing the original made this abundantly clear. The quality of the different inks used had been different, and that obviously showed up in the manuscript. It seemed that the ink used for writing on parchment went through various stages. At first, a mixture of carbon and glue was used, but the problem was always which liquid should be used to galvanize the glue in the mixture. Different metallic salts were later added to the mixture, which would allow the ink to be absorbed better in the parchment, but at the same time these metallic salts could cause the ink to eat away at the parchment, a highly destructive effect over the long term. This process, too, can be halted temporarily, regardless of which ink was used and in the short term, even an expert would find it difficult to tell the difference between the inks used. However, it is totally impossible to match up inks precisely. The result is that over the course of time they decay with different rapidity, which makes it easy to spot the various inks employed. Thus, every such correction will become apparent at some point in the future.

Interestingly enough, the composition of the ink led to a dispute among the sages of the Talmud. The addition of vitriol makes the ink more durable and improves its appearance, but makes it much harder to use in correcting manuscripts. Rabbi

Meir permits the use of vitriol, while the other sages forbid it, and Jewish law follows the sages.

Elijah went through the manuscript word by word. He was totally familiar by now with the exact content, except, of course, the unique seventh line of each scroll. He heaved a sigh of relief when he found that in almost every instance, his hypotheses had been correct. Alfred came in a few times to offer him food and drink, but Elijah declined each time and almost ignored his presence. He completed his review of the entire manuscript and felt a sense of jubilation and accomplishment.

Here, as in the other manuscripts, the seventh line was different! This was to be expected, and he would have been bitterly disappointed had such a change not been made. He took out his flashlight camera, and secretly photographed the relevant passage.

Alfred came in again. "Professor, you've worked for three hours straight without rising from your chair!"

Elijah looked outside and saw that the sun was indeed setting.

"I wanted to ask you something," Alfred continued. "There is another section, but I'm not sure if it's part of this manuscript. Would you be willing to glance at it?"

"If it's a Hebrew manuscript, I'd be delighted to see it," replied Elijah immediately.

184

Alfred brought another section. Elijah took a look at it, and made sure to use his flashlight camera to illuminate it. A few clicks, and he had a number of photographs of this section as well. If there had been any doubt regarding the connection between the Hong Kong manuscript and this one, he found the connection here. The section was written in the same style as the other one, and showed no corrections. It stated that this was one of the seven copies that Nehemiah of Peki'in had made for Elazar ben Rabbi Simon, who had heard it from his father, who had heard it from Rabbi Akiba, who had heard it from ben Horkenos, who had heard it from Rabbi Johanan. At the bottom of this section Elijah saw two faint signatures and decided to investigate them later.

"This one is not particularly relevant," said Elijah, who was already accustomed to lying with a straight face, as he returned the last section to Alfred. "I don't think I'll include it in the opinion I was asked to offer." Elijah thought he caught a measure of disappointment in Alfred's eyes, but the man recovered very quickly. Alfred invited him for dinner at a restaurant on the banks of the Bosporus. After first declining politely, Elijah accepted the invitation, with the provision that it would be a moderately priced restaurant.

They drove back to the city, this time in Alfred's luxurious car. Along the way, they stopped at one of the bridges above the Golden Horn of the Bosporus that link the Asian to the European side of the city. On both sides of the inlet, dozens of fishermen were plying their trade. Alfred pointed out the floodlit palaces of the sultans and the numerous mosques scattered throughout the city.

They picked up Ozlem, who had just locked up the store, and arrived at the banks of the Bosporus. On the way to the restaurant that Alfred had chosen, they passed many places that looked like cafés or coffee shops. In each of these, young men and women sat on low stools and smoked *narghiles*. Some of them were playing backgammon. Elijah noted that the holy crusade against smoking had not yet reached Turkey. Nowhere in the city had he seen a single no-smoking sign.

Alfred had selected a restaurant opposite the Spice Bazaar with a pastoral ambiance. Elijah thoroughly enjoyed the food, which reminded him of Israeli cuisine, and the conversation was animated. Ozlem was more interested in Israel and its inhabitants, while Alfred wanted to know about the prices of rare Hebrew manuscripts.

The meal ended very late, with Elijah satiated both in terms of food and everything there was to know about Turkey in general and Istanbul in particular. They wanted to drive Elijah back to his hotel, but he decided to take a cab, both because the hotel was in the opposite direction from their home, and because cabs were inexpensive. He entered his hotel room and dropped, exhausted, on the bed. Here, at least, he could be confident that no one would wake him in the middle of the night.

He lay on his back and began to analyze all his recent experiences. He needed to find some sort of framework for everything that had occurred, some overall perspective that would allow all the data to fall neatly into place.

As he lay there, his eyes followed the shadows that drifted in through the window into his room. He was reminded of Nash's game theory, which the legendary John MacDonald had also used in a most succinct form to explain the human race. There are systems that reach a point of equilibrium that is disturbing to them, but from which they cannot escape. The most famous of these is the dilemma of the prisoners. Let us assume that two criminals robbed a bank. The police arrested both and locked each up in a different cell. The police do not have an ironclad case, and if each suspect insists that he was not involved, the police will be forced to release them. The most they can be convicted of is being in possession of a deadly weapon, the penalty for which is two years in prison. If both confess, each will be sentenced to four years in prison. However, if one confesses and the other does not, the one who confessed will turn state's evidence. The one who confessed will then receive a one-year sentence, while the other will receive a seven-year sentence.

When The Ottoman Empire Conquered Jerusalem

What is the best course for each to take? Each is in a solitary cell and has no idea what the other will do. He also has no way to influence the other. The best course for each to pursue is simple. If his friend confesses, it would be best for him to confess as well. Otherwise, he risks incurring a seven-year sentence. If his friend does not confess, it is still wise for him to do so, because then, as state's witness, he will receive only a one-year sentence. That is Nash's point of equilibrium. That is the point that all the players will reach. The best course is for neither of them to confess, and then they will only have to serve a two-year term for weapons possession. However, they both have to confess, due to the fact that they cannot communicate. This point of equilibrium is not the best choice for the prisoners, but it is the one they will choose, whether they like it or not.

Nash's equilibrium point is valid when it is in the interest of all parties to act in a particular way but other factors cause them to act differently, and the result is that their choice is not the best one for them. And just as in a moment of inspiration Nash had come up with his theorem, Elijah had an epiphany of his own: *That's it! I can understand it at last! Eureka! I've just discovered the significance of the* Even Shetiyah!

Nash's equilibrium point is what underlies the story of the heart of the world, which lies across from the Even Shetiyah and the fountain! When the heart is at the top of the mountain, it sees the fountain and can live. If it descends along the slope of the mountain, it no longer sees the fountain and dies. There is no way the heart can ever bridge the gap between itself and the fountain. That is the idea behind ultimate redemption, in mathematical terms!

In other words, dear Mr. Norman was seeking a way to bypass Nash's equilibrium point, or, in less scientific terms, the fool wanted to bring about ultimate redemption all by himself. Furthermore, according to the Kabbalists, redemption-wise, this year was a very auspicious one. Norman was seeking the formula based on the Kabbalah. The formula was to be found in the ancient manuscripts, in the hints planted by Nehemiah of Peki'in, and Elijah was the one flying around the world assembling the hints for Norman. It could be an extremely dangerous enterprise! Elijahhad to find some way to prevent Norman from going through with his scheme! *We've had enough false messiahs in our history!* he thought.

Elijah bought Orna a few pieces of jewelry from the bazaar in Istanbul. Orna was thrilled with the jewelry, and even more by how their bank balance kept growing. Elijah sensed the difference that had taken place in her. She was calmer, and her face radiated joy. The girls fell asleep, and Elijah sat himself next to Orna and embraced her. He concentrated on the text he had found in Alfred's manuscript. He would have to bring it to Norman tomorrow. There was no way he could conceal it, as he had with the manuscript of Rabbi Batzri.

Finally, he blurted out: "Orna, I need to ask you a question."

"That's what you're thinking about now? After you fly abroad and leave your wife all alone for three whole days?"

Undaunted, he went on:

"Let's see if I remember how it goes:

"Ten Sefirot out of nothing, and they are ten in extent beyond limit. Their end is infused with their beginning, and their beginning with their end like a flame attached to a glowing ember. Know, think, and imagine that the Creator is One and there is nothing apart from Him, and before One what do you count?

"He created reality from Tohu and made His existence out of His nothingness, and He hewed great pillars from the intangible air. He created four elements and arranged them according to three mothers.

"Twenty-two letters: He carved them, hewed them, refined them, weighed them, and combined them, and He made of them the entire creation and everything to be created in the future."

"The last section is simple," replied Orna without pausing, her medical training clearly showing. "That's a crude description of the DNA double-helix."

"What?"

"Genetic characteristics are transmitted through what is referred to as the double-helix. Let me try to explain it to you in simple language. One can regard this helix as a very long film whose units are connected to one another. The number of units is enormous, but there are only four basic types of unit. Each sequence of three units is referred to as a 'word' or letter, which relates to a single amino acid. Amino acids are the basis of everything alive. If you want to see what the helix is doing, you simply need to add an amino acid to every three units. All the amino acids combine with proteins, and all together form a person. Simple, no? There's something like three billion of these units. Theoretically, if we could arrange them one after the other and use the proper formula, we could easily make a replica of the human body. Where did you bring your riddle from? Turkey?" She thought her question was hilarious.

"How many amino acids are there?"

"Twenty," Orna answered curtly.

"I find that somewhat puzzling. Had there been twenty-two, that would have paralleled the number of letters in the Hebrew alphabet."

"Actually, there are indeed twenty-two," said Orna, as she played with his hair. "There are twenty amino acids, but if you try to join one to the other, you wouldn't know where one ends and the other begins. So, there are two markers to mark the beginning and the end of each protein, so that there are, in reality, twenty-two items."

"Whoa! Are you telling me that all I am is a mixture of amino acids?"

Orna laughed. "Without going into details, the answer is yes."

Elijah thought back to the text and realized that it indeed referred to four elements and three mothers.

"And these twenty amino acids are all that's necessary?"

"Twenty acids are enough to produce billions of different proteins. In any event, it's much more complex than that. Certain sections of the helix apply to specific parts of the body, while others don't. There are many sections that don't seem to fulfill any function. Sometimes, you find more than one unit for a given acid. Do you want to know what I think? I think that whoever posed that riddle to you wasn't really familiar with the concepts. He read a little bit there and another bit elsewhere, and figured that was enough to make him an expert."

While Orna's answer seemed brilliant, Elijah couldn't understand its significance. What would this have to do with the redemption of the world?

192

Everything Elijah had heard from Orna, added to everything else he had heard and seen, churned about in his mind. He felt himself totally lost as he fumbled in the dark, trying to understand what the *Ari*, Bar Kokhba, and Rabbi Simon ben Yochai had understood, but it simply escaped him.

The next morning he arrived at the university library early to check out various details regarding the extra section that Alfred had shown him, but which he had claimed was insignificant. After dismissing it as inconsequential, Elijah had been unable to investigate that section in depth, and now he had to rely on his memory of it. He was finally able to work out that the two signatures had been those of Shabbetai Zevi and his disciple, Nathan of Gaza.

Throughout the centuries, there had been false messiahs - both male and female - who had arisen among the Jewish people. Some of them had drawn a large group of disciples around them. The vast majority had brought nothing but grief and woe to the Jewish people when they were ultimately unmasked as - at best - deluded individuals, if not downright charlatans. They had disappeared along with their disciples, crushed and broken, the nation's dreams that the end of their troubles was nigh, crushed, too. Elijah found a number of books about Shabbetai Zevi and the movement he had founded. He found that quite a large number of believers in Shabbetai Zevi had maintained their belief in the man even after he was forced to convert to Islam, and that some of these groups exist to this very day. The Turks refer to these groups as "*donmeh*". These people, while ostensibly Muslim, keep various Jewish laws and customs in the secrecy of their own homes and closed communities. Elijah recalled hearing someone whispering that word behind his back, as he was on his way to Alfred's store. That person had evidently wanted Elijah to know that Alfred was a member of that sect, and that would explain why Alfred had not said whether or not he was Jewish. Of all those who had emerged from the Jewish people to form other sects, the only one surpassing Shabbetai Zevi in his influence had been Jesus.

Alfred's copy had evidently been in the possession of Nathan of Gaza, who was born in Jerusalem and moved to Gaza, and that was probably where this copy had been found. Elijah had noticed that there were comments on Alfred's scroll which had been added at the time of Shabbetai Zevi, and which had evidently been written by him or one of his disciples. If Alfred was one of the *donmeh*, that might explain how the scroll had come into his possession.

The fact that Shabbetai Zevi had attempted to solve all the world's problems merely increased Elijah's fear that Norman was attempting to follow in his footsteps.

Very reluctantly, he returned to the Institute, but didn't know what to do with himself there. On the one hand, he had to

194

report back to Norman, but, on the other, he felt that under no circumstances should Norman find out what he had seen in this copy of the manuscript. He decided that he would send Norman only the added notes he had seen on the scroll and which he had not read to Orna, and would refrain from mentioning the part he had read to Orna the previous night. He sent this extra section in an e-mail.

> *Two stones build two houses. Three stones build six houses. Four stones build twenty-four houses. Five stones build one hundred and twenty houses. Six stones build seven hundred and twenty houses. Seven stones build five thousand and forty houses. Go out and calculate what the mouth is unable to say and what the ear is unable to hear.*

Norman called him shortly afterwards.

"Thank you for sending the latest text," said Norman.

Taking advantage of Norman's call, Elijah asked, "Would you have any idea what this is all about?"

"All I know is that it's a type of mathematical calculation," replied Norman.

"Yes, yes - I can see that. But what's the basis for the calculation? I tried to come up with some sort of formula, but it totally escapes me."

"It's known as factorials. In mathematical terms, a factorial is noted by an exclamation mark after the number. For example, '3!' would mean "three factorial". A factorial is the entire series of numbers, starting from one up to and including the factorial number, all multiplied together. That means that '3!' would be 1 x 2 x 3, while '6!' would be 1 x 2 x3 x4 x 5 x 6, and so on."

"OK, but what does all that mean?" The impatience in Elijah's voice was palpable.

"What it means is that if you have a certain number of objects, the factorial of that number is the number of possible ways those objects can be arranged. For example, if you have two objects, then '2!', which is 2, means that there are two ways the objects can be arranged, namely A and then B or B and then A. If you have four objects, where '4!' gives us the number 24, then there are 24 different ways of arranging four objects."

"Marvelous. Your explanation couldn't be clearer. But what do all these numbers actually mean? That's what I want to know."

"Who said there is any meaning?" responded Norman. "I have no idea. Still, be that as it may, we need to figure out whether it's worth our while to purchase Alfred's manuscript. Would our buying the manuscript provide us with a better understanding of Jewish history, and would it help the Institute financially? Keep up the good work, Elijah. Goodbye."

Norman had brought the conversation to an abrupt halt, and Elijah was left holding the phone in his hand.

Elijah had realized by now that Norman was not really interested in buying any more copies of the manuscript. All he wanted was to obtain the seven allusions left by Nehemiah of Peki'in, one in each of the seven copies. Elijah was terrified of what Norman might do once he assembled all the information contained in each of the seventh lines and reconstructed the ancient message contained within them. He assumed that Norman was no less an expert than he in dealing with these ancient manuscripts, and that the only reason he had sent Elijah to obtain the information was because his failing eyesight made it impossible for him to read them himself.

As the day wore on tediously, Elijah became ever more concerned about the possible dangers involved in this project, but when he read his e-mail that night, his concern was raised from possible to real and immediate. He was as tense as an over wound spring, and tossed and turned the whole night long. Even when Orna embraced him, he could not shake his agitation. From that point on, he basically stopped eating, and his sleep was limited to at best to two or three fitful hours each night. The purple bags under his eyes grew more and more pronounced. Orna saw what was happening, but was powerless to help. She was afraid that Elijah was coming down with some mysterious illness.

An email message from Mei-Ling had left him petrified. It was terse, but terrifying. "My grandfather fell from the third floor of his bank and died on the spot. The police are investigating. It does not appear to be accidental. My grandfather was the most cautious man I had ever met. You and I both know who was responsible for this. Eliyah, take care!" Elijah tried to relieve the tension and wrote back to her: "Just keep your spirits up. I'm sure I can arrange for help from here. Take care of yourself and don't cross the street on your own."

He had no doubt that this was the work of the Chinese Mafia trying to blackmail Norman, but would their arm extend to Israel as well? If so, he himself was in very grave danger! And what about Norman himself? What was he really up to? And wasn't Elijah equally at risk from whatever Norman seemed to be doing? Wherever he looked, all Elijah could see was that he was somehow in the direct line of fire.

Elijah began to vomit. Anything Orna persuaded him to eat, wound up being spewed into the lavatory bowl. In his heart of hearts he was glad that the only information he had given Mei-Ling about himself was his untraceable email address. Hopefully, that would keep the Chinese Mafia away from him - but who could tell? Their power could well have extended to locating him here, in Israel.

A few nights later, Orna arranged to have someone take her shift, and returned home. As soon as Elijah opened the door, she attacked him. "Who is that whore in Hong Kong?"

"Orna, what on earth are you talking about?"

"And she even has the gall to call you 'Eliyah', no doubt a lover's nickname. Look at yourself. You're obviously head-over-heels in love with her. You're out of your mind. You're sick. If you want to carry on an affair with someone in Hong Kong, that's fine, but I will not tolerate lies. Let's talk the whole thing over and then we can decide what to do with the girls."

"Orna, what are you talking about, for God's sake?"

"I'm talking about your email correspondence with Mei-Ling."

Had Elijah not been so ill from lack of food and sleep, had he not been suffering from frequent dizzy spells and acute anemia, he might even have regarded the accusation as a compliment.

"You're out of your mind! Have I ever struck you as a sex symbol? Would you believe that someone would fall in love with me after a two-day acquaintance in Hong Kong? Whatever gave you the idea that I'm having an affair?"

"I can read between the lines. All those imaginary troubles she writes about are really a kind of code between you enabling her to form a dependence on you, while you are the white knight in shining armor rushing to her defense, just like in the movies."

"I've never heard anything so preposterous in my entire life, and I'm especially surprised to hear it from someone as intelligent as you. And I've always felt myself to be naive and inadequate compared to you."

"That's exactly the point. You need to compensate yourself for your feelings of inadequacy, so out you go and find some cheap little trollop to whom you can come across as the hero. Elijah, I know you too well. You're totally transparent to me. I have absolutely no doubt that you're hiding something from me."

"Come with me," said Elijah, and in a totally atypical action on his part, he more or less dragged Orna over to the computer and sat her down next to it. As soon as he logged on, he heard the distinctive sound indicating that new email had arrived - from Mei-Ling.

Without even bothering to see its contents, Orna jumped at him again. "You see, you write only to her."

Elijah clicked the e-mail open.

"Dear Elijah, Rabbi Batzri collapsed outside the synagogue after the prayers. An ambulance took him to the hospital; he died on the way. According to the official version, he died of a heart attack. Elijah, I beg you, tell me what to do. Should I come to Israel? Yours, Mei-Ling."

Elijah recalled the dream he had had of the two of them - he and Mei-Ling - flying over Jerusalem. Maybe the dream had foretold what seemed to be happening now?

"So?" said Orna, as if she had proven her point. "Does it seem logical to you that every time she writes to you she informs you of someone else dying? And at such short intervals? Now she has the gall to want to come to Israel!"

"Orna, I've got something to tell you."

Orna missed a few heartbeats as she waited for him to go on.

"There's no affair here. It's much worse than you could possibly have imagined." And even though he had signed an agreement forbidding him to discuss anything related to the Institute with anyone, Elijah broke down and told Orna everything that had happened ever since he had started to work for Luzzato. He told her of the murder of Kim in Hong Kong, of the Hong Kong crime syndicate with the naïvely romantic name "White Lotus", of the pursuit of the different scrolls, of Norman with the American accent who was nevertheless totally adept at writing Hebrew in the southern Italian style. To top it all, he admitted - albeit reluctantly - that he had almost been kidnapped by the Chinese Mafia.

Orna was overcome with emotion, "You mean the Chinese Mafia almost managed to nab you?" It was impossible not to see her new found appreciation of him. All her anger had dissolved magically, and her concern focused on ways to protect him. "I can see now why you've been receiving such astronomical sums of money. Our finances have been going up exponentially, but everything has a price, and we have no way of knowing when you will be required to pay that price."

"I never thought about it like that," said Elijah, which just added another woe to the pack of troubles he was already carrying.

"I bet that's precisely why they chose you for this job. You're a very naive man, Elijah."

"Orna, the fact is that I am not the only one in danger, the same applies to you and the girls. That's why I'm so worried. I'm terrified that they'll stop at nothing."

Orna was a very pragmatic person, with absolutely no connection to the Kabbalah. "I have a theory," she said. "Your Mr. David Norman - together with the Chinese Mafia - is in a race to find the treasures that were hidden at the time of Bar Kokhba, possibly including the Temple treasures. Elijah, how many scrolls have you already examined?"

"Four."

"Why don't you write down everything you've found out up to now, and let's see where that will take us? Let's see if we can beat Norman to the punch and find the treasure before he gets to it."

"I've been thinking along those lines, too, and I have a slight advantage over him. I examined one scroll whose existence he doesn't even know about. Nor do I intend to enlighten him."

"I want to help you."

"What I've managed to understand so far is that the seventh line of each scroll refers to both the cosmological realm in regard to the creation of the world and to the world as it is here. In other words, if we piece together all the seventh lines, this should tell us both when and how to bring about the ultimate redemption. One of the scrolls talks about the *Even Shetiyah*, which is across from the heart of the world. Another states that the *Even Shetiyah* is located on the Temple Mount in Jerusalem."

"That means that we have to find some very high place which is opposite the Mount, one where, if we descend from it, the Temple Mount can no longer be seen. That must be the reference to the slope. Go on."

"The third clue states that redemption should come during one of those years specifically suitable for it. This year is one of them."

"And roughly when in the year should that take place?"

"In the summer."

"In the summer? We're at the beginning of the summer right now. Can you pinpoint it any more closely?"

203

"No, I have no idea."

"Alright then. What else?"

"Then we find the reckoning of the factorials. This evidently must be related to various letter or word combinations, which evidently constitute some type of Divine code. These have to be recited at a certain tempo, and one must stop saying them at a certain time. We don't know any more details."

"I still maintain that the genetic code is somehow involved here, but I can't figure out how to connect it to the other clues."

"There are a few more things you should know about David Norman. He is able to write easily using an ancient script, is interested in the Kabbalah, can foretell the future and read minds. He is the owner of Luria Investments, and runs the Luzzato Institute. Both 'Luria' and 'Luzatto' are the names of famous Kabbalists. In his to-do list, he prophesied the death of Kim, and was willing to accept this with cruel equanimity."

"Elijah, you already have enough pieces of the puzzle."

"Not really. It's like a patchwork. We don't know exactly when, where and how this is supposed to take place. I don't know who John McDonald is, or Odel Weiss. Her first name, too, is connected to the Kabbalah, and it was she who wrote that article which seems to have disappeared after its recall by the magazine publisher. And, of course, there is one other name involved here. Norman's list included 'Visit Gardi in the hospital'. Who is this Gardi?"

"Well, to me, Gardi sounds Yemenite. If he's still in the hospital, I'll see if I can locate him through our computer at Hadassah Hospital. I suggest you continue going to the Institute and act as if nothing has happened. I daresay Norman will send you to see other manuscripts."

"Well, tomorrow I'll pay a visit to my friend Shlomo Nehorai, CEO of Text-Com, who was also mentioned in Norman's list. Maybe he can give me another clue."

"Now why does that name sound familiar?"

"We were at high school together and have been friends ever since."

"I am absolutely fascinated to see how you've changed suddenly from a scholar who deals with ancient documents into a private investigator," Orna remarked with her usual cynicism, but primarily to alleviate the tension in the air. "I have one basic question, though. Tell me, do you actually believe in all this mystical mumbo jumbo?"

"I believe that Norman believes in it and that, to me, makes him a person who is out of control. However, given the three homicides and other potential homicides that surround the whole case, any association with him is highly dangerous. Second, don't forget that Isaac Newton was also very interested in alchemy and other strange phenomena, and he is considered the father of modern scientific thought. Now it's my turn to ask you a question: Do you believe me now about my ties with Mei-Ling?"

"Absolutely."

Elijah embraced her. "Do you know what Rabbi Akiba would have had to say about this?"

"And since when are you suddenly a disciple of Hasidic rabbis?"

"I'm trying to find out everything I can about the Kabbalah. It's said that Rabbi Akiba was a great Kabbalist, and I'm curious to know why he gave orders to have all the copies of *Sefer Yetzirah* burned. However, that's not what I wanted to discuss right now. One of Rabbi Akiba's statements concerns the grounds on which a man may divorce his wife. According to him, 'Even if a man found a woman who is more attractive than his wife, he has the right to divorce her'."

"Yes, I figured that she must be very pretty. I felt that in the way you responded about her," Orna remarked bitingly. Deep down, Elijah felt a certain sense of satisfaction at this turn of events.

Orna continued, "I believe you, but that doesn't mean I'm going to let my guard down. If a woman does too many shifts at the hospital, it makes it much harder for her to keep her husband." Elijah was delighted. That would mean that from now on the burden of caring for the little girls would be distributed more equally, even though she was a medical doctor and he was only a doctor of ancient languages. Indeed, the next morning he was able to take the car to his meeting with Shlomo Nehorai.

Elijah had often passed the high-tech industrial park in Jerusalem, but had never actually driven into it. From the outside it was very difficult to see what the individual buildings looked like, but as soon as he drove in he was impressed by their beauty and elegance, and noted that each had its own individual character. Shlomo's company was located in a building known as the Ivory Building. The elevators were all glass-enclosed, and large picture windows faced west. As with most large buildings in Jerusalem, this one was built on the slope of a hill, and it was difficult to estimate the number of floors it contained, which explained why it took him a while to locate Shlomo's office. At least those few extra moments gave him the opportunity to look around and admire the architecture. The building was encased in white marble that made it glitter in the sunlight. It had been built on an incline, and each floor had its own private terrace with grass and shrubbery. Many of these gardens were even graced by modern, mostly marble, artistic sculptures. He eventually arrived at the right floor and walked over to the woman at the front desk, whom he took to be the receptionist.

"Good morning. I would like to speak to Mr. Nehorai."

Without even bothering to look up from the document she was working on, the young woman mumbled, "Fourth door on the right."

As he walked along the corridor, Elijah noted that the doors to all the rooms were open and that all were the same size. Shlomo was indeed in the fourth room on the right, as a plain sign on his door indicated, without even giving his title as CEO. He was deeply engrossed in the data he was reading on his computer screen.

"Elijah!" Shlomo called out warmly and got up from his chair. The two men shook hands and embraced, thumping each other on the shoulder, as if trying to beat the dust out of the their clothes. Elijah could not but note - with a clear sense of superiority - that Shlomo had gained a lot of weight since their last meeting over ten years ago, whereas, he, Elijah, had kept the same weight for years. *That's very uncharitable of me*, Elijah thought to himself as he sat down.

"Let's not waste time on formalities: I'll ask you 'How're things,' and you'll say 'Fine,' and neither of us will have learned anything of value," said Shlomo. "All I can tell you is that I can't spend much time with you, as I have another meeting scheduled soon."

"That's fine with me. In fact, I have a very specific question to ask you: How have you managed to program artificial intelligence to analyze ancient manuscripts?"

208

"I'll tell you briefly," said Shlomo. "The first generation of programmers tried to have the computer mimic human thought processes when they play chess - but they had no way of knowing exactly how people think. They used brute force by having the computers analyze every possibility and then come up with a move. What this meant, though, was that the computers became so bogged down with the millions of possibilities that their moves were not always the best under the circumstances. Well, the programmers soon realized that people do not work that way at all. A chess player - unlike a computer - will not examine all the possibilities. Intuitively, he will examine three or four lines of attack and decide which one to use. It was only when this analysis was made and the computers were programmed to react the same way people do in playing chess, that the computer was able to defeat a human opponent. We adapted these techniques in analyzing documents."

"Now that computers have reached a high level, is it still necessary for them to emulate the human brain and select only certain lines of thought?" asked Elijah.

"It may take another forty years for computers to be able to do that. If we look at the number of cells in the human brain and especially at the number of neurons, we are talking about billions of cells. And then we have to consider the links between them, which are the basis of all human thought. A number of years ago, a computer analyst laid down a 'law' -

Moore's Law - which states that computer power doubles every eighteen months. This, indeed, has been the situation more or less since the invention of the computer. If we can maintain that 'law,' it will take about forty years for us to develop computers with the capacity of the human brain. Of course, Moore's Law is subject to changes in both directions. It's possible that a major breakthrough will take place that will accelerate the process tremendously, but by the same token, it's possible that unforeseen difficulties will impede the process."

"That means we won't be around to see it," Elijah muttered, half to himself.

"And it will be better if we aren't," said Shlomo immediately. "Imagine what would happen to us. I can already visualize demonstrations by the 'Committee to Liberate the Computer' with demands for equal rights for computers."

"You mean the 'Committee to Abolish Modern Slavery'," Elijah prompted him. "There'll be demands to give computers their personal freedom, equality, pensions, free upgrading and repairs at the expense of the state. And don't forget a fair shake for old computers, and a prohibition against just junking them."

"Exactly. And imagine what would happen if one of these computers becomes a prophet named Karl Marx Comp, and enters into a jihad against the carbon-based creatures that are destroying the environment. By that time, there'll be many more of them, and they'll be far less vulnerable and more powerful."

"It'll be easy for computers to destroy us in a few seconds," Elijah chimed in. "If they unite, they'll be able to cut off all our water and electricity supplies. And, of course, they can launch several nuclear weapons."

"All we can do is to ask for an honorable surrender," said Shlomo as he waved his hands in lieu of a white flag. "That is, if they even deign to speak to us. I'm already depressed about the future of mankind. It's best not to talk about it at all."

Both laughed, and Elijah went onto the next stage.

"Do you, by any chance, know someone by the name of David Norman?"

Shlomo looked at Elijah long and hard. "I guessed that was the reason why you wanted to see me. I only met him once and I spoke to him once on the phone, but he's the type of person who is very hard to forget. He heard about the program we had developed to examine Torah scrolls. As you know, the Torah scroll has to be hand-written on parchment and must be perfect. If a single letter is missing or a single extra letter appears in the scroll, it may not be used. According to Jewish law, after a Torah scroll is written it must be examined three times for accuracy. We developed a program that mimics the actions of those scroll-checkers. It checks that each letter is within the parameters of acceptability in terms of Jewish law, that each letter that should be present is indeed present, and that there are no superfluous letters. For example, by Jewish law, each letter has to be of a specific shape. Let us say that a particular letter has to have a specific horizontal line at the top. In the course of time, the ink of a handwritten letter might crack, so that there isn't a solid line at the top of the letter. That would invalidate that letter - and hence the entire Torah scroll. Our program will check that as well."

"Let me guess. I bet the rabbis were opposed to this program."

"Of course. However, we also found another use for our program. As Torah scrolls are hand-written, each one is totally unique. By using our program, we're able to build up a database of each individual Torah scroll. If a Torah scroll is ever stolen, it is a simple thing to apply our program to it and identify its actual owner."

"And Norman is somehow or other involved in this," sighed Elijah. "I suppose you can use the same technique to identify other manuscripts."

"Elijah, of course you are concerned with your specialty, but in the long term we can use our program for many other applications in various fields. For example, if a computer program is somehow deleted, it's important to be able to reconstruct it exactly as it was before. A single misplaced comma in the program can prevent its reconstruction and can

212

even, in some circumstances, lead to the destruction of the computer itself. Norman was looking for an infallible way to reconstruct material."

"And you developed such a program for him?"

"We explained to him that in order to do what he wanted, he would need two supercomputers."

Elijah sat up straight. He remembered the two supercomputers that Luria had tried to smuggle out of the United States.

"And what did he say about that?"

"That he owned some of the most advanced computers in the world."

There was something strange about that. According to Gabi Moldovan, Luria had failed in its efforts to export the supercomputers from the United States, but according to Shlomo, Norman had nevertheless found a way to obtain access to such computers.

"Do you have any idea where these computers are located?"

"In my opinion, they're not in Israel, but that's only based on bits and pieces of hints I've picked up. No one in the high-tech community in Israel is aware of any such computers in the country - but then again, we might be wrong."

"Well, did you complete all the programming?"

"Tell me, wouldn't you work night and day if you could earn millions of dollars?"

"Shlomo, that's perfectly legitimate. There's no need for you to apologize."

"Isn't that what you're doing with him right now?"

"You mean earning millions of dollars?"

"No, working night and day. Norman is not the type of person you can say 'no' to."

"Actually, he offered me a job, and I came to you to hear more about him. I must tell you that from what I hear from you, things look very good."

"I have to go. Take my advice: work for him and build up some savings."

"One last question," said Elijah. He had evidently seen too many episodes of 'Columbo' and was beginning to fancy himself as a more modern version of that detective. Orna had once said that Elijah was a mixture of naivety and ineptness. "Would you have any idea where the funding came from?"

"I received my checks from Cordoba Investments, and they were signed by the company's CEO, John MacDonald."

The Seventh Sphere

When Titus Conquered Jerusalem

In the year 823 after the founding of Rome, which was 70 C.E., Titus Flavius Vespasianus conquered Jerusalem. The conquest was far from easy, and Titus's victory over the rebellious Jews was one of the primary reasons why the Roman Senate granted him very special honors. Officially, it was noted that it was only through his father's advice and the help of the gods that he had managed to subdue the Jewish people and destroy the city of Jerusalem. All who had tried to conquer this city had failed. While this account is historically inaccurate, it does indicate the importance with which the Romans regarded this triumph.

Three separate Jewish forces combined against the Roman might. Simon Bar Giora controlled the Upper City; Johanan ben Levi of Gush Halav was encamped on the Temple Mount itself, and Elazar ben Simon and his men were in the Temple court. These three - freedom fighters, according to one account, but the leaders of gangs of thugs according to another

- were engaged in a murderous internal struggle among themselves for the control of Judea. However, they all joined forces when Titus besieged the city.

After a siege lasting five months and following a number of vain attempts, the Romans finally breached the city wall and razed the city to its foundations. For Jerusalem to be conquered was nothing new. Even the wanton and wholesale slaughter of men, women, and children was not extraordinary in those days. In fact, under the Hasmonean rule, Jerusalem had been taken a number of times.

But Titus surpassed them all. He consulted with his senior officials as to what was to be done with the Temple; for all but a seventy-year interregnum between the First and Second Temples, the two Temples had stood for a thousand years. In fact, the Second Temple had been thoroughly renovated only a few decades earlier by King Herod, and now stood there in all its glory. Titus sided with those who wished to demolish it, and decided to raze it to the ground and utterly destroy it, something no other conqueror had done for over 500 years.

The aim of those seeking to destroy the Temple was clear. According to them, the Temple was the source of all Rome's problems with the Jews. It served as a symbol of the Jews' pride and rebellious nature, and it was the Temple that fostered their gall in being willing to oppose the might of Rome.

*Destroying the Temple would be akin to breaking the Jews'
backbone. All resistance would collapse, never to rise again.
Just as the other nations in the area - the Ammonites, Moabites,
Philistines, etc. - had lost their original identity, the Jews, too,
would simply disappear as a nation and become part of the
global Roman Empire.*

*The Temple was not used only for various ritual
ceremonies, even though these took up a great deal of the time
and included sacrifices: lighting candles, burning incense,
singing the world-renowned song of the Levites, blowing the
shofar and trumpets on various dates throughout the year, and
other religious rituals. It also served a number of other, no less
important, functions. The priests offered religious guidance to
Jews from all over the world, the scribes and religious leaders
taught the Word of God, the Sanhedrin and the Great Bet Din
sat in judgment, while all matters concerning the economy and
the state of the Jewish people both in the Land of Israel and
throughout the rest of the world were determined there. Jews
throughout the world were taxed a half-shekel a year toward
the upkeep of the Temple, and these taxes were all brought to
the Temple annually. Beyond all these purely functional
aspects, Jews would come from all corners of the globe to the
Temple to see it and to experience its sanctity. It was the nerve
center of the Jewish people at the time. Should the Temple
disappear, reasoned the Roman officials, the Jewish people*

217

would remain a body without a heart, and would soon wither away.

The sanctity of the Temple was so great that even the priests were not permitted free access to it. The entire priestly clan was divided into twenty-four watches, and each watch was assigned a weeklong stretch for serving in the Temple. We assume that there must have been certain priests who remained in the Temple on a permanent basis to ensure continuity, but the vast majority only served during their watch. The constant flow of people to the Temple, the institutions located in it, and all the tourists present, made a visit astounding. It was all these factors that accorded the Temple its special luster and stature among the Jewish people.

When the Temple was destroyed, there were those who refused to eat meat or drink wine, symbolic of their mourning for the Temple. There was a feeling of a religious and national crisis, and no one could foretell how or when the crisis might be resolved. For many Jews, this was the end of the world as they knew it. They were not at all sure whether the Jewish people would ever rise again.

Yet, just at that most crucial time, a group of scholars arose that effectively halted the decline. Rabbi Johanan ben Zakkai, Rabbi Eliezer ben Horkenos, and Rabbi Akiba ben Joseph were among the most prominent members of this group, which totally changed the direction of the Jewish religion. They redirected all the spiritual input that had been directed toward the Temple into prayer and good deeds. Various national, religious ceremonies that had taken place in the Temple were decentralized and transformed into local and personal ceremonies that could be held anywhere, and so on. As part of this transformation, they removed certain works from the public eye and deliberately caused some of them to be forgotten. Other works were made freely available, as part of the group's various considerations. Among others, they sought to suppress various mystical works and concepts, which dealt with the realms of mysticism, messianism, and the apocalypse, topics which were very popular before the destruction of the Temple. We are not sure why they did so, but we do know that they were quite successful in their quest. Judaism underwent a major change in its entire orientation, but as a result, it did not disappear.

Elijah found a note from Norman when he arrived at the Institute, asking him to call as soon as possible. First, he brewed himself a cup of strong coffee. The past few days had taken their toll and he needed the caffeine to keep going. His hair had begun to fall out, probably, he felt, because of a combination of extreme tension and genuine malnutrition. Maybe what he needed, he thought, was some type of food supplement, as he compulsively pushed back his forelock and found a few more hairs in the palm of his hand. In reality, there wasn't much for him to do at the Institute, except to await further instructions. He sent a high-priority email to Norman, expressing his concern for Mei-Ling's life.

Elijah looked out the window and was entranced by the different birds perched in the trees. His thoughts again turned to Rabbi Akiba. Rabbi Akiba had occupied his thoughts quite frequently in the past few days, for somehow or other he sensed that if he could understand Rabbi Akiba and the varied accounts of his character, he would be able to understand what Norman was plotting, why Kim had been killed, and whether he, Elijah, was slated to be the next victim.

Rabbi Akiba's statement, "Even if a man found a woman who is more attractive than his wife, he has the right to divorce her," which he had used to infuriate Orna somewhat and to arouse her jealousy, seemed quite strange. Rabbi Akiba did not specify that the grounds for divorce had to be finding a better woman, or a more righteous woman, but a more attractive one! Was that the way for a religious leader to express himself? After all, in order to find a more attractive woman one must go looking for one. Is that what Rabbi Akiba meant? And how is it that no one in the Talmud disagrees with this viewpoint? Nor was this written in the 21st century. According to the School of Shammai, adultery is a valid reason for divorce, and according to the School of Hillel even a woman who is unable to fulfill her household duties properly may be divorced - but just because the man found a more attractive woman? Add to that the fact that the Talmud tells us that Rabbi Akiba loved his wife dearly, and that it was because of her that he became such an illustrious scholar. Indeed, the Talmud tells us how, out of love for her, Rabbi Akiba bought his wife, Rachel, a golden pendant with a model of the city of Jerusalem.

Elijah opened the window, took out the pack of cigarettes he had bought that morning, and lit one. He was not generally a smoker, but he hoped that cigarettes might help calm his frayed nerves. Of course, as soon as he took his first puff he broke into a paroxysm of coughing, but he nevertheless persisted in smoking the entire cigarette, inhaling deeply each time. He found Rabbi Akiba's moral views to be strange and contradictory. After all, he had grown up with the words, set to a melody, that *"Rabbi Akiba said: 'You shall love your neighbor as yourself' is an important principle in the Torah."*

221

Yet only yesterday he had come across another passage, by the same Rabbi Akiba according to which:

> "If two people are walking in a desert and one has a flask of water, and if they divide it up both will die, while if one drinks it he will survive and reach a settlement. Ben Petora says that it is better that both drink of it, rather than for one to witness the death of his fellow. Rabbi Akiba came and taught: "From the verse 'Your brother shall live with you', we learn that your life takes precedence over that of your fellow."

Now, from a strictly legalistic point of view, Rabbi Akiba's ruling might be correct, but what about concern for the other person? How can we relate this to "You shall love your neighbor as yourself"? Isn't it possible that if they both drink of the water and work together they might find more water, or dig a well, or seek aid? If they do not split the water, the one with the flask will be preoccupied with ensuring that the other person does not take the water from him, and how will he have the will to take the initiative in seeking water? He will be unable to turn his back on the other person for so much as an instant. In essence, this amounts to a cold-blooded battle for survival between the two. It is strange that so esteemed a Torah scholar as Rabbi Akiba would adopt so egotistic a view. This aspect of

Rabbi Akiba's views was obviously not encapsulated in the song Elijah had been taught as a child.

He was deep in thought about this puzzling contradiction, when the incessant ringing of the phone broke the silence, startling him no end.

"Hello," he managed to splutter, before another coughing spell began.

"Hello. Is that you, Professor Shemtov?" the voice asked.

"Yes, yes."

"Are you ill?" It was Norman, and Elijah almost threw up at Norman's exaggerated courtesy.

"No, no, I'm fine, thank you."

"Don't worry about Mei-Ling. She'll be flying to Australia, out of harm's way."

"I'm very happy to hear that."

"Elijah, I've found what I've been looking for! I'd like you to come over to verify that what I've found is the original before I buy it."

"Fine," replied Elijah, "but where and when?"

Norman briefed him about the technical details. The flight would leave on Sunday. Elijah would arrive the same day, and they would begin work immediately. While Norman did not foresee the work taking any great length of time, Elijah should take into account that more might be required. The return flight would leave at noon the following day. Elijah marked down the details.

"But why can't I fly there directly? And where is this place - Formentera?"

"It's a small Spanish island. Years ago I bought a house there. The island does not have an airport of its own, so you have to fly to Barcelona and from there to Ibiza, where I'll arrange for you to be picked up." Norman hung up, and Elijah returned to his ruminations.

Rabbi Akiba was one of the leading spiritual leaders of the Jewish people after the destruction of the Second Temple.

He decided to follow a different train of thought. If the Temple Mount is the key to everything holy, we have to reexamine the destruction of the Second Temple. As a result of the destruction of the First Temple, the Jewish people went into exile in Babylon. The exile in Babylon clarified a lot about Norman. What could Elijah learn from the destruction of the Second Temple?

His mind seemed to have hit a mental block. He couldn't answer the question in any meaningful way. All he could think about was the parallel between that time and the way the Jews of the 21st century are split and how deep are the divisions within the Jewish people. Evidently, there had been no great change in that regard. Elijah was weak and exhausted, and was afraid that all this was because he had started working for the accursed Institute. He went home, but there, too, he was unable to unwind.

Elijah and Orna were fully aware of the risks involved in the trip to Spain; the closer Norman came to locating the next scroll, the greater the danger to Elijah.

"Don't worry. Norman will keep you safe so long as he hasn't deciphered all the clues," Orna said, in an attempt to reassure him. "I'll be rooting for you from here and will continue to search for this Gardi fellow. So far, I haven't located anyone with that name in any Israeli hospital. For all we know, he could have been discharged from the hospital after that note was written."

"Unless he died - from natural causes, or otherwise." Elijah's comment reflected his gloom.

"In any event, I plan to start working backward chronologically until I find him."

"Thanks, Orna dearest," he said, trying not to show how worried he really was.

Early on Sunday morning, Elijah arrived at Ben Gurion Airport and made his way to the Spanish national airline counter. The woman at the counter smiled at him with one of those smiles reserved for important passengers, a smile which one just had to revel in. As expected, his flight ticket was waiting for him. It was for Ibiza via Barcelona; arrival time

10:00 am. The return flight was Monday at 11:00 am. Not surprisingly, the letters "VIP" had been stamped on the ticket. *Well, well, I've become a Very Important Person*, he thought to himself, but found no comfort in the fact. He could not stop worrying. *How long will I continue to remain important?*

At Barcelona, a representative of the airline was waiting for him, and she led him to the domestic flights terminal. It was a short flight, and half an hour after leaving Barcelona, he landed in Ibiza. As he had almost no luggage with him, he passed through Customs with no problem and was the first passenger to reach the outside reception area.

"Good morning, Professor Shemtov," he heard a woman's voice behind him. Even from those few words, he realized that the person spoke English with difficulty and with a heavy Spanish accent. He turned to see who had called him. The woman must have been about thirty years old. She had large black eyes and long, curly black hair. She wore a short white dress that accentuated her slim figure. *She really is very pretty*, thought Elijah to himself.

"I'm pleased to meet you. I am Ruth, Mr. Norman's housekeeper. I've come to pick you up."

"It's my pleasure. I'll follow wherever you lead."

Ruth smiled, and they walked out of the terminal. As soon as they stepped outside, the torrid heat and bright sunshine took him by surprise. He was used to heat, because Spain's climate was much like Israel's, but as a resident of Jerusalem, he was used to its cool, dry climate. The high humidity here seemed to seep through every pore of his body and made him sweat profusely, caused him almost unbearable discomfort. Yes, Tel Aviv was no less humid, but people who lived in Jerusalem were spared it. The two entered a taxi that was waiting for them at the curb. He was delighted to find that the taxi was air-conditioned. Ruth said something to the driver in Spanish, and they drove off.

"Is this your first visit here?" she asked Elijah, with a bewitching smile.

"Yes."

"Ibiza is one of the four large islands of the Balearic Islands. We are close to the Spanish coast, and there are a number of other small, uninhabited islands in the area. The large islands are Palma de Mallorca, Menorca, Ibiza, and Formentera. Until relatively recently, they were isolated and the people subsisted on agriculture. In the 1960s, many American hippies came here, but in the last thirty years the islands have become vacation resorts. Formentera is a small island. It is great to live here in the winter, when there are no more than five thousand residents on the entire island. However, in the summer we are swamped with tourists."

"Well, shouldn't that justify building an airport?"

"The island is so small that there isn't even room for an airport. There are only two gas stations on the entire island. The only way to reach Formentera is by sea. There is a ferry, but it is easy to reach the island by motorboat. We are going to the port, where a small boat awaits us. You'll enjoy the trip."

The drive to the port took very little time. To Elijah, the port seemed minuscule. The taxi drove into the port until it reached a locked gate. A guard stood at the gate and he and Ruth broke into a heated argument.

"He refuses to let you enter. He says we need a special permit, which has to be obtained a week in advance. The taxi driver will drive you to a different place, where I'll be waiting for you with the boat." Every kind of alarm bell went off in Elijah's mind, along with revolving blue police lamps. Everything pointed to imminent danger. He didn't say anything, but he certainly did not radiate any signs of joy.

The driver took Elijah to the end of the dock and signaled to him to leave the taxi. The driver didn't know a word of English, and Elijah was unable to communicate with him. He left the taxi and was again subjected to a blast of humid heat, which seemed to smother him. A man approached him and stood by his side, stared at the water and lit a cigarette. The man began speaking to Elijah in a soft undertone. Elijah didn't understand a word. If he had been worried up to now, all the bells in his head seemed to explode in a raucous cacophony of sound. The man was clearly stronger than he, and much taller. Elijah sized up his opponent and instinctively backed off, taking care not to get any closer to the water. If a car came and tried to kidnap him, what would he do? Was Ruth one of the gang that intended to kidnap him? His thoughts were interrupted by the sounds of a boat approaching. Ruth waved to him, and the stranger left.

"Did you receive any interesting offers?" Ruth laughed. Elijah smiled nervously. He couldn't understand the local humor.

"This island is full of gays and lesbians. He is one of them," Ruth explained, and Elijah relaxed. The so-called "boat" which Ruth had promised to bring was, in reality, a four-seater yacht equipped with a bedroom, a kitchen, and a toilet. Ruth steered the yacht skillfully, as if driving a familiar car. She dialed a number on her cellular phone and handed it to Elijah. The line was rather noisy, but Elijah could still hear Norman's voice.

"I have the scroll," said Norman. "It's waiting for you. You'll be here in about forty minutes, and then we can work on it together. I'm anxiously awaiting your arrival."

"By the way," said Ruth cheerfully, "my friend Isabel, whom you probably will meet tonight, is bisexual."

That set Elijah to thinking in a different direction: was Ruth a lesbian? That might or might not be relevant. He needed

229

to assess every single fact and its implications carefully, because he felt his very life depended on his ability to do so speedily and accurately. He would somehow have to overcome the problem of his total ignorance of the Kabbalah, and the different texts that he had been gathering for Norman were an enigma to him.

The trip itself took about half an hour. At least as long as they were sailing, the strong breeze dissipated some of the effects of the scorching sun. The dock on Formentera was very small and showed gross signs of neglect. Ruth weaved her way into the port and soon moored the yacht. A young man of possibly eighteen ran over and tied it down. Ruth had a brief conversation with the young man before she and Elijah got into a jeep parked nearby.

"Emmanuel maintains the yacht when it's in port," Ruth explained casually.

With Ruth at the wheel they drove off, soon driving along the single road through Formentera. On both sides of the road, he could see the ocean; the strong sunlight blinded him, forcing him to squint. Now they started ascending a hill. The scenery naturally changed. Dense vegetation on both sides - trees and bushes - gave one the feeling of driving through a forest. Numerous unpaved roads leading to private homes branched off from the main road; some of the houses were near the road, others further off.

"We're here," said Ruth.

Elijah looked around, but could see no path or building. Ruth turned suddenly onto a dirt path, indiscernible among the surrounding vegetation. Only when they were actually on it, could he see the faint outline of the path. She drove for about twenty yards, sometimes pushing aside foliage that blocked the way. Suddenly, ahead of them Elijah saw an old, simple electricity-powered barrier, and a small yellow sign proclaiming "Private Property." Ruth pressed a remote control button from inside the jeep, and the barrier came up. Once past the barrier, they drove for another thirty yards among the trees and before he realized it, Elijah found that they were driving on a superb asphalt road, although it was quite narrow and suitable for only one car at a time.

Ruth drove slowly for about a hundred yards, as the road kept twisting and turning, finally stopping in front of a white two-story house, which appeared to be a very modest abode. Close to it was a large single-story structure, whose purpose Elijah could not even guess at.

They entered and immediately found themselves in the large, circular living room. On the walls were clusters of small windows, through which light poured in to light up the interior. Four strategically placed sofas effectively divided the room into distinct areas. Throughout the room there were bookcases stuffed with books. The impression given was of coziness and

Elijah felt tempted to sit down on one of the couches. When he looked up, he saw that the room's ceiling consisted of a perfectly symmetrical dome.

"I shall go and call Mr. Norman. Meanwhile, what type of music would you like to hear?"

"Whatever you think is appropriate," said Elijah, as he took a seat on one of the couches. Because of the way the room had been built with its domed ceiling, every word that anyone said was echoed back and forth. Elijah was surprised that Norman was willing to put up with so poor an acoustical area.

Ruth opened a cabinet in one of the corners and pressed a number of buttons. To Elijah's surprise, one of the walls slowly opened to reveal a picture window. As the wall opened, so did one half of the dome. Elijah took in the breathtaking view. Facing him was the Mediterranean and to the left the lower part of the island. Ruth chose a track that combined a Gregorian chant with Hasidic soul music, ethereal music. Elijah examined a large map of the area hanging on the wall. On the map, Formentera looked like a kid with a long neck that drank from the waters of the Mediterranean, while Ibiza watched on patronizingly, like an older brother. Elijah closed his eyes and let his imagination carry him away.

He had almost dozed off when he heard Norman's familiar voice. "Professor Shemtov!" He opened his eyes, startled, and noticed that the music had stopped. Norman was dressed simply, in black slacks and a blue short-sleeved shirt. He appeared to be even more nearsighted than ever, as he put out his hand to shake Elijah's. Elijah stood up hastily and shook the man's outstretched hand.

"I think I must have dozed off," he apologized.

Norman led Elijah through the furniture in the room, and it seemed to Elijah that his host was unable to see the different pieces but had memorized their locations. In one of the corners, which had been hidden by a square wooden beam, stood a spiral staircase. Norman climbed it, feeling his way with the help of the banister. Elijah followed. The room in which he found himself, evidently a study, also had a domed ceiling, made of clear glass. The view was spectacular, and there was a feeling that the desk was positioned in the middle of the woods.

Norman pressed a number of buttons, and the dome was concealed by white curtains. Next he opened a drawer and carefully drew out a wooden box.

As Elijah looked at the scroll that Norman had removed from the box, Norman played around with the computer on the desk next to him. He spoke into a microphone, and the much-enlarged computer screen image was projected onto the wall.

"I have an invention which enables whatever I say to be translated into text on the computer screen - a voice recognition program," Norman volunteered.

They worked efficiently, with no unnecessary chatter. Elijah analyzed the text on the scroll using a magnifying glass, the ultimate low-tech antithesis to Norman's display of computer pyrotechnics. Elijah went through the scroll letter by letter. As he verified each letter, Norman spoke it into the microphone, and it appeared on the wall, enlarged. By now, Elijah almost knew the entire text off by heart. He waited expectantly, though, for the seventh line, and when he got there he made sure to repeat the letters in the same monotonous tone, so as not to alert Norman of his knowledge of the codes embedded there.

Not unexpectedly, the seventh line was unique. What it stated was different from anything in any of the other scrolls: "When you reach the pure marble rocks, do not say, 'Water, water.'"

Elijah continued reading the text, a task that took another hour to complete.

There was a soft knock on the open door. Ruth waited outside. Elijah noted that she had not even considered entering the room.

"This appears to me to be an original scroll, written by Nehemiah of Peki'in," said Elijah, even though he knew that his statement was totally unnecessary. There was no doubt that the scroll was genuine, and Norman was fully aware of that fact.

234

Elijah had only been brought there to read the text because of Norman's problem with his vision.

Norman was satisfied. "Well, that's that. Ruth has come to invite us to lunch."

Lunch was served in the dining room, which overlooked the Mediterranean. It was a vegetarian meal consisting of mushrooms, fruit, and various juices. The food was served by Maria, a woman about fifty years old.

Elijah saw Norman and Ruth exchanging glances, and wondered about the relationship between them. Norman was a good forty years older than Ruth, but Elijah was convinced this was not a normal employer-employee relationship.

Norman and Ruth chatted away in Spanish. Elijah didn't understand a word, but this was the first time he had heard Norman speak it, and to his unpracticed ear it sounded like Norman spoke it like a native. Again Elijah wondered about where Norman had originally hailed from.

After lunch, Norman suggested that Ruth give Elijah a tour of the island, after which they would pick up Ruth's friend Isabel in Ibiza and return.

They drove but a short distance before stopping at an old windmill.

"Many hippies lived here during the 1960s. You see that house next to the windmill? Bob Dylan lived there for two months. This entire area was built up about 250 years ago. The windmill still works to this day, and it is one of the oldest functioning ones in Europe."

Elijah looked at the house in which Bob Dylan had lived. The house seemed quite unimpressed by that fact.

"The local residents always lived here in relative tranquility. For example, the Inquisition never came to Ibiza, and certainly not to Formentera. Even the Spanish Civil War was not felt here. During the Franco era, this was one of the few places that managed to evade censorship and dictatorship, which is why the hippies discovered and were drawn to it. It was remote, far from anywhere else. You could even say it was cut off from the rest of the world." She seemed to be carried away by her own voice.

Suddenly, in front of the house that Bob Dylan had used, another piece of the puzzle snapped into place. There just had to be a connection between the hippies, Odel Weiss, and John McDonald. In her article, Weiss had hinted that McDonald had wandered through Spain. Would a hippie such as he comes to Spain to take part in the Civil War? No way! He would come here to chill out. And if Bob Dylan too had been here, it was a clear indication that this place was not that much off the beaten track.

The tour of the island was brief, and immediately afterwards they sailed back to Ibiza. In Ibiza, Ruth took him to one of the famous beaches.

Toward sunset, they walked along the beach, and Elijah kept glancing - and immediately glancing away in embarrassment - at the European women with their very scanty bathing suits, either sitting or lying on beach chairs or on the sandy beach. They sat down in adjacent chairs, and Elijah sighed.

"What's that all about?" asked Ruth.

Elijah did not know how to answer the question. It was a typical Jerusalem sigh, which in Jerusalem would not even be noticed. He thought that the sigh might be in reaction to all the pretty girls out there, but decided that this was hardly something he could tell Ruth.

"There are different interpretations," he answered. "Some say it is a sigh of despair at the world. Cynics might interpret the sigh as regret for being unable to sit here each evening, watching the sunset. Doctors would say that sighs have a medical purpose, in that they cause you to breathe more deeply and thus inhale more oxygen. Jewish mothers would say it is brought about by guilt – for feeling no guilt for not having any feelings of guilt. Sociologists would no doubt interpret it as a typical Jewish sigh."

Ruth laughed and Elijah felt at the top of his form. Further down, aging hippies sat on the rocks singing, accompanying themselves on tambourines. The evening gave way to night, and the hippies celebrated the night of the full moon. When it was late enough, Ruth and Elijah went to collect Isabel at one of Ibiza's famed discotheques.

When Ruth had told him that they would be going to a discotheque, the closest parallel Elijah could envision was one of the student lounges at the university, which he had entered every so often as a student. He could not believe his eyes when he finally stood at the open door of the discotheque. It was packed with people shoulder to shoulder, and the clothes they were wearing were either extremely revealing or bizarre - or both. The sound of what was evidently supposed to pass as music was deafening, and he covered his ears with his hands. He was in total shock. Ruth moved into the discotheque and almost disappeared from view. This must be the trap they had set for him! Now, finally! They had done a good job of camouflaging their intentions until this moment. He had to do something to save himself!

He finally spotted Ruth and made a dive to reach her. Frantically, he clutched her hand. He tried to speak to her, but the noise made it totally impossible. With very great effort, she was able to decipher what he was trying to communicate by screaming into her ear. "If you leave me, even for an instant, I am lost! I am unable to navigate in unfamiliar places." She nodded that she understood and led him, using hand motions, through the crowd of people. He followed her blindly, the noise crashing around his ears. They crossed the hall and wound up at a flight of stairs at the other end, which they climbed slowly, having to flatten themselves to the side to allow other people to descend. They eventually reached a sort of balcony, which overlooked the entire hall. One part of the balcony was open to the Mediterranean night, and Elijah breathed the relatively purer air there deeply. Here too the music was extremely loud, but it was at least possible, with great effort, to hear what the other person was saying.

He found a seat, while she disappeared for a while and returned with three bottles of beer and a bottle of juice.

"I'm going to look for Isabel, but she will probably come up here looking for me, as this is the place we normally meet. It is best that you remain here." Elijah was delighted not to have to make his way through the sweating, heaving crowd.

He looked down onto a minuscule stage surrounded by a fence, on which an almost nude woman was dancing.

Among the entire hubbub, he suddenly heard a female voice speaking excellent English, but with Spanish accent.

"Hello, Professor Shemtov. I'm Isabel, Ruth's friend." Elijah turned around to find where the voice was coming from. Isabel was a young woman with short, very curly black hair. She wore very narrow glasses. He could sum up her look very easily: student; feminist; fighter for the environment and against the intellectual dictatorship of white, dead, European males.

"Yes, I'm Professor Shemtov," he admitted. "How did you recognize me?"

"From the photograph that Mr. Norman gave Ruth. How do you think she recognized you at the airport? Did you think it was some type of divine inspiration? Thousands of people fly in every day."

Isabel sat down next to him, and he noticed that she was drunk. He tried to think of where Norman could possibly have gotten a photograph of him.

"Are you a professor of mathematics, like Norman and the others?" she asked, and his ears perked up. He realized that in her inebriated state it might be easy to pump her for information, but he had to do so before Ruth returned.

Norman a professor of mathematics? That was news to him.

"Are the others also going to come? How about John McDonald? Will we be meeting him as well?" he asked.

"You already have!" she answered.

He tried to process that bombshell in a hurry. "Are you telling me that Norman is John McDonald?"

"Of course! He changed his name after he was placed on the Wanted List during the Spanish Civil War. Did you meet Maria? It was her mother who saved him from death. They say that he arrived in Spain when he was still a young boy, and he was found searching through all sorts of dark, dusty monastery

240

attics. He was almost put to death by the Republicans after he tried to steal the treasures of a church that had caught fire. His claim that he was simply searching for old manuscripts was received with scorn. He was saved by his youth and the pity of a woman named Rosa, who interceded on his behalf. Rosa was Maria's mother."

If that's the case, Elijah reasoned, the scroll I have just seen must have come from that church. Norman's claim that he had just found the scroll was a pack of lies. It appeared that what was written in this scroll was one of the links in the chain of hints.

"And what is this about the mathematicians?"

"Norman wound up in the United States, where he studied mathematics. These were evidently friends of his from those days. In the past six years, Norman has only brought three guests: a woman and two professors of mathematics. I never met them, but I did see photos of them, each with a black border around it, because Ruth said they had died a short while after visiting here. I hope you're not the next in line," she added. Elijah was understandably distressed.

Isabel looked at him with the same look a drunk gives an electricity pylon in trying to gauge if he can beat it in a fight. "Didn't Norman tell you how he found Ruth?"

"Tell me."

"Ruth is Norman's housekeeper the same way Madame Pompadour was the housekeeper of Louis XIV."

As Elijah did not know the relationship between Madame Pompadour and Louis XIV, he chose discretion as the better part of valor.

"I've known Ruth since she was thirteen. We were in high school and university together. Did you know she's a medical doctor?"

Elijah could detect a certain strain of envy in her words. He wondered why he was always attracted to doctors.

"She was my brother, George's, girlfriend. One summer, she went to work on some farm in southern Spain. Norman happened to visit the farm. He asked Ruth to come to Formentera for a month, to take care of a sick guest who was staying there. I have no idea how he managed to bewitch her, but she came to him and she hasn't left him since. Six years!"

"How do you fit into the picture?"

"He pays me enormous amounts of money to come here. Whenever he travels, I come here to keep Ruth company. He doesn't like leaving her on her own. Ruth can spend as much as she wants on anything she wants. But what kind of life is it for a young woman? To stay here with an old man? To my mind, he must be over eighty years old. To this day I have no idea where his money comes from. Do you know where he was born? Where his family is from?" Elijah got the impression that Isabel

242

too wanted to find out as much as possible about Norman before Ruth returned. He waited, and she continued:

"She worships Norman and follows him blindly. That word is a bit of a misnomer, because if anyone is blind, it is he. Maria comes in once a week by plane from Barcelona to cook and clean for them, and she is not exactly a friendly person. Sometimes she sleeps over and works another day, flying back at the end of the second day. Ruth, though, is totally isolated."

"Have you ever tried to speak to Maria?" Elijah asked.

"Sure. She's never answered a single one of my questions, and then she goes to Norman and Ruth to complain that my nosiness is disturbing her work. Ruth yelled at me. Do you know that Ruth never enters Norman's study, so as not to disturb the privacy of the genius at work? It's enough to drive you mad. Whenever Norman isn't there, Maria locks up his study. I once actually entered the holy of holies. Maria had been cleaning it and had gone down to the kitchen for a few minutes."

"And did you find the secrets of man's existence there?"

"I'm glad you have a sense of humor, but I found nothing at all, except for the black-bordered photographs I told you about. Ever since that time, Maria locks herself in when she works in the study and locks the study from the outside as soon as she steps out of it. It's totally unbelievable. You're the only person I've ever met, besides Maria, who knows Norman. Now it's your turn. Tell me what you know about him."

He thought to himself. What indeed did he know about Norman? He had even been surprised to find out how old the man was. He certainly did not look like a man who was over eighty. In the few minutes he had spoken to Isabel, he had found out more about Norman and Ruth than he had in all the time he had been working for the man. He decided to remain silent. He had his own problems, and Isabel's revelations had not made things easier in any way. On the contrary - now he had an additional element of fear. The three people who had visited Norman had all died soon afterwards. What he did remember was that often the best way to deal with a problem is to simply ignore it. Indeed, problems often have a way disappearing of their accord.

Isabel, though, did not go away, but now devoted herself to the task at hand - polishing off two more bottles of beer - when Ruth came up behind her.

The two embraced, and Isabel asked Elijah, "Would you like to dance?"

He shook his head vigorously from side to side and the two women disappeared. His mind worked in slow motion, as if in a trance. And there, with all raucous noise of drums and guitars and the wild gyrations in the discotheque, he remembered an ancient legend he had learned in school about

Rabbi Akiba and three other great rabbis who had become involved in studying the Kabbalah. Rabbi Akiba had warned the other three great rabbis, Ben Azzai, Ben Zoma, and Elisha ben Avuyah, and had made the cryptic comment: "When you reach the pure marble rocks, do not say, 'Water, water.'" His warning had not helped. The legend goes on to state that because of their studies of the Kabbalah, Ben Azzai died, Ben Zoma became insane, and Elisha ben Avuyah became a heretic, rejecting everything to do with Jewish belief. Only Rabbi Akiba had emerged intact after his encounter with the Kabbalah. The warning Rabbi Akiba had given the other rabbis was identical to the seventh line of Norman's manuscript. Could this story have been what the manuscript alluded to? But try as he might, Elijah simply couldn't see the connection. And could whatever the three dead people in the black-rimmed photographs been working on provide the key to their subsequent deaths?

About twenty minutes later, Ruth and Isabel returned, dripping with sweat. Elijah was delighted when they finally left the discotheque and headed for the port in the jeep. Elijah helped Ruth and Isabel untie the ropes securing the yacht to the dock, and they set sail.

"Do you like Trance?" Isabel suddenly asked Elijah.

"I really am not used to that type of music," replied Elijah.

"If you listen to Trance, you can be elevated spiritually. It enables people to free themselves from their unnatural preoccupation with their ego. If you immerse yourself in this music, you can cast off all your chains. In a Trance session, everyone concentrates on the music like a single beating heart."

Elijah was totally amazed. He had never imagined that anyone could reach so sweeping a conclusion about the excruciatingly loud noise he had just been subjected to. Isabel laughed.

"I think I'm just too old for that type of music," he finally commented lamely.

"It has nothing to do with age," said Ruth. "Norman is older than you, and he loves to listen to it. It is a question of being open to new thoughts and ideas."

"Your Norman is the greatest genius of our age," said Isabel. "I'm surprised that God doesn't come to him each night for advice as to how to run the world."

Elijah suddenly felt unbelievably tired. It was the end of a very long, very wearying day, and all he wanted was to sink into a comfortable bed. Ruth led him to his room like a lamb to the slaughter. He plopped down on the bed, and hoped to have a full night of restful sleep.

But it was not to be. He tossed from side to side while sleep eluded him. He dozed off for a while, but never entered a deep sleep. He found himself neither sleeping nor fully awake.

He was too tired to get up, but too awake to fall asleep. He kept picturing in his mind's eye the scroll he had seen earlier that day, with the image of the Ibiza beach superimposed on it. Everything he had experienced during that long day appeared in his mind as a hopeless jumble.

Thinking back, Elijah recalled having seen the mark of a rubber stamp and a signature on the other side of the scroll, but he had not paid attention to them at the time, possibly because Norman had been so insistent that they finish as soon as possible and that Elijah should go out and enjoy himself. Altogether, the whole day had been strange. He tried to concentrate on everything he had seen. Soon it came back to him, as if the reverse side of the scroll was before his eyes. This scroll had been copied from the scroll collection of the Templar monastery in Geronda. Permission to copy it had been given by Cardinal Pedro Reuchlin, who sold holy works to the Templars in Spain. Reuchlin's signature appeared on top of the rubber stamp of the monastery.

Who needed to receive such permission? Elijah knew that if he racked his brain he would remember the answer to that question. After all, he knew a great deal about the Templars from his study of the Crusaders. *Now, who needed the Cardinal's permission?* He finally remembered - someone who was not a member of the monastery, and especially if the matter concerned internal monastery documents. *A Muslim or Jewish*

247

scholar would certainly need such permission before copying anything. The chances of a non-Christian scholar being given access to any church document were very slim to nonexistent, unless - wasn't there always an "unless" - a considerable amount of money changed hands. And the one thing Elijah knew from the time he had started working for Luzatto was that money was absolutely no object to the Institute. With that thought in mind, he finally dozed off.

All of a sudden, he jumped out of bed as if bitten by a snake. With no idea what had awakened him, he went over to the window and looked outside. The light of the full moon illuminated the garden outside. He suddenly noticed two people, dressed in white, walking, and their backs to him. They looked like ghosts. At first he was terrified, but when he looked more closely he saw that the "ghosts" were Ruth and Norman, walking hand in hand. Elijah wanted to beat a fast retreat from the window, but soon realized that was unnecessary, as there was no way they could see him. The room itself was pitch dark, and the only light reaching it was from the outside. From afar, he saw Norman whisper something into Ruth's ear, and he heard a faint laugh from her. For a few seconds he felt a twinge of envy, but that thought soon ended. He saw the two entering a room in the garden near an ornamental pool; they closed the door behind them.

Suddenly, for some reason he could not fathom, Elijah wanted to see the scroll again. But of course, Norman's study was locked - so Isabel had said. Yet something impelled him, and he decided to try his luck anyway. He hurried to Norman's study with his flashlight-camera in hand. The distance to the study seemed immense, and the noise made by his slippers seemed deafening. The door was closed, but was it locked? Gingerly, he tried the door handle. The door had not been locked! An oversight? Well, whatever the reason, he now had access to the study.

The room was dark, and Elijah didn't dare turn on a light. Isabel was sleeping somewhere in the house, and Maria might also be there. As he entered the room, he saw that the computer was in standby mode. He tapped a key and brought it back to life. On the desk were four picture frames, which had not been there when Elijah was invited into the study that morning. Elijah looked at the first, and his blood ran cold. It was a picture of Norman embracing an elderly woman whose beauty was still discernible. From the surrounding scenery, he saw that the photograph had been taken in Formentera, near the lighthouse. On the photograph there was an inscription in English in a small feminine hand. The signature was clear: Odel Weiss. Odel Weiss smiled at Elijah from the photograph. Odel Weiss had also been on the island, and was dead!

Elijah looked at the next two photographs. Both were of a group of people whom Elijah could not identify, together with Norman. He assumed these must have been the guests that Isabel had mentioned. The last frame did not contain a photograph, but a letter. It was hard for him to identify the handwriting. With great difficulty, he realized that the script, very small and compact, was a Hebrew script known as *nuskalam*– "half reed".

Elijah photographed all four items. He made sure to photograph the letter several times, from different angles. He opened the drawer from which Norman had taken the wooden box containing the scroll. As he had imagined, there were seven such boxes there, one for each scroll. He saw his life contained within those boxes. As soon as the boxes had all been filled, he assumed that he too would be dead.

He stepped over to the computer and examined the different icons. One, which was written in ancient Arabic, would never have caught his eye, but after seeing the framed letter he decided to click on it. He was not wrong. Pressing the icon made the computer run a program named "Golem", written in the same ancient Arabic. For a moment Elijah's blood froze. The program looked like a normal database program, with people's names. However, there was only a single entry in the entire database, and that was for "Professor Elijah Shemtov". Everything was written in Hebrew, but using ancient Arabic script. The numerals, too, appeared in the Arabic notation rather than the more common Latin one. Elijah read the entry carefully. Almost everything he had ever done in his life was listed there: his names, his parents' names, his daughters' names, everyone's birth dates, the schools he had attended, the universities where he had taught, etc... details, long forgotten, were all there on the screen.

On the right side of the screen was a large square, which read "Run". Elijah clicked on the square. The computer churned away for a few seconds, and then words in large letters appeared on the screen. Elijah read a list of names of people, and next to each was a grade. In the first place was Elijah's name, way above the others. A number of them had been tagged and marked "not suitable". He knew almost all the people on the short list. They were among the foremost experts in Hebrew manuscripts. Elijah breathed heavily. He began to understand how Norman selected his people and what factors made them unsuitable. It was evidently due to some type of Kabbalistic calculation of the person's name. Now he remembered how when he had first come to the Luzzato Institute he had been pressed to give his full name. He returned to his own name and added a few letters to it. The same words appeared, but in the square the words "not suitable" appeared. That proved his point! There were Kabbalistic factors involved.

As he thought about it, the computer began to beep. He thought he heard footsteps. He acted totally hysterically, shut down the computer in a hurry, grabbed the camera-flashlight, and rushed out of the study toward his own room. He had no idea if he had moved things around, and only hoped that Norman would not remember if there had been any changes. He was out of breath when he finally reached his room, and it took him many long minutes before he could breathe easily again. If there had been any footsteps, they were no longer audible. He fell onto his bed and tried to reconstruct what had just happened.

Why was he no more than an aesthete of letters? Why had he never been interested in the content? The seventh line kept coming back to him. He had to find out, as soon as possible, what was meant by "When you reach the pure marble rocks, do not say, 'Water, water.'

The Eighth Sphere

When The Crusaders Conquered Jerusalem

In July 1099, the Crusaders conquered Jerusalem. An assemblage of princes devoid of a king and without a ruler came to reclaim the City of God. With them came a ragtag rabble drawn from throughout Europe. Godfrey of Bouillon attacked the city from the north, while Raymond of Saint-Gilles attacked from the south. Near what is now the Nablus Gate, the troops broke through the wall of the city and the Christian troops poured in through the breach. Tancred was the first to reach the Temple Mount. He locked the gates to it, and as a sign of his extreme devotion systematically looted all the treasures contained within it. Hundreds of Muslims, who had paid a huge ransom to save their lives, were clustered on the roof of the Al-Aqsa mosque, to be slaughtered a short while later. The Jews locked themselves in their synagogues in the Jewish Quarter and beseeched God to help them. They were burned alive, along with their Torah scrolls. Contemporary accounts tell of the Crusaders' horses having to wade through blood up to their bridle reins, about the heads and limbs piled in the streets, and of the lethal combination of religious fanaticism and lust for booty and plunder. Again Jerusalem was witness to a terrible slaughter, which came to an end only when the Crusaders had killed everyone they could lay their hands on. Thus the mighty Christian warriors proved that, unlike Islam, which prided itself on forcing itself upon others by the sword, they - the religion with a message of mercy and of turning the other cheek - could wallow cheerfully in the blood of innocents.

Twenty years after Jerusalem was conquered in the First Crusade, two French knights, Hugues de Payens and Geoffrey de St. Omer, set up the Order of the Templars. They and seven other knights who joined them took a vow of poverty, chastity, and obedience, and pledged to devote their lives to battle the enemies of God. At the head of the order was its Grand Master, whose full authority was unquestioned. Under him was an advisory council of elders, whose recommendations were not binding on the Grand Master. Very seldom, though, did the Grand Master act against these recommendations. At the request of the order, King Baldwin II of Jerusalem granted the Templars land on the Temple Mount, where the Al-Aqsa mosque had stood. The building that the Templars erected on the site was called Solomon's Temple, because of the (mistaken) belief that it had been the actual site of Solomon's Temple.

The Templars scorned death, and the order soon grew to be the best organized and strongest in the entire Crusader realm. Unlike other monastic orders in the Middle East, the Templars were interested in the esoteric beliefs of the other religions with which they shared the area. They learned both Hebrew and Arabic, studied Greek geometry, investigated the secretive Druze faith, took an interest in Jewish Kabbalah and sequestered themselves with Muslim Sufis.

The main center of the Templars was in Jerusalem, until that city fell to the Arabs in 1187. Then its center was moved - at first to Acre and then to Caesarea, and even later to Antiochia and to Cyprus. When Acre fell in 1291, the Templars returned to Europe. The order, which had originally been extremely poor, became one of the greatest landowners in Europe. It owned fortresses, estates, fields and vineyards throughout the continent, and as religious functionaries, its members were exempt from paying any local taxes and were subject only to the Pope.

The Templars transferred large sums of money from Europe to Palestine and from Palestine to Europe. In order to accomplish this, they developed a banking system that was highly advanced for its time. They were the first to introduce the idea of travelers' checks. A Christian knight who wished to travel to the Holy Land could go to any of the offices of the Templars in France or Spain, deposit money there, and receive a receipt. When he came to Jerusalem, the local office would then honor that receipt and pay him the amount in question.

But there was a fly in the ointment. As the Templars flourished and became more and more wealthy, opposition to them arose. One of their greatest opponents, who also owed them a great deal of money, was Phillip IV of France. On Friday, April 13 1307, Phillip's soldiers attacked the Templars in France, seized all their holdings, and imprisoned every Templar on whom they could lay their hands. Ever since that time, Friday the 13th has been considered an unlucky day.

The Grand Master, Jacques de Molay, and senior officials of the order were tortured, as was customary at the time. According to Phillip, they confessed to a long string of crimes, including Satan-worshiping, homosexual orgies, the sale of the Holy Land to Muslims, black magic, and plotting to seize France.

According to the rumors that swept Paris at the time, the Grand Master was able to bribe one of his jailers, and received a number of magic books of the order. De Molay then proclaimed his innocence and claimed that the confessions extracted from him and others had been under torture, and that their only sin had been in confessing to have done something they had not done. Phillip reacted immediately. On March 18

1314, de Molay and other Templars were burned at the stake outside the Notre Dame cathedral. On the stake, de Molay cursed the Pope and King Phillip, and promised that by the end of the year both would join him in Heaven. Indeed, a month later, on April 20, Pope Clement V died suddenly, at the age of fifty-four. Phillip died in November that year, at the age of forty-six.

The people of that generation interpreted these deaths in various ways. The Templars' opponents viewed this as conclusive proof of the Templars' satanic powers, whereas their supporters saw it as proof of the Templars' innocence.

Most modern historians believe that the allegations against the Templars were unfounded. The claim that they had engaged in black magic was based on their ties to the members of other religions and on their famed collection of documents, and was simply used as an excuse to appropriate their considerable property. That was exactly how Phillip treated the Jews: he banished them from France and seized all their assets.

Somewhere, Elijah heard a noise. It took some time for him to realize that the noise would not go away by itself. He focused, and finally realized that someone was knocking on his door. He had evidently finally dozed off.

"Yes?"

Ruth entered the room. She was more beautiful than ever.

"Professor Shemtov, I accidentally overslept. Norman is still asleep. It's already 10:00 am, and your flight is due to depart from Ibiza at noon. We have to leave immediately. The problem is your connecting flight to Tel Aviv. If you miss your connection to Barcelona, you'll have to stay here for a few days longer."

Elijah jumped out of bed. It took him but a few moments to be ready. At Ruth's suggestion, they skipped breakfast and he found himself shaving on the yacht that took them from Formentera to Ibiza, trying to keep his balance and hoping Ruth would steer them through safely without overturning the boat.

Ruth steered with one hand, while holding a cell phone in the other and carrying on conversations with different people.

"I'm trying to get them to hold the plane," she explained. There was a taxi waiting for them at the port, and they half-ran to it. Elijah was breathing heavily, as he tried to move as quickly as possible. Only when they were about ten minutes from the airport did he regain his equanimity.

"The plane has been delayed for thirty minutes. We'll make it easily."

Thirty minutes stretched into forty-five. They had time for a long, leisurely breakfast at the airport.

Ruth's cell phone rang. "Elijah, it's for you. It's Norman."

"Good morning, Professor Shemtov. I just got up. I'm sorry, Ruth did not wake me up in time." As usual, Norman's voice was sweet and reassuring. "We'll continue to work on the scroll by correspondence. I'll be coming to Jerusalem soon. Very soon. You'll be the first to know about it."

Elijah said goodbye to Norman and then to Ruth, and boarded the plane to Barcelona. Because of the delay, he had very little time to wait before boarding the plane to Tel Aviv.

Throughout the flight, Elijah was engrossed in himself; his comfortable First Class seat was totally wasted on him. Norman was familiar with every tiny detail of his life. What did he know about David Norman? How could he have agreed to work for a man about whom he knew so little? Why was Norman living under an assumed name and running two investment firms simultaneously? Was the man an international swindler? Elijah felt his life was still in very real danger. Granted, the execution itself seemed to have been postponed, but for how long? He swore to himself he would find out everything there was to know about David Norman, come what may.

During the flight he was obliged to rely on his memory, which he needed to do in order to process whatever information he had on the race for the scrolls. How had the scroll reached Spain with the stamp of the Templars? Elijah assembled all the information in his mind and began to try to cross-reference it with what he knew about the conquests of Jerusalem. He realized that what, until now, had only been a hobby of his - the study of the different conquests of Jerusalem - had come in very handy a number of times in enabling him to understand certain aspects of the overall puzzle. He wondered if he had mixed up cause and effect; maybe it was not he who had chosen this area as a hobby, but rather that this hobby had chosen him. He remembered that the Templars had been granted an area on the Temple Mount, within the Al-Aqsa mosque. There had been several unconfirmed reports of manuscripts that the two founders of the Order had found there, manuscripts the existence of which the Templars had never admitted and whose very existence they had attempted to conceal.

Suddenly, another piece of the puzzle slipped into place, and Elijah jumped out of his seat. The flight attendant came over immediately and Elijah ordered a cocktail, to celebrate the brilliance of his insights in detective work. Both in the Templar conquest and in the hints found in the scrolls, Al-Aqsa was a key element. And the scrolls themselves! Elijah had no doubt that they had found some of the scrolls of Nehemiah of Peki'in, almost 900 years after they were hidden on the Temple Mount. That might even be the reason why the French persecuted the Templars for being involved in black magic and mysticism. There was no doubt about it! The Templars had found the secrets on the Temple Mount and tried their hand at word combinations, God's secret codes. Most historians claim it was just an excuse to put them to death and seize their assets. But then, what do historians know about secret word codes? The fact is that de Molay had cursed both the French king and the Pope, and his prediction that both would die that year had indeed come true exactly as he had specified.

The flight landed at Ben Gurion airport at night.

After a short sleep, Elijah's first stop was the university, to print the digital photographs he had taken. He hoped that Orna would not remember exactly when he was due back, or if she did remember, she would understand the pressure he was under and the urgency of what he had to do.

The photograph of Odel Weiss had a simple inscription: "To John, the one and only. There is no one like him, and there never will be. Odel Weiss." In the second photograph, with the sea as the background, John could be seen embracing a much older man. Based on John's apparent youth, the picture must

have been taken when he was still a student. The other man had
a shock of white hair, an old-fashioned shirt, and eyes, which
even in the blurred photographs, seemed to suggest infinite
wisdom. The inscription again added a piece to the puzzle: "To
John, who carried the banner of Nash's equilibrium point." The
signature was illegible. In the third picture, Norman was shown
next to a short, stout man with a ponytail and the face of a
hippie who had never grown up. The man held his hands behind
his back and appeared surprised at having his picture taken.
There was no inscription on the photograph.

Elijah ran to the library, logged onto the Internet, and
tried to identify the two men in the pictures. All he knew about
them was that they were mathematicians who had died in the
last few years. In spite of the lack of information, the Internet
search soon yielded results. He found them on a web site that
dealt with famous people who had died, and provided their
pictures.

The man with the shock of white hair was evidently a
mathematician named Marcel Gardosh, one of the most
productive mathematicians of the 20th century. Elijah read his
biography with baited breath. Professor Gardosh had been born
in the early 20thcentury into an assimilated Jewish family in the
Austro-Hungarian Empire. Gardosh had almost no material
possessions: no home, no family, no property, and certainly no
fixed abode. From time to time he would arrive at another

mathematician's home with two half-full suitcases, and announce: "I'm here," and the other mathematician would see to all his needs. In return, he would share with the mathematician various profound mathematical insights. Every so often he would receive a prize for his mathematical work or he would receive payment for a lecture or royalties from the sale of his books. He would use the money to support mathematicians in need or donate it to organizations that dealt with mathematics.

The second photo was of Professor Larry Wolford, a very shy man who specialized in computer sciences at UCLA. Wolford was one of those who had set up the protocols for the Internet, dealing with principles, standards, names and concepts that enabled the Internet to become what it is today. His primary contribution was in utilizing the unexploited power of computers.

Elijah found that Wolford had been one of the primary initiators of a computer project named "Links Right Now". His premise was simple: most computers in the world are inactive for most of the time. All this tremendous computer power should somehow be harnessed for the good of mankind. If all the computers were effectively linked in real time, they could be utilized without their owners losing any computing power. All this excess computing power could be transferred to those places that were in need of it. The analogy made by the

proponents of this idea was to unused electricity production.
Unless the excess is somehow "siphoned off", it is a total loss.
Wolford left academia in the 1960s and became a hippie. He
never married, never had a family, spoke little, and very few
people knew him personally. Of course, by harnessing all this
excess power, one could possibly emulate the power of a
supercomputer. Could that have been Norman's interest? Here
was an idea that was well worth considering, at some point.

Elijah sighed. Norman seemed to fit in perfectly among
such extraordinary people. What bothered him most was how he
himself fit into the group. He tried to find some common factor
that would link him to these great minds. He went to the
bathroom in the library and took a long look at himself in the
mirror. What he saw was a rather ordinary, somewhat rounded,
everyday kind of face, with old-fashioned glasses, and rapidly
thinning hair. Most of the people who saw him assumed he was
a teacher or a university lecturer, and they were right. No one
had ever mistaken him for a great army general or a scientist
who would leave his mark on humanity. As opposed to the
interesting biographies he had just been reading, his own was
nondescript and uninspiring. He had attended an average high
school, had served in an army unit, had graduated university
cum laude, gone on to graduate school, married the right girl
from the right family, and was now a university lecturer
struggling to obtain tenure and to eventually receive a decent

pension when he retired. No, he could find no common element linking him to these giants, and he was convinced that in future generations his own photograph would not appear in any of the search engines.

He returned to the letter he had photographed and tried, slowly, to decipher it. It was an extreme example of *nus-kalam*. In this script the letters are all joined together. Even experts found this script difficult to read. It was developed primarily by the Jews of North Africa and the Arab lands. Wealthy Syrian Jewish families used it to communicate with each other over their extensive business enterprises, using it as a means for denying customs officials and others an understanding of their affairs.

The letter had been written in the 20th century, and not necessarily at its beginning. As it had been written with the kind of fountain pen that was not manufactured before the 1920s, the letter was obviously written during or after the third decade of the century. The handwriting was extremely clear and consistent, which would seem to indicate the work of a professional scribe. The person was obviously well acquainted with this type of script, and Elijah found it remarkable that anyone alive was still using it - and evidently very skillfully. By the early 1900s, the use of this script had been curtailed. Even then, there were a few left who still used it, and they were all in their eighties. Elijah felt a certain surge of pride in realizing he was probably the youngest person in the world who was still able to read this script fluently.

He sat down to work. In his work he used specially lined paper, which enabled him to write the original text on one line and the deciphered text on the next. He used only a pencil, as constant revisions necessitated erasing and rewriting sections. Where he knew what the word was, he added the appropriate vowel points to it. Often, when working, he would practice imitating the writing style of the original writer. Sometimes, to obtain the proper effect, he would use the same writing implements the original scribe had used: a reed pen from the Atlas Mountains, a quill from a Polish duck, a fancy pen with a metal nib, apple-flavored tea… Using the same instrument often gave him an understanding of what the original pen strokes had been, the rate at which the ink flowed, and the various shapes of a particular letter. For example, when a stylus is used, it is difficult to make a stroke from the bottom to the top, and as a result this type of script is generally slanted.

He had worked for a good hour when the effects of not really having slept since leaving Israel finally caught up with him. His eyes were smarting, his stomach churned and he decided to go to see Orna at the hospital. On the way, he tried to come up with some hypothesis with regard to the role these mathematicians had played in Norman's life. First, he knew that Norman was a brilliant economist. Elijah was not sure whether

266

this was due to his knowledge of economics or to his psychic ability to foresee the future and read minds. Anyway, Elijah, too, was familiar with the Nash equilibrium point. The question was what bearing it had on Norman's dark deeds. He wished to know what interests and factors were involved in considering the Nash equilibrium point. What factors prevent someone from maximizing his profits, and force him to work against his own best interests? What people are ensnared in the prisoners' trap? And where was Wolford's preoccupation with the underutilized time of computers leading? He wondered if computer power was what was needed to combine the different holy names in all their various combinations. The big question was if Norman had killed those people after having extracted what he needed from each of them, and if so, why? And was he, Elijah, next on the list?

He entered the hospital's Ophthalmology Department, hoping that Orna was not operating at the moment and that he would be able to have a brief chat with her. He peeked into the lounge where off-duty doctors rested, but there was only one doctor there, with his back to Elijah, and making himself a cup of tea.

"Sorry, sorry," Elijah said apologetically. The man turned around to see who was speaking. He looked very familiar, but Elijah couldn't place him at first. Elijah was sure he had seen the man before. Just then, Orna walked in and he

remembered who the man was. It was the driver who had come
to pick up Norman from the Luzatto Institute on Elijah's first
day of work. What was he doing here? And why was he
wearing a white hospital gown?

"Eli! You're back!" Orna called out, her face lighting
up.

Elijah hugged her tightly and whispered to her, "Who is
that man?" He realized that the man could be helpful in his
search, because he might know Norman. On the other hand, he
might know nothing at all about him.

"He happens to be Professor Manoach, the chief surgeon
in our department, a world expert in eye surgery, especially for
corneas and retinas."

"Are you sure he's not a cab driver?"

"Are you suggesting that a famous surgeon would be
moonlighting as a cabbie? Have you taken leave of your
senses?"

"Please introduce us," Elijah asked Orna.

"Professor Manoach, I'd like you to meet my husband,
Dr. Elijah Shemtov."

"It's a pleasure."

"My pleasure too. Haven't we met before?"

"I rather doubt it. You might have seen me when you
came to pick up your wife, because we often operate together.
Alternatively, I might have operated on you."

"Don't be so modest, Professor Manoach," Orna chimed in. "It's a well-known fact that you remember every patient you've ever operated on since you started working here in 1948." Nonetheless, Elijah was one hundred percent certain he had not made a mistake and he had the distinct impression that the cab driver had recognized him as well, but for some reason, he refused to acknowledge it. Elijah found it hard to regard this man as a famous surgeon rather than a taxi driver.

"Orna, could you walk me to the staff car park?" Elijah asked, "And please tell me everything you know about Professor Manoach."

"To all his patients, Professor Manoach is a saint. They can almost see the halo shining around his head. Among the hospital's movers and shakers, he's known for his reticence; he won't ever breathe a word about any of his patients. Of course, plenty of jealous people reckon he's just a snob, but the consensus is clear as to his skill as a surgeon. I've operated with him on a number of occasions. He's a stickler for detail and he double-checks everything. He treats every operation as if it was his first, and prepares himself accordingly. When it comes to faces, he has a phenomenal memory."

They took the elevator down and left by the rear door, straight into the staff car park. Something caught Elijah's eye, and he stood still for a moment. Orna waited patiently, figuring that he would tell her what caused the delay. Suddenly he started running between the cars, dragging her along with him.

"According to gossip, he operated on King Hussein of Jordan, the Shah of Iran, various Saudi princes - and that's to name but a few. His patients worship him, not least because he's discreet even after their deaths. He's unbelievably devoted to his patients."

"That's it! I told you!"

"You haven't told me anything."

"That Mercedes - it's his."

"Of course it's his. Everyone knows he drives only a Mercedes. It's like his trademark. Tell me, is that why you thought he was a cab driver?" Orna was unable to suppress a smile.

"Listen! I know Norman. On my first day at Luzatto, I saw him come to drive Norman to the airport. I agree that the man is totally devoid of charisma, but if he's so important a surgeon, imagine what that says about Norman's status - having an esteemed surgeon driving him around!"

"Didn't you tell me that Norman has major eye problems? Surely the link between the two is obvious."

"Orna, tell me, do you think that Dr. Manoach has operated on Norman?"

"Or will be operating on him. At any rate, you've told me Norman only settles for the best, and Dr. Manoach is the best in his field. He must be Norman's personal physician."

"That would mean that Norman must have a file in the hospital computers."

"I would assume so."

"Great! Orna, can you get a copy of it for me? Time is working against us."

"I'll get it for you."

"Orna, you've really shed light on the whole subject."

"Look, I'm an eye doctor, aren't I?"

"You open the eyes of the blind. Do you think I married you just for the sake of it, without an ulterior motive?"

"Between you and me, Dr. Shemtov, you married me because of my beautiful eyes, thank you very much." Orna laughed.

The Ninth Sphere

When Absalom Conquered Jerusalem

About 440 years after the Exodus from Egypt, at nearly 1000 B.C.E., Absalom conquered Jerusalem. It was a relatively easy conquest, as his father, the aging King David, had no intention of contesting his beloved son. Rather than do battle, David fled to the desert with his few loyal servants. Thus he spared himself the sight of the masses cheering his son, who had plotted to kill him. Absalom came from Hebron and ascended to Jerusalem from the south, and again David had to fight for his life.

The historians of that time puzzled over why Absalom forgot the most basic move of every coup d'état: first and foremost, kill the dictator! That is a fundamental lesson known to every power-thirsty novice in the Middle East. If a revolution breaks out, do not invest in destroying the king's army, taking control of the power centers, controlling the media, winning the people's *hearts and minds, recruiting foreign powers to join your cause, and other unproven measures. Instead, recite in your mind the traditional and highly effective means, the necessary and the only means: kill the predecessor as soon as possible! Kill him! Kill him! Kill him!!! Everything else is marginal. As befits the biblical explanations, the blindness was explained as an act of God that prevented Absalom and his people from seeing the writing on the wall.*

One of the people involved in this saga was Ahithophel the Gilonite, David's advisor, who, for unknown reasons, had reversed his loyalties and joined Absalom against David. The people were afraid to take sides, lest the father and son become reconciled at some point, and David would take revenge against those who had joined Absalom. The first piece of advice that Ahithophel gave Absalom was to deepen the rift with his father by taking David's concubines. Absalom took his advice, and publicly took David's concubines as his own, a deed which no feelings of remorse could ever absolve.

After he took Jerusalem, there were two schools of thought as to how Absalom should proceed. The first, that of Ahithophel, was to have Absalom pursue his father and kill him. The second, by Hushai the Archite, was to first mobilize greater forces and then use their superior numbers to crush David and his entire camp. For some reason, Absalom preferred the

273

second suggestion, that of Hushai - a secret supporter of David – which was a disastrous mistake on his part and led to his ultimate downfall.

As soon as Ahithophel realized that his advice had been rejected, he knew that the revolt was doomed and he acted accordingly, by making rational use of the little time remaining to him on earth. As the Bible tells it: "When Ahithophel saw that his counsel was not followed, he saddled his ass and arose and went to his house, to his city, and gave charge to his household, and hanged himself, and he died; and he was buried in the sepulcher of his father."

Ahithophel strangled himself a considerable while before the final battle between Absalom and David, in which Absalom was defeated and was killed by Joab the son of Zeruiah, David's chief of staff. In doing so, Ahithophel violated one of the most sacred tenets of statecraft. Nothing in politics can be anticipated, certainly not who will emerge victorious in any battle. Ahithophel, though, had received his education in the university of hard knocks and not in a modern institute of academic learning, which might be why he ignored these high-sounding principles.

Elijah's nerves were stretched to the limit and beyond. Feeling that everything was closing in on him, he decided the safest place for him was a coffee shop in the city center. Who would dare go after him there? He sat at a table and ordered a double espresso. Following the quantities of caffeine he had consumed in the last two weeks - enough to bring down an army - he would subject his body to more poison. He took out the printout of the photographed letter from Norman's desk, and began to decipher it. Its letters combined to form words, which in turn formed sentences:

"To my beloved son Joseph Absalom,

"May He who dwells on High guard and protect you from all evil, Amen. May the Lord, Master of all angels, send you His angels, Pediel, Sariel, and Raziel, the helpers of Metatron, and may He guard and protect you.

"Ever since you left and did not answer, I pine for you who are not here. Your letter arrived on Friday, and I was both happy and sad. I was happy that you are alive and well, but I am concerned because you are in a land at war, and what does this have to do with you? Do we not have enough troubles that you thrust your head into a country where each one swallows the other while still alive? I know what you are looking

275

for, but your path is not a proper one. I am afraid
that what I did was not wise, because I wrote you
things which should not be written, and I
revealed to you secrets of the Torah which
should not be revealed, and I taught you the
Ma'aseh Merkavah - the deepest of the deep of
the Kabbalah - which one may not even teach,
and only one who is capable of studying it
himself may learn it. Nor did I wait until you
grew up and became wise and reached the age of
understanding. I did so because one never knows
one's day of death, and I was not well and was
afraid that you would remain alone."

The enormous effort required of him to decipher the
letter up to that point had made Elijah's eyes smart. He signaled
the waitress that he'd like another double espresso. By now, he
was unable to see straight and felt slightly dizzy. That made
reading even more difficult. He took a break and looked at the
people strolling about. The letter stirred his soul, and he
continued reading:

"Even though I know you will not change your
mind, I would like to ask you to consider your
actions carefully, lest you sin against God and
Man. As you well know, our Sages tell us that
one who seeks to know what came before all and

what will come after - it would have been better had he never been born at all. How much more so is this true for one who tries to change the natural order of things? We have had no greater profits than Elijah and Elisha. Yet, even they - who had the power to change the very course of nature - did not do so except in the direst of circumstances, as when the prophets of Ba'al would have removed belief in the One God from the Jewish people. Elisha too, sent one out in a moment of acute distress, but for the rest of his life he regretted that action.

"You, my beloved son, remember how Rabbi Johanan ben Zakkai regretted his whole life that he had used these powers, and on his deathbed he was not sure if he would even enter Heaven because of that act. You, no doubt, know that the author of the work *Ketem Paz*, whom our ancestors relied on, stated that the use of these matters might even be forbidden by Jewish law, and who can tell what damage they can cause? It was thus not in vain that Rabbi Akiba removed all these scrolls from circulation, and did not even show them to his beloved Bar Kokhba. My son, remember the story of the Mystic de la

Reine, who wanted to use this for good purposes - as a blessing - and in the end it turned into a curse, as a result of which thousands of innocents suffered. And you, my beloved son, do you think that you are more holy than Rabbi Isaac? More pure than Rabbi Israel Ba'al Shem Tov? More righteous than Rabbi Elijah of Vilna? More ascetic than Rabbi Nachman of Bratslav? All of these considered use of this for years and decades, and after consulting with the Forces on High made sure to keep far, far away from these matters.

"Furthermore, those before us were giants, while we are but puny ants in comparison. They, with their mighty vision, saw that the time has simply not come and the die has still not been cast. And you, my son, feel that you are able to roll the rock off the well single-handedly and bring salvation? Will you be the one to bring the fountain to the heart? This is something that, with our intellect, we are not even able to fathom. Let the Master of the World take care of it in His time, but you must leave this alone. Remember that Satan lays waiting in the dark, and a single misstep can plunge you to your death.

"Know further that our group is not pleased with the fact that I even keep in touch with you. They also begged me and implored me to promise not to contact you without informing them and receiving their consent, but I refused to accept that restraint. I informed them that the agreement we signed was conditional on the documents existing and for that time. Then, if the documents no longer existed, the society no longer exists and there is no leader. They lodged a complaint with Rabbi Elazar, and he justified me. They nevertheless asked - and I consented - that I be involved in certain procedures to save you from the Pit of Destruction.

"As to myself, even though I have such a very strong desire to see you before I die, I am afraid, my son, that I will not see you in this world. My disease is getting the better of me, and I believe that I will soon be joining your late mother. God will, of course, do what is best. If, indeed, I never see you again, I beg of you, my son, to listen to the words of your father and of all the previous generations. Desist from what you are

279

doing, while you are still able to do so, because
you are playing with fire.

"I am very much concerned about your health
and welfare, for our Sages say that anyone who
delves into these matters is lost. Indeed, some of
our greatest rabbis who were involved in these
matters - such as Rabbi Isaac Ashkenazi, Rabbi
Moshe Luzzato, and Rabbi Nachman of Bratslav
- all died prematurely, and did not live out their
days. Leave what you are doing, find yourself a
wife, and live a long and happy life.

"I have sent this letter to the address on your last
letter, but I fear it may not reach you because of
the perilous times. I have given a copy of the
letter to Judah Gardi, and I have made him swear
to guard it like the apple of his eye, but not to
keep it in his home. I am sure that when you can,
you will meet him and receive the letter from
him, for God will surely ordain that.

I sign with tears,

Your father who loves you,

David ben Joseph Moreno, S.T."

Again a reference to Gardi! Elijah did not understand
most of the contents of the letter, but he noted that certain
concepts mentioned in it could also be found in the scrolls, and

he had managed to decipher those references. He tried to put together whatever facts he could, so as to understand the letter. He noted that the signature was written out in full, and was not an abridged version of the writer's name. He noted the "S.T." added at the end, which the accepted wisdom understands as being an abbreviation for "*Sefaradi Tahor*" - a pure Sephardic Jew, namely that the family had a genealogical lineage tracing back all the way to the expulsion of the Jews from Spain in 1492. Elijah, though, knew that that attribution was wrong, and that the abbreviation really stood for "*Sit Ve Tin*", which in Arabic means "dust and ashes", thus an indication of the person's humility, first introduced by great Sephardic rabbis; the type of humility that only a truly great person can allow himself.

Elijah made himself a new list: the water and the marble, the heart and the fountain, the four ways of studying the Torah encapsulated in the Hebrew initials '*Pardes*', Rabbi Akiba and the scrolls, the age when one may study Kabbalah, the *Ma'aseh Merkavah* and the "Other Force", namely Satan. These were all Kabbalistic ideas, which he understood. He also knew the names of the great Kabbalistic sages.

Now he tried to fathom the relationship between the father and the son. He felt the great love, the pain and the reprimand of the father toward his son. While the father's name was David, his son's name was Absalom. It was impossible to ignore another father-son combination with those names, the biblical account of King David and his son Absalom. What could he learn from that biblical story? After all, that was one of the more dramatic conquests of Jerusalem... in the revolt of Absalom against his father, there were all the elements of a Greek tragedy: love, hate, jealousy and sex.

Elijah then thought back to the oft-used Modern Hebrew expression that translates as "the advice of Ahithophel". Indeed Ahithophel's advice to Absalom was very sound, and if Absalom had but heeded Ahithophel's second assessment, he would have become king. According to the Bible, "as if a man inquired at the oracle of God; so was all the counsel of Ahithophel". The people of Jerusalem at the time were able to evaluate Ahithophel's advice correctly. Historians are puzzled as to why Absalom overlooked the most elementary rule when someone rebels against a monarch. The very first thing to do is to kill the monarch! Absalom's blindness to this obvious rule is seen as being God's intervention in history, which prevented him from seeing the writing on the wall. Had Norman also opposed his father? And if so, why?

Elijah ordered another coffee. His throat burned. He had found no direct link between the biblical story and the letter he had just read and realized that he now had to find out whatever he could about David Moreno and his son Absalom. He ran the names through his mind and even wrote them down. Whenever his mind hit a blank wall, he would write down the names as well, an absent-minded habit of his since primary school. He again wrote the name David Moreno, once from right to left and again from left to right. He couldn't believe what he now saw: in Hebrew, scrambling the letters comprising the name "Moreno", he got "Normo" - Norman! This surely was no mere coincidence. He had to get out in a hurry. Leaving the waitress the cost of the coffee and a huge tip, he rushed out and hailed the first cab he found. He had no doubt that Nissim Toledano, or, as he used to refer to him, "Uncle Nissim", would be able to answer a few questions.

Nissim greeted him warmly and effusively, in the style of the Middle East: "Distinguished doctor, hello! How are you, Mr. Shemtov? How're things at the university? How are Orna and the girls? Come, sit with us." He rose from his chair. "Welcome to our humble abode. Greetings, my friend and honored guest."

"Thank God, Uncle Nissim, everyone's fine. How are you?" The two embraced.

"Thank the Lord, we live and breathe, and speak to those of our friends who are still alive. Everything else is unimportant. The only thing that matters is good health."

Nissim Toledano was a distant relative of Elijah's mother. He was always immaculately dressed, and even today, at the age of eighty-two and with a serious heart condition, he wore a light-colored suit and tie. He was a tall, dark-skinned man with a perpetual smile and a completely bald head. He was inordinately proud of the fact that an ancestor of his had arrived in the Holy Land immediately after the Spanish Inquisition when the Jews were expelled from Spain, hence the Hebrew surname Toledano, "from Toledo". As a child, he had been sent to the Christian Terra Sancta School, where he had achieved total mastery of both literary and spoken Arabic. In the army, he had served in an intelligence unit, and after leaving it he had been involved in numerous governmental assignments whose nature could not be divulged. He had been less successful in his personal life. His wife had been a sickly woman who died very young, leaving him with their daughter, whom he had raised single-handedly. His daughter had married, then divorced, and had offered him no joy. At the age of eighty, he had entered a retirement home, where he was a star among the many widows. Elijah had found him in the lobby of the home.

"Uncle Nissim, I bet you knew all the Jerusalem old-timers who spoke Arabic."

"Of course, doctor!" replied Toledano, falling into Elijah's trap. "In my days, Jerusalem was a small town, with possibly forty thousand Jews, and I knew them all." Toledano realized he had gone too far, and backtracked somewhat. "Let's say that I knew the Sephardi Jews, or at least the vast majority of them. I really did not know the Ashkenazi Jews."

284

"Did you know Rabbi Moreno?"

"Which Moreno? There were a number of them. There was one who was a scribe, one who was a rabbi, Moreno the Kabbalist. All of them were members of the same family."

"What do you know about the Kabbalist?"

"He wasn't someone I knew well, but all knew of Rabbi David Moreno, head of the Kabbalistic Yeshiva. He was a quiet man, a very learned rabbi, but he had a hard life. During World War I he fled from Turkey so as not to be drafted into the Turkish army, and wound up in Aleppo, Syria. There he married the daughter of a famous Kabbalist. His wife died young, leaving an infant son for him to raise. He never remarried. His son was reputed to be an incredible genius; everyone said he would go very far. This son, though, was a wild one. I don't remember his name. Rabbi Moreno was loved by all the rabbis of Jerusalem. Guess why."

"How should I know?" sighed Elijah. "Was it because he was a very great scholar?"

"Not only was he a great scholar, but he knew how to behave. Before he met a great rabbi for the first time, he would find out which works the rabbi had written, and would then proceed to study these works. Rabbi Moreno would come to the rabbi and ask him a basic question about his books. The rabbi would be pleased that he had finally found someone who had read what he had written, and would spend hours talking to

Rabbi Moreno. Rabbi Moreno would just sit there and nod his head periodically. The rabbi would then tell everyone how great a scholar Rabbi Moreno was, even though he had not uttered a word..."

Uncle Nissim laughed at the guile. He suddenly stopped talking, as if considering what to say next. When he finally started speaking again, each sentence hit Elijah like a bombshell.

"You, too, are a descendant of a very famous Kabbalist."

"I am?"

"You, Elijah Shemtov, are one of the descendants of Moses ben Shemtov de Leon."

"Moses de Leon? The one who brought the *Zohar* to the attention of the entire world?" Elijah found himself trembling uncontrollably.

"From Acre to Castile, from Provence to Salonika, from Fez to Baghdad, all praised the work of Rabbi Simon Ben Yochai. The fact is, though, that even during de Leon's lifetime - and he was a bookseller by profession - there were disputes as to the authorship of the *Zohar*. Rabbi Isaac of Acre, in his memoirs, writes that he met de Leon outside his city, and he claimed that he had copies of old letters in his possession. He even promised to show them to Rabbi Isaac when he returned to his home, but de Leon took ill on the way and died before he returned. On the other hand, it was claimed that the wife of Rabbi Joseph de Avila met de Leon's widow and his daughter, and both claimed that the author was de Leon himself, who attributed the work to Rabbi Simon Ben Yohai... And there is also another secret," said Uncle Nissim, who seemed to be almost in a dream world.

Elijah was tense as he waited to hear what else the old man had to say.

"Your middle name is Metatron, one of God's trusted angels."

Elijah was aware of that embarrassing fact, but had successfully hidden it in all his encounters with others. Here, though, was an opportunity to find out the background of that name.

"Why was I given that name, Uncle Nissim?"

"It was the Kabbalist Moreno who chose that name for you. Your grandmother, Esther, went to him and asked for a blessing for you. He gave her a blessing, and suggested that you be given that middle name at your circumcision ceremony. He suggested that when you were given your name, the middle name should be whispered, so that no one except the one who named you would hear it. Under no circumstances was anyone else to know about it. Only your grandmother, your mother, and the one who named you - I was the one who did so - were aware of it. Even you were not to be told until you turned thirteen. You, too, were not to divulge your name. If you followed these instructions precisely, you would be blessed, would have a good life, and would help many people. You can thus say that Moreno influenced your life."

"My mother said it was nothing but some old superstition, but she didn't want to argue with Grandmother Esther, so she went along with it. It really didn't seem to make a difference anyway, because no one knew about the name. I only found out about it at my Bar Mitzvah, when Grandmother Esther revealed the secret to me. To me, it was indeed terrible. My grandmother always wanted me to become a doctor, because then I could help others. She died ten years ago, and I'm sure that my mother forgot the whole incident. Now only you and I know the truth, and I know that you would never tell anyone. Only now have I begun to understand the significance of the name."

Elijah remembered how he had always concealed his middle name, even though he was not quite sure why he had done so. Maybe his life had been saved by the fact that he had kept the bargain and never told anyone his name. Sitting in the lounge of the retirement home, Elijah started daydreaming. He did, though, have one last question for Uncle Nissim.

"And what about Rabbi Moreno's son? Did he indeed go far?"

Nissim sighed. "Even the best of intentions are ruined by reality. After the Arab riots in Palestine in the late 1920s, the child simply disappeared. The Arabs evidently killed him. To this day, no one knows exactly what happened to him. His father never abandoned hope of finding him. Poor man. All the Kabbalists of the Holy Land, of Aleppo, of Babylon, all prayed for him. For the child's first eleven years his father took care of him, pampered him, taught him - and then he disappeared."

Elijah was disappointed. Was that the end of his beautiful theory about "Moreno" and "Norman"? He wound up his visit, said goodbye to Uncle Nissim, and went home, where Orna was already waiting for him.

"Eli, I found David Norman's medical file. He's scheduled for surgery on the 21st of June. However, he refused to be hospitalized the day before, as is customary, but he promised to fast the day before, and to check in at 5:00 am in preparation for the operation. That's very strange, especially when the surgeon feels that his condition is critical and that he might lose his eyesight altogether. It might be mere coincidence, but I noticed on the calendar that the 21st of June is the longest day of the year. I think that that day is..."

"For heaven's sake! Do you know what today is?" Elijah shouted out, his face covered in a cold sweat.

"Yes, I know that's two days from now. I hope you aren't upset with me about that fact."

"No, no. I'm sorry I raised my voice. That is vital information, and it was you who spotted it. I'm really upset at myself because I still don't quite know how to begin. I don't have so much as a single starting point from which to move forward."

"Well, maybe I can give you one. It took me ten days of intense searching, but I finally found Gardi's file and I know where to find him."

"Are you serious?"

"He's in the David Home."

"But that's a psychiatric hospital!"

The Tenth Sphere

When The Persians Conquered Jerusalem

In 614 C.E., the Persians took Jerusalem from the Byzantine Empire. At first, they tried to persuade the inhabitants to surrender peacefully, without a battle. Patriarch Zechariah agreed to surrender, but the masses refused point-blank. The Persians chose to besiege the city in the summer, in order not to subject their troops to the rain and cold of the Jerusalem winter. For twenty days the Persian troops made as much commotion as possible, to attract the people's attention away from the noise they made digging tunnels beneath the city walls. At that point, the wall on the west simply collapsed and Jerusalem fell into their hands like ripe fruit. Having been forced to fight because of the intransigence of the Jerusalem residents, the Persians had no qualms whatsoever in venting their anger on them. For three days they slaughtered everyone they came across and plundered whatever was worth plundering. Special targets of theirs were the Christian monasteries and their monks. The monks were killed and all the valuables in the many religious edifices were taken away, including the Holy Cross, upon which, by Christian tradition, Jesus had been crucified. Even that holy relic was shipped to Persia.

The Jews greeted the Persians joyfully. Ever since the declaration of Cyrus of Persia, which had proclaimed the end of the Babylonian exile, the Jews had regarded the Persians as friends. At this time, the Jews regarded the Persian conquest as God's redemption of the Jewish people, and large numbers of them joined the Persians. A Jewish force from Galilee attempted to take Tyre on behalf of the Persians, but was unable to do so. However, it did succeed in capturing Acre for the Persians. An attempt was made to restore the sacrificial cult on the Temple Mount.

A short time later, for internal political reasons, the Persians switched their allegiance to the Christians. An official decree forbade Jews from living in Jerusalem. All the various attempts through gifts, bribes, pleading and begging were in vain.

In 630 C.E., the Byzantine King Heracles vanquished the Persians and reconquered the Holy Land. In order to obtain the support of the Jews, he signed a treaty with their leader, Benjamin of Tiberias, gave them a signed deed of protection, and even swore personally to uphold this agreement. Under the influence of the heads of the Church, Heracles violated his solemn agreement. He killed many Jews in Galilee and Jerusalem, and forbade Jews from living in Jerusalem or within a radius of three miles from the city. In order to prevent Heracles from having to suffer for breaking his solemn word, the heads of the Church accepted the punishment themselves. To this day, those who follow the Byzantine Christian tradition, namely the members of the Greek Orthodox Church in Syria and Jordan and the Copts in Egypt, have a special fast day in penance for Heracles' broken promise.

Elijah jumped out of bed at 6:00 am, June 20th, the day before the longest day of the year. It was not as if he had been sleeping; he had lain awake the whole night. His single, sane lead was to a man in an insane asylum! His life was in danger, he knew, but he had no idea from which direction the peril would come. He felt utterly helpless, but knew that he had to do something.

He drove to the David Home in Ein Kerem and turned off the car engine. The peace and quiet in this pastoral setting, which at other times would have been enthralling, did nothing to still his fears. Ein Kerem is in a valley and is an island of greenery just a few minutes away from the hubbub of the city. The houses are all small and made of stone, and the local residents want nothing more than peace. It could have been a veritable Garden of Eden to Elijah - if he could have just calmed down a little. The main building of the David Home stood right in front of him. The window frames were all painted a sky blue, as if the heavens themselves had invaded the different rooms. Elijah fell in love with the place and, for an instant, thought how pleasant it would be to live here, to forget all his obligations, to wipe from his memory the thousands of letters and words he had processed. Why, of all the people in the world, had Norman selected him? And based on Norman's computer, was even his selection an error, not having taken his middle name into account? What did Norman want of him? Up to a few weeks ago he had been a nonentity, a minor university lecturer, one who blended into the Jewish landscape and disappeared into it and for all he knew, as of tomorrow, he would be no more than history.

He stood at the door, terrified of entering a world that was so utterly unfamiliar to him. Elijah was a man devoid of the tools necessary for contending with the aberrations of human nature. Accustomed to living his life among the gifted, among doctoral students who aspired to become members of the exclusive club of full professors, he had neither the training nor the background to deal with the insane. In his head dozens of possible scenarios played out dramatically, each more bizarre than the last.

What on earth are you afraid of? He rebuked himself. *After all, the building is crawling with armed guards; and if it's the feeling that your life might be in danger that's bothering you, well – it's in danger already, whether or not you decide to enter the building.*

He forced himself laboriously out of the car, locked it and double-checked that it was locked so that no one would tamper with it in his absence, made sure he had not parked too far from the curb, and after running out of excuses to delay his entry, squared his shoulders and walked toward the gate.

At the reception desk, he asked to speak to Mr. Gardi. The nurse on duty asked him to wait, and disappeared into the interior of the building. A man dressed in pajamas came over and tried to take off his shirt. "Are you new here? Are you the new guy? Here, we all wear pajamas. Let me help you. You're new here. Yes, I can tell you're new. Tell me that you're new here. Would you like to sleep in my room, on my bed? I won't mind. Come and sleep in my bed with me." Elijah remained glued to the spot, as if someone had nailed his feet to the ground. He felt totally powerless. The man in pajamas kept tugging at his sleeve, until a male nurse came and led him away. Elijah felt his blood pressure rising to a level that made a heart attack imminent. The nurse finally returned.

"Are you the guy who's looking for Judah Gardi?"

"Yes."

"He's in the dining room, but I would really appreciate if you could please wait outside. It's treatment and breakfast time right now and we don't usually entertain visitors at 6:45 am."

"It's an emergency."

"What do you mean by 'an emergency'? The man has been here for the past forty-five years and will remain here until the day he dies. So what's so urgent? Please wait outside until I call you."

Elijah went outside and sat on the edge of a bench, trying to imagine that this was just another day in his rather dull life. Had he been a patient here, he would probably have gone outside to sit in the garden, too. A group of men dressed in green passed him. They were all speaking Arabic and laughing about something.

Elijah walked over to them. "Do any of you know Gardi?"

"I'm his attendant. What do you want to know?"

"May I speak to you for a few minutes?"

"Why not?" said the man, as he moved away from the rest.

"I'm pleased to meet you. I'm Professor Nash."

"Likewise. I'm Naeel Suleiman."

"Are you from Jerusalem?"

"Actually, I'm from Nazareth, but I obtained my nursing degree at the Hebrew University in Jerusalem. For the past four years I've been Gardi's attendant."

"Only for the last four years... I'd very much like to ask you a few questions. Please take this envelope. I believe it will be fair compensation for the time you spend here with me." The nurse took the envelope and Elijah felt encouraged.

"Who was his attendant before you?"

"Someone named Mualem was with him for forty years."

"And what happened to him?" Elijah was afraid to hear the answer. "Did he die?"

"He did, actually, he died three years ago."

297

"From what?" asked Elijah, almost shouting.

"Look, Mualem cared for him until Mualem turned seventy. He was pensioned off, and died of old age."

"Do all patients have a personal attendant?"

"No way. There is a special trust fund abroad for Gardi. He gets royal treatment here, unlike the other patients. He has his own private room and a private attendant throughout the day. At night, too, there's a special attendant on duty. Actually, I thought you must be from the Foundation."

Elijah caught on immediately. "Well, not exactly. Unless, yes, you could call me that. I'm not an official representative; I'm here unofficially. The person funding the Foundation is a relative of my wife. She asked me to come and see how Gardi is treated. Between you and me, she asked me to come incognito, so that no one should know about my ties to the Foundation. That way I can see how things really are, without anyone trying to put on a show just for my benefit. I was also asked to find out if any other relatives come to visit."

"Almost no one comes," said Naeel. "He used to have a cousin who came every few months, but the man died. I have a feeling the other relatives are delighted that he's out of their hair. Mualem, who took care of him for so many years, told me that a certain American comes every so often to visit him, and he's overjoyed when the man arrives. However, after every such visit, it takes Gardi months before he returns to normal."

298

"Why? What happens when the American comes?" Elijah was very perturbed.

"He starts telling all kinds of stories."

"Well, telling stories hardly seems so unusual."

"You don't understand. His stories relate to what is known as the 'messiah syndrome'."

"I don't understand what you mean. I wonder if you could tell me what it's all about. Does he say anything about the American?"

Naeel suddenly became very suspicious of Elijah's behavior, his body language, his demanding tone. "I don't know if I'm allowed to say anything. We're not permitted to reveal any information about our patients. Maybe you should check with the department head. He also deals with Gardi on an individual basis."

Elijah decided that he should calm down and improvise something that would put Naeel on his side.

"The American you referred to was the husband of that relative of my wife's. He was Gardi's benefactor, but he died about a year and a half ago. His widow is still considering whether she should continue to send money. I have to report to her about how things are and whether she should continue with her support."

Naeel's manner changed immediately. "I'm sorry to hear that. I didn't know he'd died."

"OK. Could you tell me what you meant by the 'messiah syndrome'?"

Naeel was happy to oblige. "In France, a large number of insane people are convinced they are Napoleon. In England, they think they are the king, while in Italy they think they are the Pope, or at the least Michelangelo. In Israel, it's the messiah. Pregnant women claim that the baby in their womb is the messiah, while men are convinced that God is about revealing Himself to them, while others tell us that they have been entrusted with saving the Jewish people."

"Does Judah Gardi claim to be the messiah?"

"He says he's able to perform miracles just by his utterances, and that he knows word combinations that can bring about miracles. He claims he's the one who suppressed the 1929 riots with his words. These are his exact claims, and he also claims that as soon as he recovers from his illness, he will bring the messiah. For the first few years after he was admitted here he refused to take any medication. He kept repeating over and over again that none of us here was normal and that only he was normal. But that, of course, is what all patients here believe. He's already over seventy and has basically stopped speaking to anyone. Each night at sunset he tells his story to the trees and the rocks."

"I'd like to ask you to bring him out here to me. I've never been to this place before, and I daresay you appreciate my reservations. Once you enter the building, you are no longer master of your own fate."

Naeel nodded his agreement and a few seconds later he entered the building. After what seemed like hours, but was actually only about fifteen minutes on the clock, he came back pushing an old man in a wheelchair. The man had a dark complexion and white hair. His head was bent forward, almost touching his chest.

Naeel stopped the wheelchair and said, "You have a visitor. You stay here for a while and I'll be back soon to take you inside again."

The old man seemed totally engrossed in himself, as if he saw and heard nothing of the outside world. Elijah moved a little closer, and when he saw no reaction he got up and effectively blocked off the sun, which had been shining on Gardi. The old man realized that there was something blocking the sun. He looked up, saw Elijah, and seemed to look right through him.

Gardi was wrapped in a *tallit*, a Jewish prayer shawl, and murmured words or parts of words. From time to time he looked in the book of Psalms that he had in his lap. Naeel sat a few yards away, reading a newspaper.

Elijah said, "David Norman sends his regards."

Gardi stared at him, but made no comment.

"David Norman - of the Luzzato Institute? Don't you remember him? He's the only one who comes to visit you here. Try to remember. It's very important. You just have to remember him... David Norman, the American. Don't you remember?"

Not a sound, not a gesture. Nothing. Elijah plucked a leaf from a nearby lemon tree, and sat down. He played with the leaf, but was at a loss as to what to do next. If Gardi did not speak, all was lost. Maybe he should just sit and listen to the man's meaningless mumbling. Maybe that was the answer...

Minutes passed, and nothing changed.

"Judah Gardi!" Elijah cried out in desperation, a cry that caused both Gardi and Naeel to sit up. Gardi was seized by a coughing spell that shook his frail body. His face turned red, and Naeel hurried over.

"I have to take him in and give him an inhalation."

"But please bring him back."

"We'll see."

"You have to!"

Naeel gave him a stern look.

Elijah had to appease Naeel after his outburst. "I'm sorry. It is really vital. I won't raise my voice any more. I just thought maybe that way I could stir him up and get through to him."

Naeel had already brought the wheelchair to the edge of the path. He turned around and repeated, "We'll see."

Elijah felt as if a giant steamroller had just run over him. He was utterly crushed. How could he have blown the only opportunity he would have of approaching Gardi? How does one talk to a person who has been certified as insane? Things were, finally, coming to a climax in a few hours, and the world turned around as usual; everything at its own tempo. Elijah persuaded himself that he absolutely had to calm down. He had to match his tempo to that of the asylum and to try to figure out how things operated here. Otherwise, he was lost.

He tried to empty his mind of all thoughts, as if meditating, but he was unable to do so. His head was burning up.

Think of one of the conquests. Which conquest did you like best? Concentrate on the conquering of Jerusalem. Maybe then you will be able to calm down. Elijah, choose a conquest. How about that of Titus? No way! OK, so which conquest was the most significant in your eyes? He asked himself. *Let's see. A number of the conquests were heroic, but which was the most significant? I know: the conquest by Persia.*

'Very few people will agree with you, Elijah.'

No, but I can prove it.

'Prove it.'

Mentally, Elijah began to lecture his audience – which consisted this time only of himself. The only others present were the trees and rocks. No one was in the garden. *If Gardi can talk to the trees and the rocks, so can I,* he thought to himself.

At first, the Persians tried to persuade the inhabitants to surrender peacefully, without a battle. The masses refused point-blank.

Elijah was unable to concentrate. It was already noontime and the sun beat down on him mercilessly. He forced himself to think about the conquest.

All the valuables in the many religious edifices had been taken away, including the Holy Cross, upon which, by Christian tradition, Jesus had been crucified. Even that holy relic had been shipped to Persia. *OK, how does that help me now?* For the first time in his life, Elijah thought that his obsession with the different conquests had been nothing but a waste of time. *That's a strange way to show your patriotism. Maybe I'm crazy.* He decided to stop thinking along these lines, but all the different conquests that he had thought about so often simply refused to let him go.

Some people think the conquests by Babylon and Rome were the worst, because in both cases the Temple was destroyed. Elijah, on the other hand, believed that the worst of all of Jerusalem's conquests was that of the Persians. Ever since the Persian conquest, for all practical purposes the Jews had abandoned any further hope of a natural redemption based on reclaiming the land acre by acre. And with it, all hope of reconstituting an independent Jewish state had crumbled. In fact, from that time on, until the beginning of the 20th century, there were no further Jewish attempts to rule the Holy Land, or even just the holy city of Jerusalem. That, to Elijah, was the worst consequence of the Persian conquest.

In reality, the situation then in a way very much parallels the situation today, thought Elijah. *Then, too, there was constant friction with our neighbors.*

One of the other consequences of the loss of all hope in reconstituting a Jewish state by natural means was the opening of the field to every type of messianic idea, no matter how wild. This included all those who believed that the only possible avenue of redemption was through miraculous means, outside the normal realm of the historical process; for redemption could not come through natural means. On the other hand, there were those who objected - and many that object to this day - to any human intervention in the Divine plan.

Throughout his life, Elijah had developed a theory that Jewish mysticism had only begun after the Persian conquest. Only one who really understands the different conquests of Jerusalem can appreciate the originality of this theory. If there were any mystical elements present before that time, Elijah believed, they were only marginal. He found support for his theory in the large number of works in this area, which appeared after the Persian conquest. He thought of the classic case of Shabbetai Zevi, who arose at a time when the Jews seemed to have lost all hope of being rescued from their terrible fate by natural means.

Suddenly, at the insane asylum, Elijah realized that for the past two weeks he had been assembling all types of facts that contradicted his theory, but that had not been enough to totally demolish it. *Sefer Yetzirah* had clearly been written centuries before the Persian conquest. The Bar Kokhba revolt took place in 135 C.E., and even by that date *Sefer Yetzirah* - the oldest Kabbalistic text we are aware of - was already in existence. Already at that time, Rabbi Akiba had ordered all copies to be burned, and, in fact, the vast majority of copies of that work were destroyed. All that we have is a short section of it, totaling about 1500 words. What Norman had found was that Nehemiah had only pretended to burn the copies, as the son of Rabbi Simon Ben Yohai had bribed him to make seven copies.

Gardi's claim had evidently been that he was able to save the world simply with words. Could Gardi have known the verses of these scrolls? Elijah was convinced that it was Norman who financed Gardi's hospital care, and that he was the "American" who visited Gardi from time to time. Indeed, something to that effect had been on Norman's to-do list: visit Gardi in the hospital. Maybe Norman was indeed the son of

Rabbi Moreno, and maybe both Gardi and Norman had learned the appropriate verses from Norman's father. And maybe the Kabbalists were right in claiming that by such verses they could change the world! This was in total contradiction of what Elijah had always believed. And maybe Norman made a point of visiting Gardi because he knew that it was Gardi's study of the Kabbalah that had driven him to insanity, just as it had Ben Zoma.

In the end, Elijah decided he had no choice but to enter the building. Casting all his reservations and hesitations aside, he walked in, making a conscious effort, difficult though it was, to appear nonchalant, hoping to be inconspicuous, to avoid attracting any untoward attention. That, he believed, was the only possible way to gain access to Gardi. He believed he now knew how to accomplish this. Of course, Gardi would not know the man as "Norman". Norman was a name he had adopted much later.

Peeping into each doorway, he finally saw Gardi sitting in a chair near his window.

"Absalom Moreno, the son of Rabbi David Moreno, sent me to see how you are and how you feel."

This time it worked. That was the name by which Gardi knew him! Gardi perked up immediately and asked, "Where is he? Why hasn't he come?"

"He's not feeling well," apologized Elijah. By now, lying was second nature to him in all matters concerning Luzzato.

"They all ran away and I cried. Absalom said to me, 'Come with me and I will protect you.' We ran from the so-called Lifta gate in the wall around Me'ah Shearim, to the gates facing the Old City. All the Jews were running, but Absalom and I ran in the opposite direction. We stood and saw them running toward us. The Arabs were screaming 'Death to all the Jews!' Absalom told me what words to recite, and we said them together."

Gardi started breathing more heavily. He began to talk louder. "Then the Arabs all ran away. The Heavens fought on our behalf. There had never been anything like it since ancient times." Naeel looked in and stood at a distance.

Elijah was familiar with the story of the Lifta gate. In 1929, an Arab mob, inflamed by rabble-rousers, had left the Old City by the Nablus Gate. At its head were the rabble-rousers themselves, carrying a variety of objects to use as weapons against the Jews - swords and bayonets. Some of them had ancient hunting guns, with bandoliers full of ammunition. Their cries and gestures made their intentions very clear when they came across any Jews. Soon they approached the wall that surrounded the Jewish neighborhood of Me'ah Shearim.

"I believe you," said Elijah. "Absalom himself told me about it."

"He himself?" said the old man. Suddenly, he became very suspicious. "It was supposed to be a big secret."

"I've been busy helping him to find the scrolls. He showed them all to me."

"Including the one he stole from the Yeshiva?" said Gardi, doubtfully. "And including the one that old Rabbi Moreno was given by the old woman from China?"

"All of them, including the one which speaks about the longest day." By now, Elijah felt no reason not to gamble. He had to check out the details which Orna had found in Norman's medical file.

"None of the people here believe me. Mualem and all the doctors here are complete ignoramuses."

"They're weaklings," Elijah reassured him. "When the redemption comes, they will all come to you on their knees to beg for your forgiveness."

"Amen," said Gardi. He appeared to doze off, but was suddenly wide awake. "Where do you live? With Rabbi Moreno?"

Elijah remained silent.

"I see the wall from my window and I await the messiah," said Gardi. His head flopped backward.

Naeel rushed over. "I was afraid he's having another attack, so I gave him his medicine."

"I see that you do an excellent job caring for him."

"Thank you. Really, thank you." Naeel insisted on escorting Elijah to the exit, and this time he thanked him profusely for the envelope. He had evidently had time to count the sum of money it contained.

Never in his wildest dreams would Elijah have imagined acting like this at the beginning of that summer, before all this began. In his professional life, he was always interested in finding the true facts behind every document, and had never needed to resort to lies. In general, he had very little contact with people. Yet here he was acting like a born - maybe even pathological - liar.

It was early afternoon, and Jerusalem was bathed in strong sunshine. As he stepped out of the hospital, Elijah was almost blinded by the sunlight.

He had seen the light, the other light that surrounded the entire case in which he had become involved inadvertently. Norman was Absalom Moreno, who had rebelled against his father, just as the Biblical Absalom had rebelled against his father, King David. In 1929, he, along with Gardi, had used the verses his father had taught him to repel the Arabs who had attacked them. It is a historical fact that the Arabs retreated after the first assault. What no one knew was that two small Jewish

310

youths had been the ones who routed them, with the help of Kabbalistic verses.

The picture was finally clear, and the pieces of the puzzle were coming together. As the boys knew only some of the verses, and as they had not practiced saying them in unison, the deliverance from the Arabs had been only a partial one. Gardi had lost his mind, while Norman had been almost blinded by the forces they had unleashed. Absalom had stolen a scroll from his father's yeshiva, and that was why he had fled. His father would never forgive him for the sin of using the verses to alter reality. Such actions by impetuous youngsters explain why it is forbidden to study the Kabbalah until the age of forty. Rabbi David Moreno had made a major mistake in teaching his son Kabbalah at a very tender age. Absalom Moreno had fled from Israel, and adopted the name John McDonald. He later adopted an additional name, Norman, an inversion of the family name of Moreno. This inversion, with slight modifications, had given him an American-sounding name, and he called himself David Norman.

He had devoted his life to finding the copies of the original *Sefer Yetzirah*, which included the seven hints. In order to do so, he had employed all his considerable wealth, which he amassed as a result of his remarkable ability to foretell the future; and that ability had evidently come from his knowledge of the Kabbalah. It was his aim to put together all the different

words and word combinations, using the supercomputers he had
bought and tried to smuggle out of the United States. By doing
so, he would bring the fountain to the heart, and would change
Nash's equilibrium point. He would accomplish it in a marble
building surrounded with water, in accordance with the legends
of the *Pardes*. The computers had to be somewhere close to the
Temple Mount, opposite the *Even Shetiyah*, and this must be
done from a house from whose window it would be possible to
see the Western Wall, part of the wall which had surrounded the
Temple Mount. That house was one which had belonged to
Norman's father, Rabbi Moreno. Elijah was convinced that the
scroll stolen by Norman, the only one that Elijah had not seen,
specified the time of the equilibrium point. Elijah realized how
naive he had been in thinking that he could conceal the
knowledge of the scroll belonging to Rabbi Batzri. After all, as
soon as Norman sat across from him he could read his thoughts,
and he must have realized that this year was an appropriate one
for the redemption. Maybe the reason Norman had summoned
him to the Spanish island had not been to have him read the
scroll, but for Norman to read his mind. The puzzle was almost
complete. He was missing only one link: the seventh scroll! It,
too, was apparently in Norman's possession.

It was evidently time to confront Norman, but before
doing so, Elijah did what every good academic would. He
visited the university library and immersed himself in the

abundant literature regarding messianic movements and messiahs. He was sure that in his confrontation with Norman all this information would be vital. Only when the university library closed, many hours later, did he pick himself up and head for home. At least he felt that he finally had a framework for understanding what Norman was planning.

The Sphere of the Infinite

When King Joash Conquered Jerusalem

About two hundred years after King David conquered Jerusalem, in about 1790 B.C.E., Joash, King of Israel, conquered Jerusalem. Unlike other rulers and madmen, Joash did so almost against his will.

A pragmatic king, Joash devoted most of his efforts to freeing his country from the yoke of Aram, which exerted great pressure on the Kingdom of Israel at that time. A short while before the prophet Elisha died, Joash visited him and expressed his admiration for the aged prophet.

"My father, my father, Chariot of Israel and its horsemen," cried Joash on his sickbed. This term for the prophet, as the source of the nation's strength and as equal in power to its military might, had hereto been said only by the prophet Elijah. King Joash was the first to use it in reference to Elisha. Elisha, who had been complimented, blessed Joash and told him that he would vanquish Aram three times - and that was indeed what he did.

After the monarchy of David and Solomon, the country was divided into two kingdoms - of Judea and of Israel. For two hundred years, up to the reign of Joash, King of Israel, and Amatziah, King of Judea, the two kingdoms developed side by side. Sometimes the relationship was one of peace, tranquility, and fraternal love; at other times there were bloody confrontations. Amatziah, though, was the first to dream openly of uniting the two kingdoms. And if that could not be achieved by peaceful means, Amatziah would do so by war. He sent messengers to Joash and invited him to wage battle. Amatziah was a dreamer and, like many Jerusalemites before him, hoped that hope would triumph over experience, a hope which was dashed on the rocks of reality.

Opposed to him, Joash moved away from Jerusalem and tried not to provoke Amatziah. He would not even have come close to the gates of the city had not Amatziah attempted to realize his dream at Joash's expense.

Joash must be credited for having done everything possible to avert war. He warned Amatziah that he was in for a defeat and tried, to the best of his ability, to foil any attempt by Amatziah to wage a needless struggle.

"Rejoice and stay at home, for why you should meddle to your harm, so that you should fall, you and Judah with you?" asked Joash. However, Joash was a Jerusalemite and its stubborn climate affected him.

The armies of Judah and Israel confronted one another in Bet Shemesh. Joash gained a decisive victory over Amatziah. Not only did the men of Judah flee ignominiously in defeat, but, also, Amatziah

When King Joash Conquered Jerusalem

himself was taken captive by Joash. Joash ascended to Jerusalem, and took as booty for himself and his men the treasuries of the Temple and of the Royal Palace. In order to prevent another war, Joash made a major breach in the walls of Jerusalem and took hostages of the royal family to Samaria with him. Joash eventually freed Amatziah and did not kill him, so as to prevent a hundred-year war between their heirs.

Amatziah lived to a ripe old age after his failed attempt, but his time was not a tranquil one. Fifteen years after this war, a conspiracy was hatched against him in Jerusalem. He was forced to flee to Lachish, but was pursued, caught, and put to death. His body was dragged by a horse to Jerusalem, where he was buried in his ancestral plot, and with him his dreams, too, were buried.

In spite of his overwhelming victory, Joash never thought of uniting the two kingdoms under one ruler. He did not even want to remain in Jerusalem, and immediately after his victory he returned to Samaria. But like all conquerors of Jerusalem, Joash did not find it easy going. Like the others, he found that it was easier to conquer Jerusalem than to flee from it. The city took its revenge on Joash, and less than a year after his victory, he died the death of an ordinary mortal.

Elijah contemplated the idea of Jerusalem on High, as he wandered around Jerusalem below. Hundreds of years ago, the Old City, enclosed by the wall built by Suleiman, had already been divided into four quarters - Jewish, Armenian, Muslim and Christian - but the borders delineating each were never firm, with one quarter encroaching on another. Elijah reached the Jewish Quarter in order to search Norman's home, which he had heard was located somewhere in the vicinity.

The Jewish Quarter as we know it was, in Second Temple times, the richest and most prestigious of the city. Ancient Jerusalem at the time of David and Solomon was built on the slopes of Silwan. At the time of the First temple you had to climb up a steep and winding road, in order to reach the Temple. In contrast, at the time of the Second Temple, the wealthy would descend to the Temple Mount.

The streets of the Jewish Quarter were, as usual, crowded. Like the rest of the Jewish Quarter, they were paved with rock, and only rock. The roads were remarkably narrow, only two or three yards wide, enough to accommodate pedestrians but not cars. The roads themselves sloped inward to the center, to allow rain to drain off. Elijah walked the length of one street after another, observing each entrance and seeking in vain some kind of link to Norman or Moreno. He had no specific plan of attack and merely placed his trust in luck.

When King Joash Conquered Jerusalem

Like all cities built in the Roman tradition, Byzantine Jerusalem had a central road spanning its entire length and another spanning its breadth. The road that spanned the length of a city was always called the Cardo, and the other was called the Decumanus. These streets, which were wider than the others, were used by carts to bring in merchandise, as well as by pedestrians, and they were the commercial centers of each city. Various stores plied their business along these streets. When the Jewish Quarter was rebuilt by Israel after the Six-Day War, part of the Cardo was unearthed and reconstructed, taking care to preserve the houses above it. In order to recreate some of the atmosphere of that time, shops were built on both sides of the Cardo, most of them selling tourist souvenirs and trinkets of the Holy Land. Elijah found himself walking along the Cardo and surveying the area. On his left he saw part of an old wall, which had been reconstructed. According to a plaque posted on the wall, it dated back to First Temple times, and most of it was probably destroyed at the time of Nebuchadnezzar. Above it stood a yeshiva founded a hundred years ago, and nearby a three-century-old mosque. They all stood close to one another, but had very little mutual tolerance.

Elijah thought about the fate of the city. Old Jerusalem is one big archaeological site. Wherever you dig you will find many kinds of antiques and relics. After all, of all the famous ancient cities of the ancient Middle East, Jerusalem is the one of the very few to have survived throughout the centuries, and it is still alive and kicking today. Shushan, Nineveh, Akkad, Abeilah, Ur, Zoan - all of them have disappeared or were swallowed up by other cities. Jerusalem is one stubborn city that refuses to roll over and die.

At the end of the Cardo, as if to add fuel to the fire, stood a golden menorah, a good seven feet high. The accompanying blurb claimed that it was a true replica of the menorah that had stood in the Temple. Although it did not say so, the underlying motive of the anonymous donor was evidently to make this menorah available for the Third Temple, if and when it is built. And that Temple, according to Jewish tradition, will come down from Heaven, along with the Messiah. When he came closer, Elijah saw that the menorah was enclosed in a reinforced glass case, along with alarms and sensors. Well, that's what Jerusalem below is like, Elijah thought to himself.

Almost every entrance led to this or that institute of education, each with its own distinct ideology. There were spiritual seminars of every shape and size, available to anyone seeking them. An infinite number of *yeshivot* had opened their doors in the Jewish Quarter. Almost every building bore a sign, tracing the illustrious history of the site on which it stood. This building was built by funds supplied by Dutch Jews a century ago, the next by the Chabad Hasidic sect in the previous

century, and the third by the generous contribution of David
Tannenbaum of Toronto, and it had been completed but three
months earlier. One building had been a yeshiva in Ottoman
times, another had once been a hospital for the indigent. Elijah
read each sign, some of which had been damaged, but he did
not find what he was looking for.

He continued walking from building to building, from
entrance to entrance. By now, he felt that he could easily qualify
as an expert on building signs and their durability. "If I ever
want a memorial plaque in my name," he thought to himself, "it
should be engraved into the wall itself." Metal signs rust,
ceramic ones break, and paint peels. Moreover, signs can be
torn down. However, if something is engraved in the stone of
the wall itself, it remains for generations. Ideally, too, the
engraving should be at a height where it is not easily accessible.
If it is too low, it invites graffiti - as he had seen in various
places.

After wandering about unsuccessfully for two hours,
Elijah decided to concentrate on those houses that faced the
Temple Mount. Rather than continuing to go from building to
building in the Jewish Quarter, he descended the steps leading
to the Western Wall, assuming that from them, he would be able
to see which windows faced the Temple Mount. Along the way
he spotted a small garden, which amazed him, because probably
the most striking feature of the Jewish Quarter is the total

absence of greenery. During the Crusader era this area had once been a hostel, where Crusaders from Europe were lodged. Close to the garden, he saw three *yeshivot*. All their names contained either the word "central" or the word "world". What is it about this city that makes everyone think it is the center of everything?

He remembered the flytraps of his youth. The first time he had seen one, it was at the home of his Uncle Joseph, on a kibbutz. The trap was a simple one: a paper plate on which Joseph had placed small strips of rotten meat. Above the paper plate was an upside-down clear plastic funnel. The funnel was connected to a wooden box, which enclosed a wire mesh structure. Once the flies flew into the wire mesh, there was no way for them to escape. They would fly about frantically, beating against the mesh on one side and then the other, until they would fall exhausted. Every few days, when the mesh became too full, Joseph would empty it. In his mind, Elijah saw all the conquerors of Jerusalem as flies flitting around the entrance to the city. Like the flies, they too did not know exactly what was happening to them and what they should expect. They all shared the idea that if they lived a better life, they would be able to discover the secrets of the city. However, they, too, ended their lives buried in the ground. Each conqueror would add a layer, which would then be covered by the layer of the next conqueror.

When King Joash Conquered Jerusalem

Elijah walked slowly to the Western Wall. The severe heat had gotten to him. He remembered his first visit to the Wall after the Six-Day War, and it was only then that he had found out that the Wall was not part of the Second Temple wall at all, but of the wall that surrounded the Temple Mount. From that time on, like most Israelis, he would visit the Wall only when accompanying foreign visitors, as part of a guided tour of the city. He entered the Western Wall plaza and wandered around, totally at a loss as to how to proceed.

Here, in this holy place, he internalized the holy experience: who will be the one who moves the fountain and the rock from their inappropriate equilibrium point? It must be a saintly person, who will come down to our lowly world and who will heal the vessels. It is an extremely difficult task, which most are ill equipped to carry out.

Suddenly Elijah saw a great light: Norman's plan was much broader than he had imagined, and included the entire world, from the Big Bang to DNA. Elijah walked quickly from one end of the plaza to the other, and then climbed the steps leading up to the market. He had just spent three quarters of an hour in the hot sunshine on this segment. As he walked on, he was suddenly confronted by a simple door with a sign proclaiming that it was the "Alkabetz Institute". Beneath it, in smaller letters, was the legend: "Institute for Research into the Jewish Religious Poem." And Alkabetz was the name of

322

another of the famous Kabbalists! His heart told him that this was the correct door. He knocked on the door and rang the bell for some time. He had the impression that someone inside the building was observing him through the keyhole, but did not wish to open the door. He did not give up. The stakes were simply too high. After fifteen minutes of waiting, ringing, and knocking, he did something that would have been inconceivable to him a few weeks earlier - he tried the door handle. Amazingly, the door was not even locked, and it opened as he turned the doorknob. Norman stood there. Elijah was taken aback at the man's appearance. His face was sallow, deep rings surrounded his listless eyes, and he was leaning heavily on a cane. He was wearing an Arab *galabiyeh* and wore a *keffiyah* on his head. He looked extremely strange and his dress seemed singularly inappropriate. Norman stepped into the interior of the small building. The living room was tiny, its furniture Spartan. Elijah, who followed him in, could discern a small kitchen next to the living room. At the side of the living room there were steps leading downward. With great difficulty, Norman sat down on one of the couches.

"I must apologize, Professor Shemtov. As you can no doubt see, I'm not in the best of health. I would very much appreciate if we could postpone this meeting until tomorrow."

"Just one question," said Elijah. "Where is the seventh scroll?"

"Professor Shemtov, I hired you to decipher manuscripts. You are getting involved in an area that has nothing to do with you. How did you get here? I must ask you to leave immediately!"

"Where is the seventh scroll? What does it say? I want to know."

"I'm asking you politely to leave," said Norman adamantly.

Elijah looked at Norman. He didn't believe a word of what Norman was saying.

"Mr. Norman, or John McDonald or Absalom Moreno - whatever your name is. I doubt if it will come as a surprise to you if I tell you that many people believe that there are powers beyond the understanding of human beings, and that these powers are constantly involved in whatever we do. These are powers that we will not be able to identify for thousands of years - if ever.

"According to a Jewish tradition, everything which ever happened, is happening, or will happen in the future is to be found - in some form or another - in the Torah, the Five Books of Moses, which the Israelites received on Mount Sinai. However, the key to unlock all this data is not available to everyone. In the past, some Kabbalistic scholars were familiar with the detailed instructions needed to activate the Kabbalistic secrets when absolutely necessary. These secrets could be used to accomplish what could not be achieved by natural means. The rumor states that Rabbi Johanan ben Zakkai used it to escape from besieged Jerusalem, and to obtain permission from the Roman general Vespasian to open a major Torah study center in Jabneh. This information was relayed to Rabbi Eliezer ben Horkenos, who in turn conveyed it to Rabbi Akiba.

"Rabbi Akiba, though, felt that these means should never be used, no matter what the motivation or need. He was afraid that using these powers will cause destruction instead of redemption. Thus, he ordered that all written copies of the key be destroyed. He did, however, teach the key orally to some of his greatest disciples. One of these, Rabbi Simon Bar Yochai, taught it to his son, Rabbi Elazar. Rabbi Elazar was the one who, nevertheless, had the key written down by Rabbi Nehemiah of Peki'in. In return for doing so, Rabbi Nehemiah was given the promise that there would always be a Jewish settlement in Peki'in. And indeed, Jews have lived in Peki'in throughout centuries of our exile.

"It was because of those scrolls ordered by Rabbi Elazar ben Simon that, throughout the generations, there were those who believed that they could solve all the world's problems. In the course of centuries, part of the scrolls fell into the hands of various great individuals. For example, the *Ari* evidently tried to use the key, and indeed he died at an early age. Rabbi Elijah of Vilna, known as the Gaon of Vilna, wished to travel to the Land of Israel in order to bring about the redemption, but at the last minute withdrew from his plan. Rabbi Israel Ba'al Shemtov, the founder of Hassidism, was evidently also in possession of the texts, and bequeathed them to his daughter, Odel. She was the grandmother of the renowned Rabbi Nachman of Bratslav.

"We are not aware of all the different attempts to redeem the world, but all who tried were aware that all sorts of untoward and unexpected results might ensue. Some claimed that a failure in Spain in the 15th century led to the expulsion of the Jews from Spain in 1492.

"Eventually, great rabbis came to the realization that the task was too big for any single person."

Norman seemed to have recovered somewhat. He wanted to interject and say something, but Elijah would not be stopped. Everything he now knew came tumbling out.

"The most elaborate attempt of all took place in a yeshiva named Beit Shamayim, which means 'Home of Heaven'. It was founded in Jerusalem in 1727, and its declared aim was to hasten the redemption. For two whole centuries, its students spent all their waking hours in doing whatever they could to further this aim. They pored over all the Kabbalistic works they had, and invested much time and effort in acquiring works they did not have. This continued up to the early 1920s.

"One of the best and brightest of the students at this yeshiva was named David Moreno, an only child. He hailed from a long and illustrious line of Kabbalists. His family had lived in the Holy Land even before the Ottoman conquest. A family tradition had it that their family had never left the Holy Land, and had lived in Peki'in throughout.

"He married a lovely girl named Rachel from a Kabbalistic family too, and life was idyllic for a very short time - until Rachel came down with tuberculosis. For two years she lingered, finally succumbing to the disease. David Moreno was left alone to raise his young son.

"Had it not been for his little son, David would have been overcome with grief. Absalom gave him a reason to live and was the source of all his joy. At the Beit Shamayim Yeshiva, David continued to make great strides in his studies, and was soon known as Rabbi Moreno. Rabbi Moreno never remarried. He devoted all his time to his studies in the yeshiva and to educating his son. At a very young age Absalom showed signs of great genius. Due to the specific circumstances surrounding the family, David was able to bring his son to all the yeshiva's special events. Even though he taught Absalom fields of knowledge that one is not allowed to teach the young, no one stopped him, out of deference for the cruelties of his life.

"In the 1920s the yeshiva attained its peak. Enrollment increased, and many worthy potential students were turned away for lack of space. The fall of the Ottoman Empire and the opening to the west that followed it opened up a treasure chest of heretofore-unknown manuscripts. Added to this were certain manuscripts from the private collection of Ms. Sassoon of Hong Kong. All these factors caused the heads of the yeshiva, including Rabbi Moreno, to take steps that would hasten the redemption. 'It is now or never,' they said to one another.

"The place where they carried out their efforts is not known to us. What we know is that the appropriate prayers were said, the appropriate incantations recited, and all the details carried out to the letter. Due to pressure by some of the yeshiva's old-timers, the entire ceremony was not held in a single day, but was spread out over two days.

"The second part of the ceremony was never held because obvious signs of problems became apparent as soon as the first ceremony commenced. Before the end of that session, a major earthquake hit Jerusalem, the largest of the century. By the time the earthquake was over, the yeshiva building had ceased to exist. Not a single stone remained on top of another.

"The group reacted immediately. They realized that in the dispute between Rabbi Elazar and Rabbi Akiba, Rabbi Akiba had been correct, and that any attempt to try to 'rush things' in terms of the ultimate redemption was obviously something that was too dangerous to even contemplate. The dream would have to remain just that. The yeshiva itself was never reopened, and all suspect manuscripts were burned. As the yeshiva had made a point of keeping all its actions utterly secret, almost no one knew what had transpired. David Moreno, then one of the prominent scholars of the yeshiva, accepted the decision. If God was clearly not in favor of their work, who were they to contradict His wishes?

"The members of the group, though, overlooked one individual, Joseph Absalom Moreno, the son of Rabbi David Moreno, his father's pride and only source of joy. That might have been the reason why Rabbi Moreno taught him everything he knew, including the most esoteric Kabbalistic teachings. He had taught his son, even though it is forbidden to teach this to anyone less than forty years of age. The son, who was still under the age of Bar Mitzvah, was the only one who refused to abandon the dream. He was of the opinion that the reason they had failed was that they had not carried out the requisite actions in the proper manner. Before the earthquake, and certainly without his father's knowledge, he had copied out all the important documents. Thus, even though many manuscripts were destroyed in the earthquake and the group destroyed all the others afterwards, Absalom Moreno still had copies of all of these documents.

"In 1929, Absalom Moreno utilized his knowledge for the first time. An inflamed Muslim mob had burst through the Nablus Gate and made its way to the Jewish neighborhood of Me'ah Shearim, with the express purpose of destroying the neighborhood. The Jews, who had not expected this, were defenseless. Some of them attempted to flee toward other Jewish neighborhoods. For Absalom Joseph Moreno, this was a golden opportunity to test his abilities. But he could not do this alone and took a young friend, Judah Gardi, along to work with him. Together they recited phrases that no one is permitted to recite, and took actions that no one is allowed to take. The Muslim onslaught simply stopped cold in its tracks. No one else knew how this happened, but yesterday Mr. Gardi told me all about it.

"When David Moreno realized what had happened, he slapped his son's face for the first and only time in his life. Absalom did not react, and certainly showed no signs of remorse. His success blinded him. He was convinced that the only reason the group had disbanded was because of its ineptitude. He would not be inept, and he would be able to harness all the powers necessary for success. A few days later, the boy simply disappeared. In the confusion caused by the Arab riots, no one even missed him, except his father. Rabbi David Moreno spent whatever little he had in a futile search for his son. Years later, in the midst of World War II, Rabbi David Moreno died - no doubt from a broken heart."

At the mention of Rabbi Moreno's death, Elijah detected a tear forming in Norman's eye, but he went on mercilessly.

"The adventures of Absalom Moreno - by now he had changed his name once or twice - were enough to fill a decent-sized novel.

"Does any of this sound familiar to you?"

Norman did not need to nod, as Elijah spelled out everything he had put together about him.

"Professor Shemtov, I admire your research abilities, but I really don't feel well. Is there a point to your history lesson? I am generally exceptionally choosy about the people I work with. I can't understand how I went so wrong in hiring you."

"Norman the genius made a mistake? The kitten has turned into a tiger?" asked Elijah. "The reason is simple, Mr. Moreno. I have another name that you never discovered, which you did not enter into your computer. Had you entered it, you would have known immediately that I was not suitable."

"And what is that added name?"

"My middle name is Metatron."

Moreno, alias Norman, looked crushed. "You messed up the program!"

"Right! All I did was add in my middle name, the name of the most important angel in the Kabbalah. And do you know who gave me that name? None other than your father, Rabbi Moreno!"

"No, it can't be!" shouted Norman.

"I suggest that you stop your computers right now."

"What do you find so terrible in my work of saving the world?" Norman seemed older than ever. He added, "And if I answer your question, will you leave?"

"You're not in a position to bargain with me. I need your answer immediately!"

"I took two scrolls from my father's yeshiva..."

Elijah interrupted him. "Do you know what the Rebbe of Kotzk said toward the end of his life? 'When I was young, I wanted to change the world. When I became an adult, I wanted to change my country. As the years passed, I was content just to change my city. Today I say, 'I hope I can just change myself.'"

Norman was not impressed. Not only did he know the story, but he also knew how it continued.

"That's not the end of the story," said Norman. "The problem was that he began in reverse order. First, he had to change himself, afterwards his city, then his country, and only afterwards the world. Then he might have had a chance of succeeding. In any event, your riddle will solve itself in a few minutes. Open the curtain."

Norman wearily pointed to the curtain. Elijah went over, opened the curtain, and looked down. Beneath them, on a lower level, was a room full of electronics. It looked almost like control room in a space station. In it were the two supercomputers, with smaller computers linked to them.

332

"You have to stop it all," said Elijah in an authoritative voice. Norman did not react. Elijah began toward the stairs.

Suddenly, Norman seemed to come fully awake. Grabbing his cane, he jumped from the couch, ran after Elijah, and stood in front of him.

"Are you crazy? Where do you think you're going? I've spent my life to get to this point!"

"All those who tried to change the world have only added to its distress. Stalin, Hitler, Attila the Hun. How many people were slaughtered, burned alive, strangled, hanged, shot, and buried in order to make a better future? Norman, I'm speaking on behalf of all the common people, people who will not get into the history books. Leave us alone! Let us live our lives as we want, and don't impose your insane ideology on us!"

Elijah was breathless, partly because he had exerted himself, partly because of the emotion of the occasion, and partly because he had had to raise his voice and shout at Norman - to give the most important speech of his life.

"Norman, you obviously play with people's lives. What happened to the two mathematicians you employed in your service? How many people did you destroy in order to bring about this redemption of yours?"

Norman still did not respond. He looked up, beyond Elijah's shoulder. Elijah turned around and saw a large countdown clock. According to the clock, there were about four and a half minutes left. Elijah tried to push Norman aside, but Norman seemed to have found new sources of strength and he could not be budged. Elijah tried again, this time pulling at the cane on which Norman was leaning. Norman let go of the cane and tried to hold Elijah back with his two hands. Suddenly, though, he grabbed at his head with a sigh. Elijah took advantage of the opportunity and pushed Norman, who fell to the ground. Elijah grabbed the cane and ran down the stairs. Before you can enter an area in which there is danger of radioactivity, you are generally subjected to signs and warnings to that effect. Here, though, there was no warning on the double set of doors leading to the computers - but there were safeguards in place.

Elijah passed through the first set of doors and then the second, and then he began to understand what Norman meant. Behind the safety glass, this could almost have been any other control room, even if it was a little out of the ordinary. However, as he proceeded, Elijah realized that there must be something in the air, something that made him feel lethargic, something that made both his hands and his feet refuse to respond to his simple command to move forward.

Elijah glanced around the room, and saw that seven regular computers were linked to the supercomputers. Around each computer, seven loudspeakers were arranged to form a

334

menorah – a seven-branched candelabrum and an ancient symbol of Judaism - all facing the Temple Mount. The loudspeakers were broadcasting words that Elijah was unable to understand.

The computers and the loudspeakers worked independently of each other, but together they produced a sound that was both pleasant and terrifying, at the same time - if such a thing can be imagined. Elijah was not quite sure what was happening, while an inner voice whispered to him, *Run away! Run away! Run away*! He ignored it. The closer he got to the computers, the weaker he felt.

Elijah's body felt terribly hot, almost boiling. He thought of all the ordinary folk all over the world and simply attacked the first computer with the cane. Radiation, emitted by the computer, began to affect the entire area in he stood. His blow to the computer had been much weaker than he would have imagined or intended; his muscles had gone quite limp. Still, he kept hitting at it until he saw that the computer had stopped working. Like a madman, he ran from computer to computer, lashing about at them, one after another. As each computer stopped working, its loudspeakers fell silent. Elijah lost all sense of time, as he ran about the room frenziedly, sending sparks flying from the ruined computers. Suddenly, as he lifted the cane once again, he saw Mei-Ling before him, trying to use her hand to deflect the cane, which was aimed at

335

her head. He hesitated for but an instant. None of this was real, he said to himself. He continued running, throwing another computer off its stand and smashing it. All the events of the summer flashed before his eyes. Whenever he tried to strike at a computer, another tortured face appeared before him. He struck at Isabel, who screamed in fear. He felt he was losing his sanity. Another blow was aimed at his daughters, Efrat and Michali, who pleaded with him to stop. Uncle Nissim stood before him, his hands trying to fend off the blow. The pain in Elijah's joints was almost unbearable. Ozlem, the Turkish woman, was beaten mercilessly. He acted as if in a trance. At one point the walls seemed to have turned into ocean waves, threatening to drown him. A giant wave loomed up toward him, and he heard the sound of the sea as it raced in and over him. He was almost ready to flee, when his Grandmother Esther appeared on the opposite side of the room. "Keep going," she called to him. "It's not water. You can see for yourself that it is pure marble." He turned away and continued with his sacred mission. "When you reach the pure marble rocks, do **not** say, 'Water, water.'"

Elijah found himself in the middle of a room of smashed computers, electrical cords yanked out of the wall, monitors whose glass had shattered, loudspeakers trailing wires. He stood in the middle of the room, sweating and trembling, his hands uncontrollable. The cane seemed to be welded to his hand, and with a mighty effort he threw it across the room. He had no idea whether minutes had passed - or hours. His watch had stopped. Slowly, he made his way out of the carnage. When he climbed the stairs, he saw Norman lying on the floor, and the countdown clock had frozen at two minutes and ten seconds before the scheduled time.

In a state of shock, Elijah stepped out into the alleys of the Old City. He did not look back. In this state, he did not hear the wailing of air raid alarms, police car sirens, and frantic, hysterical voices of everyone around him. He walked all the way home, like a robot coming back to be re-charged.

At that moment in time, he had no way of knowing that on that hot June day in Jerusalem, all the control systems of all the nuclear weapons in the world had gone "berserk." They had all been programmed to enter into the fully armed state, ready and prepared for deployment and were about to take off for their designated targets. All efforts on the part of control staff worldwide to halt the process had been to no avail. The commands to prevent the missiles from being launched were all ignored. Nor were any of the hysterical calls to the opposing sides about an inexplicable nuclear launch believed.

"The end of the world is nigh. In three minutes, everything is going to explode," was the message from the command center in Nevada.

"Take it easy. We have everything under control," came the voice of the man's superior.

According to the reporters who wrote all about it later, had all the missiles indeed been launched, not a single person would have lived to tell the tale. The radioactive fallout that would have enveloped the world would have wiped out every living thing, down to the minutest single-cell creatures. The blasts would have blown open the atmosphere, letting all the world's oxygen escape, irreplaceably. In fact, the force of the blast would probably have blown the earth itself to smithereens, its pieces scattered throughout the solar system.

However, the catastrophe had been averted. The theories that emerged as to what had almost caused - and equally, what had averted - the end of the world abounded. The Internet was swamped with millions upon millions of communications, and theories, and surmises, and conjectures. There were those who noted that this Chinese year was a combination of the year of the dragon and the year of the snake, a combination full of challenges and dangers. Others quoted various texts, from Nostradamus to the *Zohar*, to prove that all of this had been anticipated, pre-destined. All the world's secret services were accused of crimes against humanity. Americans accused the CIA, the Arabs accused the Israeli Mossad and Russians thought that members of the former KGB were to blame. Tens of thousands - if not hundreds of thousands - of Internet sites analyzed every conceivable aspect of what had nearly been the catastrophe to end all catastrophes. In many places, anyone who might possibly have been involved was seized, tried, and summarily executed.

When Elijah reached home, he said he had a headache. He collapsed on his bed and slept through until mid-morning the following day.

"Eli, you're finally awake. Do you have any idea what happened while you were sleeping?" Orna summarized everything that had happened worldwide and then added. "Oh, yes. I'm sorry to tell you that Nissim Toledano died."

For some reason, Elijah was not surprised. He sat quietly, but was grateful that he had at least had the opportunity to say goodbye to the old man - the only person still alive who had known his middle name.

"Eli, what happened yesterday? You came home looking as if you had been in a major battle. And then you slept right through until now, as if making up for all those sleepless nights you've had over the past weeks."

Elijah was afraid to tell his wife the truth. He thought she might think he had lost his mind. All he told her was that he and Norman had exchanged harsh words, and that in the end they had pushed each other around, that Norman had threatened him with his cane, that he had been forced to pull the cane out of Norman's hands, that Norman had fallen, and that when Elijah had left, Norman was still lying on the floor.

Now he asked himself what his next step should be. In the end, the two decided to go to the Old City to check on Norman; they arrived at about noon and Elijah led the way to the alley where the Alkabetz Institute was located. As they approached, they saw moving men carrying out boxes of equipment that they had packed. Elijah saw a man who looked vaguely familiar. It was Orna who recognized the man as Israel Noy, the law expert, who often appears on Israel Television.

Israel Noy, a lawyer by training, was a short, stout, balding man with glasses. His bald spot was covered by a large black *yarmulke*, and he had a habit of twisting clumps of the little hair remaining on his head.

"Professor Shemtov!" Noy cried enthusiastically, and held out his hand. "I'm so happy to see you."

Elijah shook his hand and asked, "Have we met?"

"Well, maybe not in person," Noy agreed. "However, I was fascinated by your article about the point on the Hebrew letter *Shin*, although I'm not sure I agree with your conclusions. We had a big argument in our synagogue about your article. According to some people, you deliberately ignored the Yemenite script, as it did not fit into your thesis. Others reckoned that the documents you cited were from groups that had left the Jewish mainstream. In any event, there is no doubt that the article was a most stimulating one, and people will be discussing it for years to come."

Up until two days earlier, Elijah would have been deeply moved by the flattery, but not today.

"I would love to discuss it further with you, but we are in a huge hurry at the moment, and this is really out of nowhere. This is Orna, my wife."

"Actually, this is not 'out of nowhere' at all. In fact, I've been waiting for you here since the early morning. A client of mine expected you to come here and asked me to deliver a letter to you. Pleased to meet you, Orna."

Noy removed a letter from his pocket and handed it to Elijah. Elijah took the letter out of the envelope, read it and reread it, and then read it a third time. The letter was brief and to the point. The Alkabetz Institute, through its attorney, Israel Noy, was pleased to inform Elijah that the work he had been engaged to perform had been carried out fully to its satisfaction. The Institute had no further demands or claims. In return, it was paying him the specified amount, which had already been transferred to his bank account. That terminated the agreement between them. They were delighted with the work Elijah had performed, and hoped for continued cooperation in the future. They wished him the best of luck. The amount transferred was a million dollars!

Elijah read it over and over, not fully understanding what was going on. And what he did understand he didn't like. Noy interrupted him. "There is a small procedural matter to be completed, Professor Shemtov. Please sign this document." The document stated that in accepting the payment, Elijah waived any future claims against the Alkabetz Institute and/or any other organization connected to it in any way.

"I'm not about to sign anything," said Elijah, becoming agitated. "I don't understand what this figure is based on, and I do happen to have certain claims."

"I understand," said Noy. "My principal told me you would probably refuse to sign, but he has no intention of pressuring you into doing so. The money is in your account regardless. You have a reputation for being a man of your word and I believe you will agree that the amount is a fair one. As to your claims, you probably realize that I'm not the one you should address them to. I was not empowered to deal with that aspect. All I was empowered to do was deliver the letter and nothing more. For added security, we also sent a copy of the letter to your home.

"I don't understand. Who sent you? And what is this payment for?"

"Professor Shemtov, I don't ask questions. I'm a lawyer and I try to carry out assignments to the best of my ability, in the interest of my client. Whatever I don't know can't hurt me,

342

and I have no interest in knowing. However, taking into account that you are the world's expert in your field, and as I know that the Institute deals with various ancient manuscripts, I assume you provided advice which saved it a fortune."

Elijah left him without saying goodbye, and went with Orna to show her the Luzatto Institute. He was not surprised to see that the name on the mailbox had been removed. A large sign stated that the building was for sale, and listed the real estate agent. One of the agents happened to be there, and he gladly showed them around the building, which was completely empty, without as a stick of furniture in it. According to the agent, the building belonged to a foreign company named Alkabetz. The company had planned to open a branch in Israel, but due to the recession in the country had decided not to do so.

Orna was impressed with the beauty of the building and suggested, "Maybe we should buy it?" Elijah did not want to give the impression of a person who believed in superstition, but he gave her a withering look, which explained exactly how he felt.

The next day, when Orna got home from work, she told Elijah: "Norman didn't come in for the operation, but don't be upset. I checked under all the names he's used, and there has been no death reported under any of them. He must have left the country."

The summer came to an end and life resumed its normal tempo. The Shemtov family paid off its mortgage and moved to a larger apartment. Here, Elijah had a big study of his own. Whatever money was left over was entrusted to Gabi Moldovan, Elijah's childhood friend, and the one who had told him about the supercomputers that Luria Investments had purchased.

Six months later, Landau, the department head, burst into Elijah's office. It appeared that the Kim Foundation of Los Angeles had decided to fund two new chairs at the department. The budget was quite a lavish one and included funds for research assistants and the construction of new offices and laboratories. One of the two chairs was to go to a professor who specialized in studying Ancient Hebrew texts and the second to a professor who specialized in Ancient Hebrew grammar. "This position fits you like a glove, like anxiety fits a Jewish mother, as if it was tailor-made for you." When the position was announced, Elijah was named the head of the Moses ben Shemtov de Leon Department for the Study of Ancient Hebrew Manuscripts.

Life went on as normal, and Elijah's family flowed along with it. He conducted research, lectured in his field of expertise and published scholarly articles in academic journals. Three years later he was even awarded the Jerusalem Prize for his contributions in the field. As the awards committee put it, "Professor Shemtov has forged new paths and opened up new horizons in the study of Hebrew texts in Spain in the 12th and 13th centuries."

He knew that his papers would not change the world, but as he said to himself, the world must be grateful to those who do not try to change it, to those who will never enter the history books. It is because of such people that the world still exists.

Epilogue

When The Lord Conquered Jerusalem

At the beginning of time and of space, or - to be more accurate - before either time or space had been defined, God conquered Jerusalem and through it He created the entire world. According to the Kabbalistic Jewish tradition, the Torah, the Sabbath, and Jerusalem were all created before the world was created. The Torah preceded it in thought, the Sabbath in time, and Jerusalem in space.

How was Jerusalem conquered? God "compacted Himself" so as to leave room for the world, and left a very small opening, the size of a small needle, through which the light could shine in. For this purpose, He sowed a series of quanta within the emptiness, created matter out of nothing, and expanded it many times over. He merged protons and anti-protons, neutrons and anti-neutrons, and breathed life into the photons that were produced from this merger.

346

He created neutrons and surrounded them with helium nuclei. After making and arranging the elements, He transformed them into the prime building blocks. He fashioned black holes and set up giant red and dwarf white stars. He spread galaxies throughout, set up comets and moons, extracted light from darkness, and wove together strands of light as one does in weaving a fabric. He bound matter together and fashioned everything which He had created and which He was yet to fashion. Everything was conducted in accordance with a master plan, in accordance with His directions and His code. As the Jewish sages put it: "He looked in the Torah and - using it as a blueprint - created the world."

Once finished, He left a thin strand of the light of creation from Jerusalem on High to Jerusalem below. This thin strand was one of mercy, and was exempt from the fear of harsh judgment. This passed through the Even Shetiyah, *which is the center of the world and the gate to Heaven. It was on it that Jacob rested his head and from it he saw angels ascending to and descending from Heaven. It was there that Isaac was brought as a sacrifice, that God spoke to King David, that the Holy of Holies of the First and Second Temples were built, and it was from that point that the Great Shofar (ram's horn) will be sounded to herald the final redemption. Only in that one place is there a direct tie between the spiritual and the material worlds. Should that strand break, Heaven forbid, the world will come to an end.*

Whoever is closer to the Source of Truth will be answered more easily than his fellow, for he is imbued with a spirit from on High. Even if he ignores that fact, and even if he does not believe in it, he will still be answered more easily. Very special people would rise to pray early and would attempt to pray opposite where the Holy of Holies used to stand, and to combine the proper words, and to do so at a propitious time. Thus we are told, "When you pray in Jerusalem it is as if you are praying directly in front of God's heavenly throne. And when you pray in Jerusalem on the Sabbath you are like an infant begging his father. And if you use the secret prayers on the Sabbath in Jerusalem you are among those who will bring redemption to the world."